LAST YEAR'S JESUS

Last Year's Jesus

A NOVELLA AND NINE STORIES

ELLEN SLEZAK

AN IMPRINT OF HYPERION
NEW YORK

Several of these stories have appeared in earlier form in the following magazines: *American Literary Review,* "Tomato Watch"; *Crab Orchard Review,* "The Geese at Mayville"; *Green Mountains Review,* "Here in Car City"; *Portland Review,* "If You Treat Things Right"; *ZYZZYVA,* "Last Year's Jesus" (published as "Passion Play").

Library of Congress Cataloging-in-Publication Data

Slezak, Ellen.
    Last year's Jesus : a novella and nine stories / by Ellen Slezak.— 1st ed.
      p. cm.
    Last year's Jesus (or Passion play)—Tomato watch—The geese at Mayville—Patch—Here in Car City—Lucky—By heart—Settled—If you treat things right—Head, heart, legs or arms.
    ISBN 0-7868-6741-8
    1. Polish Americans—Fiction. 2. Detroit (Mich.)—Fiction. 3. Working class—Fiction. 4. Catholics—Fiction. I. Title.

PS3619.L57 L38   2002
813'.6—dc21
                                  2001057391

Hyperion books are available for special promotions and premiums. For details contact Hyperion Special Markets, 77 West 66th Street, 11th floor, New York, New York, 10023, or call 212-456-0100.

FIRST EDITION

10 9 8 7 6 5 4 3 2 1

Book design by Casey Hampton

FOR MY PARENTS, MY SISTERS,
AND THE ONLY CITY WE'VE ALL CALLED HOME.

ACKNOWLEDGMENTS

I'd like to thank the MacDowell Colony and the Illinois Arts Council for their generous support of my work. I'm also grateful to the many literary journal editors who have published my stories, especially Jon Tribble at *Crab Orchard Review* and Howard Junker at *ZYZZYVA*.

In corroborating (or correcting, as necessary) my memories of the 1967 Detroit race riots and pennant race, two books were particularly helpful: *The Detroit Riot of 1967*, by Hubert G. Locke, and *The Detroit Tigers: A Pictorial Celebration of the Greatest Players and Moments in Tigers' History*, by William M. Anderson.

These stories in earlier forms have had many readers, and I'm grateful to each of them. In particular, I'd like to thank Jane Brunette for helping me begin, Kerry Madden-Lunsford and Carol Slezak for pitching in near the end, and Susan Messer and Lee Strickland for offering insight and clarity all along the way.

Every writer should be lucky enough to have an agent as keen and wry as Laurie Liss—I'm glad she answered my call. And this book would be less than it is without the sure hand of my editor,

Leigh Haber. She asks important questions. I give her thanks, and, I hope, good answers. More luck for me, her assistant, Cassie Mayer, helps it all go smoothly.

Finally, because I'm one to save best for last, I'm grateful to my husband, Brian Hamill, who, supportive, generous, and funny too, helps me breathe easy every day.

CONTENTS

LAST YEAR'S JESUS

We stand in the rain in a long line
waiting at Ford Highland Park. For work.
You know what work is—if you're
old enough to read this you know what
work is, although you may not do it. . . .

—"What Work Is," Philip Levine

At some point in your story grief presents itself.

—*Holy Land*, D. J. Waldie

I caught up with the Passion Play just as two horses draped in purple bathroom rugs left the corner of Pulaski and Campau. The Romans and almost everybody else in the play and in the audience were Mexicans. They'd come from their home parish, Holy Trinity, about five miles south, near Tiger Stadium. The Romans brandished broomstick spears and wore helmets that might have been mistaken for wash buckets spray-painted gold. Jesus followed, his white bedsheet tunic flapping in a breeze too cruel for April. He wore a weave of broken twigs atop his head. He really needed earmuffs. Though the pageant had just begun, his bare, sandaled feet already dragged under the weight of an eight-foot-tall wood cross he'd carry on his back for the next two miles as we followed him south down Campau and then back along the Grand Trunk Western tracks to Veterans Memorial Park, where he would be crucified, die, and be buried.

Mary should have been weeping at the fate of her son, but instead she scowled, preoccupied with keeping her blue pillowcase veil from blowing off her head. Simon wore thick wool socks inside *his* sandals. How loyal was that? A dozen other Israelite mourners, men and women hugging their arms in the cold, followed a troop of Roman foot soldiers who cracked whips of frayed rope at Jesus's feet and back, urging him to get a move on.

The cold morning had started out sunny, but then a dense pack of clouds rolled into Hamtramck from the west and covered the Passion Play like a lid. We trudged under it, sad and silent and sorry for Jesus.

Just as I congratulated myself for snagging a spot up front a few feet from Jesus, a troop of pageant volunteers marched over and began organizing us, the observers. The volunteers wore white gloves and purple sashes. Most appeared to be apathetic high school kids, but a few wore the tranquilized look of the saved. The young guy and the middle-aged woman who led them held walkie-talkies. The woman quick-stepped toward me. Her bristly gray hair didn't budge in the breeze. She wore a navy blue polyester coat and brown platter-shaped shoes. She had to be a nun. I turned away instinctively, but she came at me, pushing me back. The volunteers spaced themselves evenly around the passion players, forming a human barrier that kept us, the mere people, back twenty feet. I was farther from Jesus than before, but I still had an unobstructed view.

Then, on a mission, the nun-woman descended again and pushed me farther back. She spoke as she did this, her voice low and quiet, carrying the arrogant assumption that we'd all shut up and listen. And, of course, we did, leaning in to hear. "People, let's have some consideration here—quit pushing and give the players room. The next station starts in a minute." She looked pleased with herself, like she was a saint because she hadn't raised her voice.

Her rebuke was uncalled for. As a crowd we were quiet, polite, respectful, even a little depressed, in keeping with the theme and the weather.

I almost left at that point. I wasn't even supposed to be there. Not that I was skipping class or anything—Mercy College shut down for the Easter holidays. But I was on Campau running errands for my grandmother, while she knelt at home, making her way around the rosary in preparation for more praying at church that afternoon. She always prayed in the living room, kneeling next to her spindled rocker, leaning on it to get up or down. The light was murky there as she kept the thick, rose-colored drapes closed against the sun, so worried was she that it would leech the green from her slipcovered sofa. "Our people pray," she often said. According to my grandmother, our people also give cash at weddings and work harder than anybody else.

I didn't begrudge my grandmother her prayers. She had raised me since my mother died when I was five. I never met my father. But I did wonder at the scope of her prayers, which seemed only large enough to include those just like her: Healthy Poles who knew better than to move away from home and who ate meat there three times a day.

The *Free Press* that morning said the Latino community needed a place to hold its procession because Mayor Archer was redoing all the streets around Holy Trinity, a neighborhood so close to downtown Detroit that people with money and jobs were beginning to claim it. "Bah," my grandmother said, "they'll make a loft out of a tenement and shoo all the rats and deadbeats here." My grandmother must have suspected I was curious about the Passion Play because as I left to run her errands, she said, "Get the rye from New Palace and the fresh kielbasa from Srodek's." She said, "Now don't you go to that parade Theresa Jagielski." She said, "It's bad enough the *czarnes* live here, now we'll get the wetbacks too." She said, "Don't look at me like that Miss-I-go-to-college. What do you know of anything? You didn't cross the ocean." My grandmother did not approve of the Mexicans from Holy Trinity because they did not belong to *her* one holy Catholic and apostolic church.

Or maybe it was because she believed they took the GM factory jobs that paid twenty dollars an hour. Stole them away from guys like our neighbor Pauley Nowicki, who got laid off from Cadillac Assembly a year ago and now sits home drinking all day and yelling at the TV. But it seemed to me that the Mexicans in Detroit struggled to find good-paying work just like everybody else. They lived in their barrio near the Ambassador Bridge that spanned the river to Canada, as if they knew they might need an escape route—a way to flee farther north, where life might be colder, but surely couldn't be harder.

The old ladies gossiping outside St. Florian's last Sunday after Mass said the mayor of Hamtramck only said yes to the Passion Play because his son got a Mexican girl pregnant at prom the year before and he felt guilty. "That's what the Mayor gets for sending his son to Cass Tech instead of a good Catholic school like St. Cyril's or St. Ladislaw's or St. Florian's right here in Hamtramck," they said. Never mind that each of those high schools had closed. The old ladies put their arms around my waist and rested their old lady heads on my chest after they said this. All of them widowed or alone in other ways, they hugged me so tight the smell of them—of the food they cooked, of needing more than two baths a week, of their dead husband's cigarettes from his old sweater they wore—stuck to my skin.

They liked me. Or, at least, what I let them know of me. "Our Theresa went to good Catholic schools," the old ladies said. "Our Theresa got a scholarship to Mercy College," they said. "It doesn't matter that she's not pretty," they said. "Our Theresa is a good girl," they said.

You are mean and ignorant is what I said right back. But only to myself. On the outside, on the steps of St. Florian's, I just smiled at Mrs. Pachota, Mrs. Oczadlo, Mrs. Makowski, and at my grandmother, and then I said, "Come on, Grandma. Let's go home. I have to study for a chem test." I took my grandmother's arm. I helped her down the steps.

You can see that when the nun pushed me around at the Passion Play, it was nothing I wasn't used to, but I saw no reason to stick around and endure it. I turned to leave, but as I did, the other organizer, a young guy, Mexican, twenty-five or so, came by. He motioned us all to move in closer, "Come on," he said, "it's okay. There's plenty of room." His gentle voice could have soothed a colicky baby. He smiled, especially at me, and then he even spoke to me. "You're not from Holy Trinity, are you?"

"No. I just came out for kielbasa." I winced at my clumsy response, but I guess he heard poetry.

"Well, we hope you like our play. You're very welcome here." He reached out and put his bare hand over my mittened one and squeezed it, a gesture so friendly I warned myself not to imagine it as being anything more. I did not typically take such precaution. Instead, I charged, then blundered almost everywhere, making mistakes in conversation, in judgment, in bed.

The teenage girls behind me giggled as he walked away. I heard one of them ask the other who he was. "His name is Felipe or Miguel," she stopped and thought, "or maybe it's Bob. I don't know. He was last year's Jesus."

Hearing that and having just met a man so easily, I decided precaution was not called for that morning. Call it what you will— divine intervention, fate, kismet—I had been delivered to the Passion Play. This warm-hearted man was a sign that I need not blunder anymore. I did not expect my way to be free and clear, but if last year's Jesus, beautiful and kind and sin-free, too, was an instrument to my peace, I would hike on, obstacles be damned.

I pushed a few people aside and moved in closer. And when the passion players stopped to enact the third station on the way of the cross—*Jesus Falls the First Time*—and with the crowd singing *Donde, donde, donde encontrare al Señor*, I got to work. I only had eleven more stations to make that savior fall for me.

Did I mention he was gorgeous? If Paris or Milan ever needed a runway Jesus, he'd get the call. He had neat dark hair, beard, and mustache. Tall, lean, and muscular, he looked like the result of a coupling between a pole-vaulter and a wrestler. Despite the cold, he wore a cotton jacket and thin white pants, as if he knew it wouldn't be fair to bundle up while a fellow member in the club of being Jesus trudged down Campau in a loin cloth and bedsheet. That's just plain thoughtful.

The *Free Press* described the Jesus role as a great honor and termed the competition for it fierce. The judges looked for somebody who emanated goodness, rather than somebody who tried to impress. And though the current Jesus fit that bill, to my taste he was too white and passive, more like bread dough than savior.

Man to man, last year's Jesus would blow him away. He radiated active goodness. He coaxed love from the pushy *abuela*, short as a shrub, in front of me who shoved and bumped everybody else away. But when last year's Jesus urged this Mexican grandma to let others in too, she became positively Mother Teresa–like, stepping aside so a bunch of little kids could stand in front of her. When he leaned down to thank her, she touched his cheek as if he were a talisman.

By his very actions, he told us we were worth the trouble. And specifically, that I was worth the trouble. Because he talked to me every time he came near. Right after the fourth station, *Jesus Meets his Mother*, he walked alongside me for half a block, and not only because some boys behind me had flashed gang signals.

"So, what's your name?" He looked over my shoulder at the boys as he spoke.

"Theresa Jagielski." Oh, that I could have offered a more mellifluous moniker.

"I knew you didn't live by Holy Trinity. I would have noticed you." He forgot the boys for a second and gazed all over me. "You should come to our Mariachi Mass some Sunday. I bet you'd like it."

I imagined the two of us on a Saturday night date and then sitting together in a pew the next morning at Mass, while a quartet of musicians strolled by, their harmonies softening the priest's decree, the sun warming the church. I saw colors and serapes and my own dull-colored hair wrapped exotically around my head.

Before I could accept his invitation, he excused himself and left to rein in the nun, who had just grabbed two little boys as they ducked under the barrier. He looked back over his shoulder almost the whole way, and though you might argue he was only keeping an eye on those gangbangers, I'm telling you he looked at me, taking in my body and blood. This former savior was clearly all man.

I felt so fine. I was making an authentic connection with someone good. Once I completed the stations, I was sure I could shout, "Hey everybody, I've got a date with last year's Jesus."

And I was ready for it. I'd been practicing. You see, for me dates and sex were not easy. Guys, for the most part, have always insulted, ignored, or patronized me. My height—I'm almost six feet tall—and engine block of a body probably have something to do with it. I'm also plain. Everything about me—forehead, eyes, cheeks, shoulders, calves—is broad and uninterrupted by a mark of beauty or even an interesting defect. Nor do I do well at parties. I start out expectant, sure I'll be noticed, holding out my hand to everyone I see and making uninteresting observations that are not even truthful: "I like your shoes," or "I think people watch too much TV." After I circle the room for an hour, always on the perimeter of conversation, I am noticed but for the wrong reasons: I've spilled my beer; the girlfriend I came with just threw up.

Nothing changed when I went to Mercy College. Most of the women I met there had steady boyfriends. Only a few were like me—unencumbered by men and encumbered by the heavier burdens that come of such lightness. All the brochures and magazines leading toward college talked about safe sex and how alcohol and sex don't mix and how no means no. The warnings and advice were delivered in bulleted lists of do's and don'ts with brightly colored headings. But they didn't have bullets for girls like me.

So after my first year at Mercy, I began to drink. Just a little. And to have sex. Just a little of that, too. To my surprise it wasn't so hard to arrange. I discovered that while I may be no great bargain, guys liked sex. I practiced with a few of them, preparing for the man who would transition to boyfriend. A classmate's cousin's friend here. A friend's neighbor there. These guys, besides being drunk, were curious about me. I never slept with a girl who had such big thighs, the classmate's cousin's friend said, squeezing mine. I worried a little about being too easy, yet two sexual experiences hardly made me a candidate for sluthood.

I thought I was playing up when I shared a meal, saw a movie, took a walk, and had sex on four separate occasions with a guy named Jack, who worked in the kitchen at Mercy washing luggage-sized pots and pans. Not exactly a fairy tale, but it seemed like progress. But then the fifth time, as we squeezed together in his twin bed on a Sunday afternoon, having just done it while his parents were at a fiftieth anniversary wedding party, he told me he didn't know why he'd had sex with me because he really felt it was important that he love a woman before he slept with her, and then he added, "and your breasts smell." At first, I thought, oh my god, didn't I brush my teeth this morning? Then I realized he distinctly said *breasts*, and I felt even more ashamed.

I didn't say anything, but I left right after that. I cried a little as I drove home because it seemed that even though I was only on sex partner number three, too many assholes had already stuck their dicks in me. No more sex without something else I promised myself—not necessarily love, but more than beer and curiosity.

Objectively speaking, as mortal beings, is there a road higher than sex with a man who'd been Jesus? I'm not saying I was going to give in right away—I hadn't forgotten my promise. But when we did do it, it would be a religious experience, almost a sacrament, and certainly not the usual self-flagellation.

Had my previous approaches to sex been too glib? Too stupid? Too desperate? Maybe, but all that mattered was that I did not want to become what I thought my mother must have been— lonely and compliant, inside and out. She'd had sex with my father, I'd bet, just once. She was forty when I was born, after all, and my grandmother always said she wasn't exactly anybody's first choice for a date. "Not pretty or smart" is how she described her own daughter, evidence our people are not such good mothers either. When my mother got pregnant with me, my father refused to marry her, and then he died the next week—a heart attack. Like my grandmother said, he deserved it. But, she also added, if only he'd died before everybody knew he'd refused your mother, we could hold our heads higher. She said this to me often as I grew up. I'm sure she said it to my mother often too.

I'm also sure my mother hated hearing it, but I doubt she complained. Complaints shrivel in the heat of my grandmother's devotion to her church. And despite her out-of-wedlock sexual encounter, my mother may have also been devout. I have wispy memories of my grandmother waking me in the dark and then tugging my arm to hurry me as we slipped and slid on icy sidewalks on the way to early morning Mass at St. Florian's. My mother met us there, coming straight from her night-shift job cleaning offices and bathrooms at the City County Building downtown. When she hugged me, I smelled bleach and dust on her. I have slightly sturdier memories of sitting in a church pew playing with the treasures my mother gave me from the judges' and court clerks' wastebaskets—giant paper clips that said I'M TRYING TO GET MYSELF TOGETHER and pens with a page of ink left in them still—while a priest droned on in Polish.

Or maybe my mother was not devout. Maybe she was like me. Quiet in the force of my grandmother's faith, but enduring, not believing. Perhaps, like me, she even looked forward to an hour of church as a time when her mind could wander around friends and school and TV shows, and boys and parties and sex.

When I was five, my mother died in a car accident. All these years later I find it hard to remember much more about her besides her gifts from the trash and the cold gray church.

The Passion Play procession picked up tempo as we moved south. After a few blocks, we stopped for the sixth station on the way of the cross, *Jesus and Veronica.* The loudspeaker on top of the gray minivan that trailed the players intoned, *Victoria, tu reinaras oh cruz, tu nos salvaras.*

I watched as Veronica, muslin veil framing her lovely face, sack-like tunic wound round her petite and perfectly pointy Barbie-doll body, reached up and gently wiped the face of this year's Jesus, wiped it of the sweat that would have been glistening had we been in the Holy Land. Here in wintry Hamtramck, Michigan, he shivered instead and buried his face in the cloth, sniffing for warmth. When he finally looked up, Veronica held the cloth high for all to see, doing an actressy double take at the image imprinted on it. But what she held up was not a piece of fine linen with the faint stain of Jesus's sorrow shining through, it was a T-shirt with a picture of a cartoon character savior crowned in thorns and looking more pissed off than sad.

Just then, the wind, already strong, kicked up a notch and blew the T-shirt out of Veronica's hands, and we all gasped as if a swarm of locusts had appeared. The T-shirt tumbled down the street while last year's Jesus ran after it. He grabbed it just before it settled into a mud puddle, and then he walked it back to Veronica. When he handed her the T-shirt, she curtsied gratefully in response. He blushed. Bloody hell. I could see he was smitten.

Veronica then connived to push off her veil, no doubt so the full force of her beauty could come through. Her black and silky hair framed her delicate face as she batted big dark eyes with lashes long as the bristles on a brush. Chin up, she looked over her small but stately nose, and bit the lower half of her go-ahead-I-know-you-want-to-kiss-me lips. Then, in a gesture perhaps essential in hot weather, but wholly unnecessary on that day when we all shivered, she raised her arms and gathered her thick hair together, lifting it to expose her elegant neck, tempting him to nuzzle it. That damn Veronica knew exactly how to snare a man, even the son of God.

I felt an instant and potent hatred arise in me that equaled in power his clear attraction to her. She preened and flirted with him right there in public as all Grade-A beauties do. I self-righteously condemned her brazen behavior, ignoring how I plucked and postured in private, secretly wishing I had fine feathers to display. The sad truth was that I would have traded places with her in a second.

All through the next four stations, last year's Jesus neglected his flock, by which I mean me, and his job as a pageant organizer, and attended to Veronica instead. She whispered in his ear at station number eight, *Jesus Speaks to the Women*, and before our savior fell for the third time in station number nine, while the loudspeaker intoned, *A ti levanto mis ojos porque espero tu misericordia*, Veronica warmed her hands around a cup of hot chocolate that last year's Jesus fetched for her from the New Palace Bakery, which was for sure, by now, out of the seedless rye my grandmother expected. Though clearly dazzled by Veronica, last year's Jesus looked my way every now and then, the sight of my face probably as welcome as bread after too many sweets. I was still in the game.

Not that Veronica was the only obstacle. The cranky nun screwed up the picture too, grimacing and breaking up our tête-à-têtes with nitpicky complaints about the crowd. Last year's Jesus listened to her patiently, his hand on the blue cloth back of her coat spread wide in blessing, but he never pushed us back as she implored.

By the eleventh station, *Jesus Is Nailed to the Cross*, we'd stopped walking and were gathered at the foot of a small swell of hill at Veterans Memorial Park. The horses, nervous with the crowd grown larger and gathered close around them, snorted great clouds of steam in the cold. The passion players led Jesus up the hill. A bitter north wind made the gold tassels on the Roman soldiers' shiny red uniforms swirl.

At the top of the hill, they removed Jesus's tunic, exposing his body, white as an egg. When the soldiers pointed their broomsticks at him, Jesus lay himself down upon the cross, and three Romans drove pretend spikes through his hands and feet, using leg-sized mallets. Others trussed him tight to the wooden structure. Jesus

just lay there, more rump roast than man. When they finally secured him, five, then six, then ten of the Romans raised the cross
slowly, inching it up and forward to rest in the base they'd pre-
constructed at the crest of the hill.

But this part didn't go so well. Clearly, the Romans did not
expect Jesus and the cross to be so heavy and awkward. After three
aborted attempts, some mourning Israelites joined in to help raise
the crucifix—never mind the betrayal. Simon and Mary Magda-
lene and even the Virgin Mary, his own mother, strained and
groaned and pushed with the soldiers, trying to crucify Jesus. Only
Veronica, standing to the side, stayed pretty and pure.

Herding duties done, last year's Jesus stood next to me in the
front row with the nun on his other side. We looked on, anxiously,
as the sixth attempt to raise the crucifix failed as well. We breathed
in sharply and in unison when the cross teetered. Last year's Jesus
put his arm around me, as if to steady the proceedings. So we
stood, linked, as the Passion Play played on.

It started to rain, not with any conviction, just enough to make
the ground slick. I swore to myself, knowing how my hair would
look all flat and wet, but then last year's Jesus reached over and
wiped away a raindrop that hung from the tip of my nose, a gesture
I read as romantic. So I stood there holding on to that good man,
praying my thanks to the wind and the rain and the weight of that
cross, which had brought me so close to Jesus. And I thought with
all my heart: God *is* good.

I didn't care if those players on the hill struggled forever, and
for a while it seemed they would. At long last, they hoisted the
crucifix to ninety degrees and prepared to inch it toward its base.
But the wood was slippery with the rain and when it slid out of
their hands again, this time it was serious. Jesus fell back hard from
a great height.

The ground trembled. The crowd became quiet. Even the
horses swallowed their snorts. It was dead still; everyone waited to
see what had happened to Jesus. But though his loin cloth slipped
and his crown of thorns fell off, everybody relaxed and laughed

when Jesus on the hill shouted, "*¡Dios mio!* Are you trying to kill me?" Everybody but me. I wanted to smite them all. How dare they laugh at his pain.

The last act continued when Veronica, running from the crashing crucifix, tripped and screamed. She sprawled on the ground and cried, thudding her fists on the hill, writhing, grabbing her left ankle. Bad actress that she was, you could tell it didn't even hurt that much. She just wanted attention.

Hearing her, last year's Jesus ripped his arm from around me and ran uphill. He knelt before Veronica, stroking her Cinderella-sized foot and, at the same time taking charge of the hilltop tableau, commanding those men and women, Jews and Romans alike, to lift on three. With his steady count, they raised the cross again and clamped it firmly in place. Jesus, now lashed to its pegs, loin cloth and crown in place, shivered, waiting to die, bearing his final indignities with a grace that made the moment truly holy.

But last year's Jesus, whose attention was back on Veronica, missed this blessed moment. He whispered in her ear, and she placed a hand on his face. Then he tucked his hands under her, rose slowly, and walked, arms full of Veronica, over the crest of the hill and down the other side toward the parking lot.

I stood alone, shivering at this familiar picture of myself. A fractured sound of pure hurt leaked out of me. I stiffened with embarrassment and prayed no one had heard. The cranky nun looked up and then moved two steps closer to me. I stepped away, but she moved with me. When I looked at her, I was planning to scowl, but I saw her expression, which was somber and concerned, and I shook my head, rueful, instead. She reached up and patted my shoulder with a touch more genuine than any I'd felt in months. Then she quickly shoved her hands in her pockets, holding her coat together against the wind.

Jesus on the cross cried out again, this time as scripted, "Father forgive them, they know not what they do." As he finished his lament, a shaft of sunlight broke through the leaded sky, and everyone bowed to its glare.

TOMATO WATCH

JUNE

Lucy woke to unusual silence. She got out of bed and walked around the house looking for her grandfather. He wasn't in his bedroom watching TV with the volume turned way too high or low or all the way off, depending on which way his stiff fingers had brushed against the knob. He wasn't in his usual morning pose in the kitchen slurping coffee and eating rye bread with hard crusts that softened slowly as he gnawed on them. Looking out the kitchen window, she could see that he wasn't in the backyard. She poured herself a cup of coffee and sat at the kitchen table, wondering where to look next.

Lucy had only been living with her grandfather for two weeks, but she knew his habits well enough already to realize that this departure from his morning routine was odd. He was a ninety-five-year-old man who spoke mostly Polish with a little broken English thrown in. Lucy still remembered a few Polish words and phrases from her childhood—*eat, good, cold, go to hell*—but none of them helped forge a connection between her grandfather and herself. Still, she had begun to grow accustomed to his slurps and grunts and mumbles, to his rapidly worsening deafness, to his confusion. Did he know what day it was? What time it was? She wasn't sure. His gurgly breathing seemed weighted with things he couldn't quite say.

Lucy had agreed to stay with her grandfather for the summer while her mother and her mother's husband, Jack, traveled around the country in their new Winnebago. Her mother and Jack were both sixty-two years old—proud members of AARP, who gleefully claimed their senior citizen discounts at restaurants and movie theaters. "Why we're paying for some of the gas for this very trip with the savings from our senior's discounts," Jack had wagged a finger in her face and bragged to her just the day before they'd left, as if Lucy were remiss in being only twenty-nine years old and unable to claim any discounts herself. Lucy hadn't even tried to hide her laughter as Jack struggled to back the Winnebago down the driveway, swearing at himself as he veered onto the front lawn that he tended so carefully. He had left strict instructions about the lawn— she wasn't to touch it. He paid a professional landscaping company to come out twice a week and do the watering, weed killing, and mowing that would keep it in putting-green-perfect shape.

Her mother had left instructions, too, but hers had to do with Lucy's grandfather. She told Lucy what he ate and when she should help him bathe and take him to church. She did this on a sunny afternoon as she and Lucy sat at the kitchen table. Jack had taken the Winnebago to the gas station to fill it up and check the tire pressure for their early morning departure the next day. Her grandfather had been sitting alone in his bedroom watching the Tigers play the Red Sox. Her mother described his typical day. She mentioned sleeping, praying, sitting, eating, and pacing. She said Lucy's grandfather was becoming increasingly senile. That he sometimes did or said odd things. "Like what?" Lucy asked.

"Oh, last week he accused me of stealing his rosary. And the week before that, he poured his coffee on his oatmeal. But don't worry," she assured Lucy, "most times he's very cogent." Tiger announcer Ernie Harwell's play-by-play drifted faintly down the hallway while her mother spoke, but other than that the house at midday was quiet and still, making Lucy think she was about to join her grandfather in a vigil.

The next morning, right before she left, her mother took Lucy by the shoulders to give her less practical advice. "Honey, I'm worried about you. You don't seem happy. I'm so glad you took this leave from work. Remember, you can't go over or around life's challenges, you have to work right through them." After a bitter divorce seven years earlier, her mother had discovered the self-help section in her local bookstore. She'd met Jack at a ballroom dancing class and she looked upon her one-year-old marriage to him as proof that she had healed herself and earned the right to counsel others. She doled out more canned optimism that morning, "When I come back, I want to see a new Lucy. A happy Lucy."

Her mother had removed her hands from Lucy's shoulders and stepped back looking pleased and expectant, waiting for a heartfelt confession, for transformation. "Ma, I took this leave of absence to help *you*, not me." Lucy laughed, covering up her lie. She had been fired from her job just a week before her mother called to announce the trouble she was having finding someone to care for Lucy's grandfather. Lucy had seen the timing as fortuitous—a free place to stay while she figured out what to do next.

There were two reasons why she'd lost her job as office manager for the small trucking company on Detroit's east side where she'd worked for the last ten years, since she'd graduated from high school. She'd been stealing money—small amounts, about a hundred a month—for half the time she was employed there. She never would have thought herself a person who would steal, but the physical act of stealing hadn't been hard to do. She kept the books, administered the payroll and the petty cash, and oversaw the budget for all office purchases, large or small. The first time she'd borrowed twenty dollars from the petty cash box at work, she'd intended to pay it back the next day. It wasn't until she'd

borrowed another twenty two weeks later that she remembered the
first loan. No problem, she thought, she'd pay back forty dollars
when she got her next paycheck. But when the next paycheck came
her car needed a new tire and she got a haircut and after she took
care of those things, she didn't have an extra forty dollars. What
she had, instead, was the realization that nobody knew she'd taken
any money. Slowly, she'd come to rely on the petty cash to soften
the edges of her life. It allowed her to go out for lunch once a
week, to go shopping at Lakeside Mall on Saturdays, to order out
for pizza every now and then. She didn't live large on it.

The second reason she'd been fired was that she'd had an affair
with her boss. The first time Lucy had slept with him she'd been
drunk. This wasn't an excuse, but it was an explanation. The second and third and all the rest of the times, she'd been sober. She'd
enjoyed the sex—the anticipation, the closeness, the physical release. Her boss hadn't been particularly handsome—his coloring,
skin, hair, eyes were all from the same blond-brown palette—but
nothing about him gave offense, and he'd always been kind to the
people who worked for him. He brought donuts on Thursdays and
he never expected the office staff to work past five.

He'd first looked at Lucy differently after she'd gotten her hair
highlighted. She'd noticed a change in his expression when he saw
her that Monday morning. Later that week, he'd taken the whole
staff, all fifteen of them, to dinner to celebrate Richard Flanagan's
retirement after twenty-five years as a dispatcher for the company.
When Lucy had too much to drink, he insisted on driving her
home. Then he invited himself into her apartment and he made
coffee and he reached out every now and then to push aside a
strand of blond hair that fell in her eyes as she nodded sympa-
thetically to the tale he told of his troubles with his wife. The affair
had only lasted three months. But now she could see that it had
never been worth the price of having to see him every day, to take
orders from him at work, to pretend she didn't know about the
bright white scar on his left knee or the coffee-colored stain of skin
on his right shoulder.

If she had cared about him, ignoring him at work and trying to hide their affair so that it could go smoothly and last longer would have been a worthwhile challenge. Instead, it was inconvenient. Now with a few weeks' distance from the job she'd held for so long, and the man she'd slept with for three months, she was vaguely surprised to find that the only thing she missed was the fresh-brewed coffee that somebody else made every morning.

Still looking for her grandfather that June morning, Lucy walked out the back door with her second cup of coffee. Jack had hired a landscaper for the backyard, too. The flower beds and shrubs were molded to his idea of perfection, soft curving lines, continuous and smooth, muted colors, all harmony and carefully monitored growth.

She walked to the front of the house then, to the huge expanse of lawn, her flip-flops slurping on the walkway, which was still wet from rain the night before. Once out front, she stopped and leaned against an elm tree, watching her grandfather work, admiring how the sharp edge of his spade bit the tight web of Jack's grass and turned over a clump of green to expose a rich black base. It took a few more seconds before the coffee fired up her sleep-sodden synapses and she woke to what she saw: Her grandfather was assaulting Jack's perfect lawn. She ran toward him, coffee slopping out of the sides of her cup and dripping on her T-shirt and legs. She called out to him as she approached, but he didn't hear her. It wasn't until she grabbed his spade from behind, that he turned, startled to see her. "Grandpa. What are you doing?" She spoke directly into his ear.

He looked puzzled and then he straightened, as much as his crooked back would allow, to meet her gaze. It was only nine o'clock in the morning, but Lucy could tell from the progress he'd made that he'd been at it for hours. He had engraved a shallow narrow trench to mark a rectangle about twenty by ten feet, and he was shoveling platter-sized clumps of Jack's pampered sod from its center. He pulled the spade back from Lucy's hands and pointed it at the dozens of tomato plants, each about eight inches high, in blue plastic washtubs that rimmed the front walk. When he spoke, Lucy caught about every other word in his Polish-English mix, but she had no trouble understanding his intentions. She made a half-hearted attempt at reprimanding him. "But Grandpa, Jack said you could only have tomatoes in washtubs in the backyard along the walkway by the garage." Her voice trailed off as she gave in to the laughter, imagining Jack's face come his return in September. Her grandfather smiled and pointed at the sun, the southern exposure that drenched the front of the house. Then he began to dig again.

Lucy went into the house and came back out a few minutes later, shorts and shoes on, ready to help. They worked together steadily for three hours, and after her grandfather placed his last tomato plant securely in the rich black hole he'd fashioned for it and tamped the dirt on all sides, he smiled at Lucy. She didn't know her grandfather well at all, and considering his senility and deafness and the language barrier, she didn't fool herself that this summer would transport them to some higher plain of closeness, but looking at the tomato plants growing nobly in the ground instead of in plastic washtubs, it was easy for Lucy to ignore the queasiness in her stomach that she chalked up to the pot of coffee and nothing else that she'd ingested since she woke up hours ago, and feel satisfied and hopeful instead. She leaned on her shovel and smiled back broadly at her grandfather. From that point on, she often sat on the front porch in the morning, watching him weed the patch. When the landscaping service showed up after that, the crew boss was unconcerned when she explained they'd have to work around the tomato patch for the rest of the summer—that they weren't to touch it.

The tomato patch made things different between Lucy and her grandfather. Before she'd helped him with it, Lucy had tiptoed around the house as if it were full of cranky children who had finally fallen asleep. Her grandfather, too, had been on guard, even while he ate or sat in his rocker, as if he expected her to appear suddenly and demand something from him. They were more comfortable with each other now, though their lives still didn't touch much. Most days, her grandfather stayed outside, tending his tomatoes, or just sitting in a lawn chair, keeping watch over them, while Lucy sat inside near a window, or on the porch keeping an eye on him, and fighting a losing battle against the morning, afternoon, and evening sickness that had forced her to admit she was pregnant and didn't know what to do about it.

JULY

The heavy, still air of their tomato watch broke one evening as Lucy knelt, nauseous, over the toilet. She'd plotted back to the intersection of her menstrual cycle, the last time she'd seen her boss, and the rate of failure when using a condom as birth control, and she realized she was seven weeks pregnant. She'd taken a home pregnancy test one night in late June just to confirm what she knew must be the source of her nausea and exhaustion and ended up staring at the two pink lines of positive news for an hour, alone in her room, her grandfather's snores gurgling down the hallway to her open door. Since then she'd dealt with her pregnancy by telling herself she'd think about it soon, or later, or tomorrow. Just not then.

That nauseous evening in July, she heard her grandfather's heavy step before she looked up and saw him at the bathroom door, which she'd left open in her rush to get there. He walked toward her and leaned down until his face was close to hers. Lucy leaned away to protect herself from the bristles of his beard, which were weaponlike at close range.

"You better give me back my money," he shouted, his pale eyes full of hate. He watched her retch one more time and then he went down the hallway to her bedroom. Minutes later, when she felt steady enough, Lucy followed and saw him tossing clothes out of her dresser drawers. He pushed her aside when she tried to stop him.

"You stole my two hundred dollars. Give it back, you bitch. I'll tell your mother."

"Grandpa, I did *not* take your money. You lost it somewhere. Stop. Your money isn't here."

Lucy shouted denials and then tried to soothe him, but gave up as he tore the sheets off her bed and looked under her mattress. As he left her room, he shook his fist and muttered to himself. She wished she had two hundred dollars to give him. She sat on the stripped mattress, tired.

She'd been sitting on the edge of her bed when her boss had confronted her about her embezzlement. He met her at her apartment over Srodek's Sausage shop in Hamtramck. It was a warm day, and the seasoned smell of smoked meats mingled with the lusher raw ones as they drifted through her open windows. Lucy remembered how tired she'd been of the smells that kept her rent cheap. In winter, they were carried by blasts of heat from the old furnace, the very floorboards fragrant. It was only during a month or so of spring, then fall, with windows and furnace both shut, that Lucy didn't feel amoebalike, as if the very boundary of her skin opened and closed around the aroma of the business below.

She'd sublet her apartment for this summer she was spending with her grandfather. It hadn't been hard to do. Hamtramck was becoming slowly gentrified in a haphazard way, with an old bar becoming a kitschy hangout for formerly suburban twenty-year-olds, and a new cafe wedged between a rent-to-own furniture store, which sold lamps adorned with dangling glass prisms, and a shoe store that specialized in synthetic leather orthotics. Still the *babusias* walked the streets slowly, net shopping bags bursting with the day's bread, meat, and potatoes. They remained loyal to the small storefront merchants, the New Palace Bakery, Ciemniak's, and Srodek's, or else were simply unwilling to shuffle their tired, swollen feet four more blocks to the Farmer Jack Grocery superstore that had recently opened. She wasn't sure she'd move back to her Hamtramck apartment once her mother and Jack returned. She wasn't sure of anything.

Lucy thought back to the Saturday afternoon in May when her boss had ended their affair. That was almost two months ago now. He'd driven to her apartment from his home in Grosse Pointe Farms that day. He parked his late model Ford Explorer right in front of Srodek's, between a battered old Buick and a Chevy pickup with a barking mutt tied up in the back. After they made love, as he gathered his things together, preparing to leave, he asked her to sit down. He was nervous and Lucy waited for him to tell her it was over. She began to reassure him—told him it was okay, that they'd only been together three months after all, that it had been fun but she hadn't expected it to last even as long as it did, that she was even relieved. Then she heard him. "We've found discrepancies in the books. We know what you've been doing. We want to be lenient. It wasn't that much money, but you'll have to go." He added that he was surprised it had taken him so long to notice her pattern of deception. Lucy was surprised, too. Whenever she heard him talking to his wife, she thought he knew a fair amount about deceit himself.

If she hadn't slept with him, she wouldn't have been caught. He'd taken a closer look at her work since they'd become involved. He had planned to give her a raise, to reward her for her efforts and loyalty. Instead, he had to ask her to leave. "I don't see a need to press charges if this is done civilly and quietly. I'll even give you a letter of recommendation. We're not talking about a huge amount of money after all." And it hadn't been much—a little more than a thousand dollars a year for the past five years—but Lucy understood they were talking about an amount of money just big enough to insure that she wouldn't call his wife. She accepted the terms.

He hadn't asked her why she'd done it. If he had, she would have told him the truth—that after the first few times it hadn't seemed wrong. Surely, nothing so easy could be. The money just helped her get by. She didn't live large off it. Even now, more than a month later, it was only the act of getting caught that didn't seem right. She felt worse about not stealing her grandfather's money than she did about stealing her boss's.

She got up from the mattress and went to the window and looked out at the tomato patch. Her grandfather paced its borders. In late summer, he'd have bushels of ripe tomatoes, testimony to his hard work and vision, to something he still could do. He bent down, examining the tallest plants, their leaves rich green, the edges like arrows, preparing to protect the fruit they were going to bear, then he stood straight again, slowly.

When he was a young man, he'd farmed in Poland. Her mother had described vast fields and bushels of produce. Lucy felt embarrassed for him, for the small patch he tended now. He'd emigrated to the United States in the early 1900s. He'd come for a better life, for work. He'd settled in Pennsylvania first, mining coal in countryside that had reminded him of his native landscape in southern Poland, where corn fields and coal mines butted up against each other in a tug of war over which would define the countryside. He moved to Michigan from Pennsylvania in the 1920s, again for work. This time he found it in the auto factories. He lived in Hamtramck with his fellow Polish immigrants, never needing to become fluent in English—a man's hard labor a common language all its own.

Now, almost eighty years later, he talked about going back to Poland, but he had no real understanding of how impossible that would be. He only left the house these days with Lucy on a limited, scheduled basis—church on Sunday, the bank on Friday. Whenever he did go out, he dressed carefully, in a suit and hat, and brought along something of value to him—a small wooden crucifix, a ham sandwich, a rosary, a loaf of bread. He'd start out alone, walking down the driveway, past the car. She wondered how far he'd go if she didn't run behind him, and steer him back to the car, back to her care.

That night, the night her own grandfather accused her of stealing from him, Lucy watched as he paced the perimeter of his tomato patch for an hour. He finally came inside at eight o'clock and went straight to his bedroom. When Lucy checked on him twenty minutes later, he was already asleep. He still wore his shoes.

. . .

The next morning, on Sunday, Lucy woke earlier than usual so she could help her grandfather bathe and dress for church. She gave herself a silent lecture on patience as she walked toward his room. He was awake and sitting in his rocking chair mumbling a prayer. His mouth, without his false teeth to hold it steady, wobbled and made a flapping sound as he breathed, like a flag in the wind. As Lucy approached, he looked at her menacingly and swung his rosary slowly back and forth like a hypnotist's pendulum.

"Come on, Grandpa, I'm running a bath so you can get ready for Mass. Let me help you up."

"Don't bother me, thief. I'm praying for your soul." He shook Lucy off and rose on his own.

She followed him to the bathroom. When he opened the door, thick steam wrapped around them and he clutched her arm for support. Lucy was surprised at his strength. She helped him undress and tossed his long underwear, yellow with age and urine and sweat, into the clothes hamper. She held his arm as he stepped into the tub and then lowered himself gently into the water. He sank back, eyes closed, hands folded on his chest. He looked peaceful, as if his day were done instead of just beginning. Lucy hummed "Taps," then stopped, superstitious.

Never tall to start, he'd gotten shorter with age. Lucy, five feet six inches, remembered him being about her height when he came to her high school graduation. But now he was stooped and barely came up to her chin. The curved walls of the tub cradled him comfortably like a baby in a bassinet. Lucy examined him closely as he lay before her. His fingers, once smooth, dark, and long, like good cigars, were twisted with arthritis from years of roofing houses and working in coal mines and auto factories. They looked like the roots of a tree, burrowing through the soil. His face was clean-shaven, but only in some spots. In others, hard white bristles punctured dry soft skin and stood out straight like the spikes of a thistle. His ears, the size of large potatoes, sprouted tufts of hair from within. He had a slight protrusion on the left side of his skull, about an inch above his ear—family lore said it was a bullet, lodged there when he was shot at down by the railroad tracks where he stole fallen bits of coal during the Depression. His body was blotched with light brown spots that melted together and made a map on his back and chest. His skin hung loose all over but even in the warmth and water, his joints were bent as if rusted tight. Lucy sat on the toilet facing him and thought about how much she'd give never to get as ugly as he seemed to her now. She stared at her stomach and thought of it stretching hard and tight during the next seven months.

She went to the other bathroom and threw up twice before she woke her grandfather from his cushion of water. She helped him dress in his only suit—thick black wool that smelled of moth balls and coffee. She went to her room and dressed quickly. When she returned, her grandfather sat in his rocker watching TV wrestling. The volume off, he stared at the bottom left corner of the screen as if all action took place there. He stood unsteadily when Lucy touched his shoulder and then hit himself on the side of the head with the heel of his hand. "My teeth—I need my teeth," he gummed his way through the words.

"Okay, let's find them. We only have a few minutes. Let's look fast." Her grandfather rifled through a stack of newspapers at the foot of his bed. Lucy checked the obvious places, his dresser top, the bathroom counter, the nightstand, and then she widened her search, realizing the unlikely was more likely. She went to a wood cabinet in the corner of his bedroom. It was an old piece of furniture, thick with dust, and roughly finished. When she opened the door, a vitamin smell blew out at her, and she felt nauseous again. She held her breath and looked through yellowed papers, bottles of medicine with expiration dates long past, holy cards, miniature plaster cast statues of Walt Disney characters, brittle photographs whose corners cracked as she lifted them, and a pile of brown paper bags so old and soft they felt like flannel. She found no teeth, but as she was about to close the doors, she noticed a small paper bag that didn't lie as flat as the others. When she picked it up, a stack of bills, fives and tens, but mostly ones, fell out. Her grandfather knelt down with her to pick them up, forgiving her for stealing his money and offering a dollar as a reward for returning it to him so soon. They left for church without finding his teeth.

An hour later, during Mass, while the priest delivered his sermon, Lucy's grandfather reached into his breast pocket, laughed gleefully, and then held his teeth in the air for all the congregation to see. A woman in front of them turned and said *sshh*. Lucy glared at her instinctively and then wondered if that protective streak would cover a baby. But, she reminded herself, this thing that was making her so sick and tired wasn't a baby yet. It was just a collection of tissue, smaller than her thumbnail. She didn't know yet what she was going to do about it. She probably *wouldn't* have it.

She'd gone that route once before, ten years ago when she was just out of high school. She and her boyfriend at the time had decided together that it was for the best. They sat in the waiting room at the abortion clinic with all the other pairs of people, some of the women so pale Lucy felt sure they'd faint in front of her. Then she caught a glimpse of herself in the receptionist's glass window and saw that she had the same sick sheen. She couldn't imagine being in that clinic waiting room now, ten years later, listening for her name to be called. She and all the other women around her would be looking at their feet, their arms folded defensively across their chests. The men next to them out of place, no help at all.

She wished she could ignore this baby for nine months and then watch it be magically born and disappear. No decision or procedure necessary. No tears. No labor. How could she raise a child? She had hardly any money, no job, and no wish to even tell its father she was pregnant. Nothing so loaded with difficulty, with problems, with warnings of disaster could be the right thing to do. Maybe adoption, instead. She thought of desperate couples who would be so pleased to have a baby. What would it be like to give a child away? Imagine opening your eyes to a baby, swaddled and beribboned, a gift for you. Who would swoon more in such a situation? The giver? The receiver? Lucy watched her grandfather shuffle up to the altar for communion. When the priest placed the wafer on his tongue, he walked away with his eyes closed, guided back to his pew by instinct.

After Mass, Lucy drove home slowly while her grandfather said the rosary and shouted for her to stop the car at every house that looked even remotely similar to his. "I'm sorry, keep going, yes, I think that's the way," he told her, pointing left as she turned right and down the road as she pulled into the driveway.

The next day she called and made an appointment at the abortion clinic she'd gone to ten years before. She called back an hour later and canceled. She didn't have to decide yet. She still had time.

As she and her grandfather worked together in the tomato patch all that month, Lucy realized how much she'd begun to count on this rhythm of their days. She forgot about everything else while they worked on his plants. She thought if she could go on like this forever, she would be content. At night, exhausted from all the time she spent working in the sun, she slept soundly.

Though he was generally uncertain about who she was, her grandfather seemed glad to have her around. She did whatever he asked. She wasn't squeamish. She picked the slugs off the leaves, yanked weeds, and turned compost into the soil. As the days got hotter and at her urging, he often sat in a lawn chair under the elm tree and watched her work. When she was through, he held the hose for hours, watering his plants at intervals during the hot dry days.

She helped him in other ways, too. She watched baseball with him and drove him to church and to confession as often as he wished. She cooked for him and did his laundry. She reminded him what day it was when he forgot. She opened his mail and took him to the bank to deposit his Social Security.

When birthday cards arrived for him during the third week in July, she admired them and read out loud all the good wishes for his ninety-sixth. She stood the cards up on the kitchen table, surrounding his meals like a fence, but he ignored them unless he happened to knock one down when he reached for his coffee, and then he placed it back upright, clumsily, upside down with all the good wishes facing her.

At dinner on the twenty-sixth of July, his birthday, though she was pretty sure he didn't know it, he dutifully ate the sausage and potatoes that Lucy placed before him. It was only four in the afternoon—he liked to eat early. It was hot. It would be many more hours before the heat would be replaced by the evening. Lucy sat across from her grandfather and watched food slop to his shirt—his fork had become even harder for him to handle lately. When there was nothing left to spill, he pushed aside his plate and coffee cup and began the slow rise from his chair, his knees and elbows ratcheting open notch by notch.

While he did this, Lucy went to the kitchen and then came back to him, a birthday cake in her hands. She saw him look frantic for a moment and reach for the water pitcher, but then she came closer and he must have seen that the blaze of fire was only a collection of candles on a cake, because he put the pitcher down. She set the cake in front of him and sang *Sto Lat*, "may you live to be a hundred years," loudly and off-key. She mispronounced half the words, but he smiled.

She took a Polaroid of him standing behind the cake, candles blazing. When she handed him the square of stiff paper, he watched as the muddy green chemical background slowly turned into a picture of his own face staring up at him. Then he placed the picture on the burning candles. Lucy poured water on the cake as the photo flared.

She led him away from the tomato patch an hour later. She spoke directly in his ear, reminding him about the heat. She placed a rotating fan in front of his rocker and then watched for a while as he sat there, mumbling his prayers and waiting expectantly for the ruffle of hot air that came at regular intervals as he made his way around his rosary, bead by bead.

She came back to his room half an hour later. It was too hot. She needed to leave the house. It was 6:30—there were hours of daylight left still. She placed her hand on his shoulder. She leaned down to his ear again. "Let's go for a drive. To Stony Creek. We can cool off with a swim." He allowed her to lead him to the car.

She helped him with his seat belt when he couldn't get his twisted fingers to fasten it securely. He leaned forward a little, his hands on the dashboard. They drove east to the freeway and then entered it going north. She saw how he watched the freeway exit signs carefully, his lips moving as he mumbled the exit names.

Once at the park, she guided him to the beach. She stopped at the edge of the parking lot, right before the sand began, and took off her shoes, urging him to do the same. She helped him untie his stiff, black shoes, and when he kicked them off, she saw that he had forgotten to put on socks that morning and his skin was red and tender at all the pressure points. They struggled together walking across the sand, threading their way past the towels, blankets, plastic toys, and children that crowded the beach even at dusk.

When they finally got near the water, he watched as she stepped out of her shorts and T-shirt. Her plain red bathing suit was stretched tight over her stomach and breasts and she saw him look at that, too. She waded in, urging him to join by pantomiming that he should take off his shirt and pants and swim, but he ignored her and sat in the wet sand instead, the water lapping at his bare feet.

The water was almost perfectly still and lukewarm, but it hid pockets of cold that Lucy stepped into with appreciation. The shallow area she walked away from was full of water wings and beach balls and parents splashing and floating with their children. She looked back at her grandfather. He stared at her, a sentry with only one thing to guard. With his flannel shirt buttoned unevenly and his long underwear showing through the open fly on his work-pants, his bare feet were the only hint that he was anywhere but home. She stepped farther out into the lake and dove in, enjoying the absolute relief that it offered. Her stomach settled as she swam, the queasiness that she'd felt almost continuously for the past eight weeks abating. The elements were in sync—water within and water without—making her think for the moment that her pregnancy was a way to keep things whole.

Her grandfather stood up as she came out of the water. She shook herself off as best she could—she had forgotten to bring a towel—and then stepped into her shorts, steadying herself on the arm he extended. As they made their way across the sand to the car, she held on tightly.

When they got back to the house, the sun was just setting, and the green tomatoes were gleaming in the dusk. Lucy and her grand-father sat in lawn chairs and took turns holding the garden hose, arcing a rainbow of water on the thirsty plants whose leaves drooped heavily in the heat.

AUGUST

Her grandfather's tomatoes grew and ripened as the summer crawled to an end. Lucy stared at them early one morning after she woke, shaking from a nightmare she couldn't remember. The digital clock read 4:13. She stood by the window and breathed deeply, searching for a hint of cool in the August air.

She was tired. She had helped her grandfather with his toma-toes the day before, bending and tending so he didn't have to. He stood to the side, directing her in Polish commands she now quickly followed, pointing to the fruit that was ripe enough to pick, to the leaves that were being destroyed by aphids, to weeds that needed excavation. She'd rushed into the house three times as she helped him, needing to throw up, the soda crackers she chewed dutifully doing nothing to settle her stomach.

The third time she'd run inside, her grandfather had followed her. When she came out of the bathroom, he stood in the hallway waiting for her. He put his hand on her back, patted her gently and told her that she worked too hard, that she should lie down for a while, that he could finish on his own. He'd sat in his lawn chair under a shade tree that afternoon while she looked nervously out the window at regular intervals, watching him watching his tomatoes. They'd both gone to bed early the evening before, Lucy dropping into sleep so quickly she hadn't had time to hear his usual snores.

They'd been together more than two months now. She wasn't afraid of him anymore, and he'd become increasingly more easy with her. He no longer looked defensive or embarrassed when she gently pointed out that he must try to remember to turn off the stove once he turned it on, or that he shouldn't put the milk in the dishwasher or that he had forgotten to put on his shoes or put in his teeth. He just shrugged and smiled, comfortable in his decline. He made a pot of coffee every morning as soon as he woke. When Lucy got up an hour later, it was waiting for her, still fresh and strong.

She continued to ignore her pregnancy. She didn't have to act yet. In a way, she envied her grandfather, so sure about what he wanted, tending his tomatoes in the heat, watching them so quietly, waiting patiently.

She walked back to her bed that early morning, but couldn't lie down on the twisted sheets. It was too hot. She needed to cool off. She saw her car keys on the dresser. She saw her red bathing suit hanging on the closet doorknob where she'd left it after her trip to Stony Creek a week or two ago. She remembered the cold pockets of water that had given her such a welcome ache. She should go there again. She would. She'd drive to the lake at Stony Creek for a swim. She'd be back before her grandfather woke up. She put on her bathing suit and then slipped quietly out the back door after looking in on her grandfather and seeing the mound of his body rising up and down with each slow breath he took. She had time. It was only 5:00 A.M. He'd sleep for two more hours. Like always.

Lucy drove with the windows down, the breeze clearing out the last shreds of her nightmare. She turned east again, and then north, driving fast down the empty freeway, and headed toward Stony Creek. When she arrived, the park was deserted. It didn't officially open until 9:00 A.M. She got out of the car and stretched, clenching her shoulder blades together and then letting them go in a welcome release, arching her back, which highlighted the swell of her stomach, reaching up to the sun just beginning to rise. She stepped out of her gym shorts and pulled her T-shirt over her head in one smooth and fluid gesture. Her bathing suit wouldn't fit much longer. As she swam out to the float in the middle of the roped-off swimming area, she realized she'd been awake for an hour and hadn't thrown up yet. She floated on her back, ignoring all the warning signs that told her not to swim when the park was closed.

She felt that perfect union of water on water again, and her pregnancy seemed to her at that moment a natural consequence that didn't have to be interrupted or feared. After floating for a while, she left the beach the way she came, trying to match her steps to the imprints she'd already made in the smooth sand, not wanting to disturb things any more. Driving home, the wind massaged her wet hair and dried her clothes quickly. Rush hour traffic began to fill the road. Still, she drove easily, hanging her left hand comfortably over the steering wheel and cupping her right hand protectively under her stomach.

As she neared the exit that would take her back to her grandfather's house, she glanced at the northbound lanes to her left. She could see in the distance that cars were slowing and swerving to avoid an obstacle. She looked, amazed, as the obstacle moved and she could see it was a figure walking in the center lane. Amazement metamorphosed to horror as she recognized the black hat, the brown paper bag tucked under one arm, the stooped shoulders draped in black wool too heavy for the early morning heat.

She stopped her car in the left lane, emergency flashers on, about five hundred feet past her grandfather. She crawled over the barrier that divided the north and southbound lanes and ran toward him, leaning hard to the left to keep on the thin strip of shoulder the old highway provided. Drivers swerved their cars and honked their horns. She ran faster, scraping her legs on the metal barrier.

Still a hundred feet away, she screamed at her grandfather's back, though she knew he couldn't hear. Her voice, direct and firm, focused like a laser. She knew exactly what she wanted. "Grandpa. STOP."

He turned and saw her. He smiled in the shadow cast by the brim of his hat. He stopped, raised his left hand in greeting and cupped his right hand protectively under a tomato—smooth, red, firm—that he carried. It shined like a beacon in the early morning light.

When Pete Flatte drove his pickup into Mayville late in August, county workers were running canvas banners up the eight lamp-posts that lined Main Street. They put one each in front of the Pigeon Bowl, Pedro's Restaurant, Eddie's Tru-Value Hardware, the Egg and Tuna Diner, Foodtown, Bill Kostecki's Mutual of Omaha Branch Office, Betty's Books, and the Second Cup. The banners heralded the town festival coming in October—the arrival of the geese at Mayville.

Forty miles inland from the lake, Mayville was much like any other town in southwestern Michigan, dull and modest, not par-ticularly pretty. Still, two of the county workers waved when Pete tapped his horn. He decided it was as good a place as any to settle for a while.

His only income was his disability from Ameritech (bad back) and the money he'd picked up from a big carpentry job he'd fin-ished a few weeks earlier, so he rented a two-room cabin on the old dump road about three miles west of Main Street. It had a loose and squeaky pine plank floor and a wood-burning stove for heat, but you couldn't get much for one-fifty a month, even in Mayville. He figured he had enough money to last until spring—though he was worried about his truck, dinged-up good on the outside and jimmy-rigged under the hood. He'd have to meet somebody soon who didn't mind giving him a jump every now and then and, as it got colder, every damn day.

There wasn't much else on the road—just two rusted-out trailers on cement blocks and a large, tidy cabin right across from him with a late model Chevy pickup parked out front. Pete had taken only his clothes and his toolbox when he left Barbara's farm. The way he figured it, he did Barbara a favor when he left her. She was sick—rheumatoid arthritis, the doctors said. Just aware enough to know that he wasn't making her life any easier, Pete also knew he was way short of what it would take to stay and do some good. Barbara's sudden illness wasn't her fault, but it wasn't his either.

He'd stopped at the Salvation Army in Grand Bluff on the way out and bought a TV, mattress, chair, table, radio, and a box of kitchen stuff. It didn't take too long to unload the truck once he got to Mayville. Still, he wished his new neighbor from across the road, who'd come out to sit on his porch as Pete pulled in, would step over and offer to help or at least say hello.

Pete waved and shouted to him right away, but the old guy, close to eighty by the sag of his face, just watched, not waving back. Never shy before an audience, Pete stacked up more boxes than he could comfortably carry. When he finished unloading the truck, the man was gone.

That same night, feeling restless, Pete drove into town and went to the Pigeon Bowl where six of the blue and yellow tenpins on the flashing neon sign out front were on the fritz. Pete saw the old man again as soon as he walked in, and he went right up to him and stuck out his hand, "Hi, neighbor. It's good to see you up close and to know you're a bowling man. I'm Pete Flatte." The old man offered back a hand and then mid-shake pulled Pete to him and hugged him hard. "Whoa, whoa fellow. Watch the ribs," Pete stepped back.

"Just glad to see you, boy. Come on, I'll buy you a beer and we'll bowl a few frames." The old man wore a blue and white seersucker suit, a red tie, and red, white, and blue bowling shoes— he could have been a poster boy for a Fourth of July fair.

Never one to question luck, especially when it came in the form of something free, Pete followed his neighbor to the bar. The bartender poured two drafts and then picked out two dollars from the array of bills the old man held out to him, "This will cover it, John. How you bowling tonight?"

"Fair, fair. Me and my son here are going to play a few frames now. We'll see if he remembers what I taught him."

"Sounds good. Go easy on him, John. He looks green." The bartender winked at Pete and then held out his hand, "I'm Frank Magnus. I own this place."

"Pete Flatte. I just moved here from Homer City. I live across the road from . . . what did you say his name was?"

"John. John Randall. He's a little soft now," Frank tapped his temple, "but not always. It comes and goes."

"Well, what the hell, as long as his money's good." Pete laughed alone and then turned to join John who stood swaybacked, cradling a green, marbled ball to his paunch.

John didn't talk between frames, but twice he took his ball and heaved it so that it jolted then jammed into a gutter a few lanes away. The two couples bowling there looked over, angry, but relaxed and waved when they saw John. John waved back and then hooked a strike down his own lane, beating Pete. They left together at midnight, walking first to John's pickup in the parking lot, where he hugged Pete again and told him to call his mother.

"Can't do that, John. She's been dead for almost twenty years now." Pete laughed as he spoke and then wished he could snatch back the words as John began to cry and inch away from him. Then Pete watched as John, still crying, poked around in the truck bed and brought out a box of cornflakes, got behind the wheel, and, still crying, reached in the box and ate a handful, crumbs cascading down his shirt.

When Pete moved a little closer to see if John was okay, he saw that the bed of the truck was packed with cornflake boxes, tightly fitted together like sugar cubes. Not exactly sober, but figuring he was in better shape than John, and knowing anyway that *his* old truck probably wouldn't start, Pete shooed John over to the passenger side and drove them both back to the old dump road.

Early the next morning, meager belongings unpacked, Pete stepped outside to survey his new home and tripped on an old rail tie that marked off a sandbox-sized, weed-choked, vegetable patch. He knelt down and pulled a tomato off a tangled vine that snaked along the ground. It was small and green. Just a few days before, he'd been working the harvest on Barbara's farm, acres of tomato plants laden with fruit. Things changed fast sometimes.

Barbara had inherited two hundred of her father's thousand acres when he died twenty years earlier. Her four sisters had each received the same. The five of them and Barbara's three grown-up nieces ran a farm stand stocked mainly with produce they grew themselves. The largest store around for fifty miles, the Hughes Sisters' farm stand always did well.

Pete and Barbara hadn't known each other long when they married, but they weren't kids. They knew what they wanted. That's what Barbara told her sisters when he overheard them warning her to slow down with him. For her part, she wasn't lying. She'd let Pete know flat out what she expected from their marriage: good loving, deep down support, friendship, and children too. He'd nodded yes without thinking it through, that sounded fine, entering her trust without a request of his own.

When she didn't get pregnant right away, Barbara didn't worry. After eight months, she pushed a little. She saw one doctor, then another. But besides the fact that she was forty-two and her eggs were a little shabby, the doctors didn't think she was the problem. Get your husband in here, they said.

When she told him, Pete lobbied for patience. "Aw, Barbara, those doctors make such a business of it. Let's just be natural for a while more. Do you really want to end up on the cover of one of those women's magazines holding a litter of babies that don't weigh as much as a sack of potatoes between them?"

He moved to kiss and hold her, but she pushed him away, "I want you to think about what I've asked. You know what I want. This isn't a big step—they just need to take a sample and do some tests."

"I'll think about it. I promise. Just give me time."

She understood—at first. She didn't mention it again until two weeks later, and when he said he was still thinking, she backed right off. But after two more weeks, his silence on the subject turned into a barrier, and it kept their paths from crossing. Most nights, he sat in the living room watching TV, while she sat at the kitchen table in a straight-backed chair reading magazines about babies and parenting.

It took him three months to realize that she knew for sure what he still wouldn't admit to her. He wasn't seeing any doctor, he didn't want the responsibility of raising any babies, and he wouldn't even look her in the eye and disappoint her honestly.

By that time, the barrier was so high she didn't need to stay away to be apart from him, and she came back into the living room after dinner. They talked—but only about other things. The baby magazines abandoned, she leafed through cooking magazines instead, staring at plates decorated with food the likes of which Pete had never seen—golden beets, red lettuce, lily-white mushrooms.

"Pete, I'm sick of just selling corn and carrots and lettuce and such. Look at these beets—god, they're pretty. It says here they taste good too. I think I'll try something new this spring planting."

"Well, nothing sells like corn in July and August. But you go ahead, honey. Whatever you want is okay by me."

"I'm not asking permission, Pete. It's my damn farm. I just wanted your opinion."

Barbara picked a fight no matter how nice he was those days.

"My *opinion* is that corn sells and beets should be red. You happy now?"

Pete weeded the vegetable patch and stacked a quarter cord of scattered wood while thinking about Barbara that morning. After a while, he took a break and went over to John's hoping to snag a ride into town for his truck, but the Chevy was gone and John didn't answer his call. He looked in the uncurtained windows, eager to snoop when he thought he could get away with it.

The front room seemed bare, but a closer look showed that it was only the center that was empty, cleared full out, a border of boxes stacked up against its north and south walls, furniture, stacked and fit together like a puzzle, against the east and west. The middle of the room looked like a boxing ring, empty except for a large bowl, shaped and painted like a half a watermelon, and a box of cornflakes on the floor. Pete went around back and peeked into another room that turned out to be the kitchen. A microwave oven and a minirefrigerator rested on a small table. Other than that, the room was empty except for a dozen coffee cake boxes and about twenty boxes of cornflakes stacked on the counter. When he heard the truck pull in up front, he ran to meet it before John could get out.

"Morning John. Say, I was wondering, could you give me a quick ride into town so I could get my truck?" Pete approached the driver's side.

John opened the door and stretched his legs out slowly and then used the door frame to turn sideways and lever himself out. His seersucker suit was crinkled, and he still wore his bowling shoes. His hair, stuck up and out all over, pleaded for help.

"What was that, son?"

"I need a ride into town. I left my truck there last night when I drove you home."

Walking toward his front door, John stopped and turned back, "What did you say your name was?"

"Pete. John, it's me, Pete."

"And we've met? You know me?"

"Well not so good yet, but we bowled together last night, and I drove you home. I'm your new neighbor—I live across the road. You hugged me and told me to call my mother."

"That's good advice. Sounds like me."

"So, how about a ride?"

"You live there you say?" John pointed across the road.

"Yeah."

"I suppose you came from Chicago or Detroit or someplace else to get way from it all."

"No, I came from Homer City to get away from my wife." Pete's laugh dwindled when John didn't join him.

"You shouldn't be talking about your wife that way son. I don't imagine she thinks you're any great bargain."

"Yeah, well anyway, about that ride?"

"I'll take you later. I have to soak my back right now. I think I pulled a muscle."

By three that afternoon John still hadn't stopped by, so Pete walked over and knocked on his open door, "Hey John, I'm wondering if I can still get that ride." He walked in and as his eyes adjusted to the semidarkness, he saw John lying spread out on the floor naked. He rushed to him, sure it was just his luck that his new neighbor was dead. But once at John's side, he could see his slow, deep breathing. He looked at the old man's body and then looked away, shuddering at the knobby, twisted protrusions of knee, elbow, and shoulders, the sagging flesh and age spots, all the markers of decay.

At least the old man came by it honestly. Barbara hadn't been so lucky. By the time they'd harvested the golden beets in late June, she could barely get out of bed. The doctor didn't know why the rheumatoid arthritis hit. She said the worst cases often were sudden onset like Barbara's and could be caused by a physical or emotional shock. Barbara stared at Pete when she heard that last part. He looked out the window, his back to her, but her reflection jutted straight out at him like a fistful of guilt.

The golden beets were beautiful. Too beautiful. Everybody ex-claimed about them, but hardly anybody bought them. Every Wednesday, Pete hauled out a batch that had gone soft in the store and hauled in a new batch straight from the ground. He worked bushels of rotten beets into the compost heap the first few times, but after that he dug a trench a hundred feet behind the store and buried them all at once whenever he got a waist-high mound. He hated working with the rotting vegetables and he alternately cursed Barbara and muttered "I told you so's" with every shovelful of stinking beets.

While he did this, Barbara leaned on the counter inside the store, trying to take some weight off her knees and ankles, only to feel it more in her elbows and wrists. She struggled to make it to the farm stand every morning, but most days it was afternoon before she managed to get there and she didn't last long once she did. Pretty soon she couldn't even make it for a few hours. She had severe anemia, a constant low-grade fever, and enough weight loss so that her thickening, twisted joints made her look more a tuber than a woman. Pete couldn't look her in the eye. It was really that simple—that clear-cut to him. She had help in the form of her sisters and nieces. There was no reason to stay. In August Pete buried the last of the golden beets. It seemed as good a time as any to pack his things.

Barbara was sleeping when he went in to say good-bye. He talked to her quietly. He thought he saw her face relax and expand as he spoke, softness replacing the straight edge of her features, like a vacuum pack just opened. His absence would give Barbara some peace, though he didn't suppose anybody would congratulate him for it. No matter—he knew it was time to leave.

Frank Magnus said you could tell time by the geese. He told Pete all about them at the Pigeon Bowl one afternoon in early October. He said that on any given day after the tenth of October, you could pack a lunch and stop alongside the fields and watch the snow geese and blue geese glide in and feed on the remnants of corn left in the fields along Route 52. They were on their way from the Arctic Circle down to Mexico. They stopped in Mayville and rested and fed for a week or two.

"Did you know that a goose flying four thousand feet high in the sky can see for seventy-seven miles?" Frank poured Pete another draft.

"Hard to believe a goose with that much to choose from would zero in on Mayville."

"Well, most other places probably aren't so hot either."

The Festival of the Geese was Mayville's big chance. With the first festival a few years before, Mayville attempted to draw the city folks in from the fancier lakeside resort towns, and it had worked pretty well. Last year five hundred visitors came into town during a two-week period, and that wasn't counting babies who couldn't walk yet, Frank said, though most of the tourists stayed a day at most. Since that first festival, Mayville had opened a few unconvincing imitations of city life—the Second Cup where a *glass* of coffee ground fresh from stale beans cost two dollars, and a gift shop that sold twenty-dollar pottery bowls too small to hold a cup of soup. It didn't take visitors long to realize there was nothing much to Mayville.

But come that October, at what should have been the height of the tourist season bringing seventy-five new faces into Mayville every day, the merchants on Main Street were up in arms. The geese were dying. The fields where they usually gathered to bob for corn had turned into stinking graveyards. Pete first heard about it when he was at Judy's Nip and Tuck getting a trim on Saturday morning and then later that afternoon when he stopped for a few beers at the Pigeon Bowl. He left the bar after hearing three versions of how the geese were dying. Lily Hamlin said they had bullet holes through the backs of their heads; Frank said they were losing their feathers; and as Pete left, a tourist from Chicago piped up, though nobody asked him, and said it was poison.

Pete drove John's truck home. He'd more or less taken it over since his own truck had died for good two weeks ago. He still *parked* John's truck at John's place, but he used it whenever he wanted. It worked out just fine as far as Pete was concerned. He took John to the grocery store and to church on Sunday.

Pete went to see the dead geese for himself the next day after Mass at St. Luke's. He waited for John in the parking lot during the service. Sitting quietly, coffee and donut in hand, staring at the blacktop was religion enough for Pete. He'd had his fill of church when he was a boy. Said enough prayers, or pretended to, back then to keep himself covered for the rest of his life as near as he could figure—assuming God kept track of that kind of thing. His mother was always dragging him to church, urging him to pray against one thing and for another. She held out prayer as a shield against everything she was afraid of, good reason or bad.

His father had usually been working when his mother took Pete to church. That's what his father did. He'd been a Detroit City cop. Pete remembered the summer of 1967 when his father had worked a crime-ridden precinct on the west side during the riots. All that summer, even before the city trouble began in late July, Pete watched his father's face turn more rigid and unwavering, his already hardened jaw gone steely. His father had been mad for a long time at everything he saw in Detroit—the busted-up businesses, his son laughing and fooling around and watching too much TV, his own wife's cloying prayers for his safety—the summer heat and the riots just brought it all out. He didn't do anything about it—he never hollered or hit—he just got quieter and stiller, like the piece of petrified wood Pete studied in science class. His father and mother moved around each other without so much as brushing shoulders. No doubt about it, their marriage was bad. The way Pete saw it, even back then, his mother should have left. Or his father. But they just stayed put, miserable together. Neither one would leave.

So Pete did. The very next summer, he took a Greyhound up to Traverse City in northern Michigan and worked the cherry harvest. He was sixteen and he was glad to be out of Detroit. Glad to be out of his parents' house. He didn't distinguish one from the other. They were both places where a riot or worse could blow up or brew without you even noticing until you were dodging bricks or bullets or going out of your mind from the stock-still misery. Why stay for any of that?

After Traverse City, Pete moved to an uncle's farm in the fertile middle of the state. And once he was eighteen and finished with high school, he moved around some more, going all over Michigan. He painted dry-docked boats in the Upper Peninsula, built houses in the resort towns that lined the lake in the northern part of the Lower one, drove a snowplow in Kalamazoo, and climbed telephone poles for Ameritech in Grand Rapids. He took any job he could do outside. Outside where silence settled, instead of suffocated. But he never moved from Michigan, unwilling to leave a state whose very shape he took as a sign of comfort, a promise that if he just stayed within its mittened borders, against all evidence to the contrary, he'd somehow end up okay.

Sitting in the church parking lot waiting for John that Sunday morning, Pete realized the dead geese probably had a different opinion on how comfortable and friendly the state of Michigan was. He looked out the window of the pickup and saw Frank and a satin-cloaked priest coming out of the church. They each had an arm wrapped around John, and Pete could see that they gripped him tightly as if they were worried John would run away. That didn't seem likely to Pete since John clutched the priest's robe with both hands. Pete stepped out of the truck and, after setting his coffee on the hood, walked to meet them.

"He won't let go of Father Jaspers's robes. He ran up on the altar during communion. He wanted Father to hear his confession right there. We thought maybe he'd listen to you, Pete." Frank unwound his arm from John's shoulder as he spoke.

"What is it your father has son? Is it Alzheimer's?" Father Jaspers had also loosened his grip on John's shoulders. He stroked John's hands as he spoke.

The priest looked to be Pete's age, and Pete looked around,

confused for a second, "No, uh no. He's not my father. He's just a friend. I don't know what's going on. You think he *has* something?"

"Well, if he doesn't have family to care for him, you should take him to a doctor. Not that there's much they can do in these cases, but try County Hospital in Littleton. They have a geriatric service."

"He has family, I think. I just run errands for him and give him a ride sometimes."

"Well, it's a good thing you're doing—caring for him."

"I'm not caring for him." Pete stepped back, waving his arms, and bumped into the truck, knocking his coffee off the hood. It splashed on his shoes. "Like I said, I just give him a ride sometimes."

Father Jaspers pried John's hands loose and pressed them into Pete's as if he were making an offering. "Just make sure he sees a doctor." As soon as the priest turned his back, Pete let go of John's hands. John didn't protest, but walked to the driver's side and searched his pockets carefully for the keys until Pete realized what he was doing and pointed to where they dangled in the ignition.

John didn't start the truck right away, but turned to Pete instead. "You're a good friend to me. You can just have this truck. I like driving it now and again, but I don't need it much anymore. I'll just borrow it when I do." John turned the key in the ignition. Nothing happened.

"Well, that's really nice of you John, but it's your truck. I couldn't do that. I'll tell you what. I'll save up and buy it from you. You can give me a good price—something way better than blue book. But for now, let's just keep it like it is. If that's okay with you, I mean." Pete pointed, "Use the clutch if you want it to start," and then offered his hand so they could seal the deal.

John shook it, "Pleased to meet you." The truck lurched, "Let's go see the geese."

John drove on the wrong side of the road much of the way down the two-lane Green Arrow Highway, and though he tried,

Pete couldn't stop him. When other cars came speeding toward them, John put on his turn signal and after checking carefully, changed lanes, while Pete screamed, "John, what the hell are you doing. You're going to get us killed." When Pete grabbed the wheel, saving them from a scrape with a slow-going tractor, John started to hiccup violently and pulled up on the left shoulder, no longer interested in the road.

They were still a quarter mile from the fields on Route 52 when Pete took over, joining a long line of cars waiting to see the geese. They idled behind a Saab with Illinois plates. A little girl, her hair held off her face with a green satin bow bigger than her head, looked out the back window and made faces at them.

The geese's resting grounds ran along either side of Route 52, a couple of acres each, four on each side of the road. As Pete approached heading north, he could see that the first two fields were spotted with large brown and gray geese, grazing on the remnant kernels from the summer harvest. Pete and John watched the geese for a while and then walked a hundred feet over to join the crowd that had gathered along the edge of the northernmost field on the east side of the road.

This field of dead geese drew all the attention. People swarmed its perimeter, held back by yellow plastic tape imprinted with LAKE COUNTY SHERIFF'S DEPARTMENT and tied on either end to a broomstick planted in the field. As if to display the sheriff's incompetence, the tape ran out from each side before the ends could meet and for twenty feet in the middle a patch job of odds and ends held people back. Pete saw three blue socks, a green plaid winter scarf, a dog's leash, and a yellow plastic belt with white daisies glued to it. He looked a little farther down and saw a brown necktie tied tight to a red sock that looked like the one he had lost in the dryer at the Laundromat a few weeks earlier. It would seem like a betrayal to break such a personal barrier. The sheriff might not be so stupid after all.

As they got closer, the stench grew strong. The little girl from the Saab was standing nearby, between her mom and dad. She held her nose and hopped from one foot to the other, tugging on her mother's jacket. When Pete and John finally wormed their way through the crowd, they saw a flock of geese spread before them like a banquet.

The geese were newly dead—Pete guessed one or two days at most—their bodies bloated but intact. Soon they'd be split wide open from the sun or be ravaged by the buzzards, raccoons, owls, and foxes that would pick them clean. Pete heard an old guy he often saw at the Egg and Tuna tell a woman that the state police, the federal department of wildlife, and the Lake County sheriff were all arguing about who had jurisdiction and until they squabbled it out, they couldn't bury the geese. Then he heard somebody else say, no, the problem was they needed to autopsy all the birds.

Pete looked at a still bird a few feet in front of him. Plump and heavy-bodied, its black wings spread open to display a five-foot wing span, as if it had been caught in mid-flutter by a stun gun. Its long gray-brown neck was straight as a yardstick and it had a stripe of white just before its bill. Its size surprised Pete. A few small elevator muscles in its wings shouldn't be able to lift a bird that big. If it hadn't been for the flies clustered around every orifice—eyes, bill, rump—it could have been an Audubon picture.

The crowd shifted and rearranged itself so that the little girl from the Saab was next to Pete, almost face-to-face, as her mother held her. Her father raised a video camera and trained it on the closest mud-colored mound of dead goose. They were all looking down, but their gaze moved up as a goose flew by, hovering over the field. Its wings straight as sheet metal, it glided in for the final stretch, banking against the wind so it wouldn't somersault uncontrolled as it landed. At the last second, the goose thrust its feet forward and began braking itself with powerful wing beats until its rump bumped the ground. Oblivious to the death around it, the bird began to graze.

It ate for a few minutes, and then began to jerk and screech, arching the horny spurs of its wing shoulders as if preparing to fight. Pete watched as its left wing flapped up and down and its head thrashed from side to side, back and forth like a cellophane pinwheel in a fickle gale. Its long thin neck bore the brunt of its convulsion. It took a while for the thrashing bird to finally lay still and when it did, its neck was arranged on the ground like a question mark.

The crowd froze quiet during the bird's jerky dance, and when it was over Pete heard everything distinctly, as if the air existed only as a perfect medium for sound—the little girl, her hair swept across her face in the wind, screaming that she'd lost her green ribbon, her mother crying, John repeating over and over with a chuckle, boy oh boy that was a big one, and the sharp edge of his own breath scraping his throat.

John fell asleep on the way home, his face blank and smooth, his breathing steady. As they sped down Route 52, Pete scrunched against the driver's side door, his attention split between the road he maneuvered and a newborn suspicion of John.

Pete chopped cherry wood that afternoon, preparing for the coming winter, hoping the physical activity would blot the twisted goose from his mind. He already needed to light a fire at night and in the morning too, to absorb the cabin's chill. A hard winter would be trouble. He'd stacked four cords so far, two each of oak and maple. It would cover him if the weather weren't too bad, but it was no guarantee. The cherry was the hardest to chop into useful size, but the dense, rust-colored wood burned better than any other—slow and deep hot. It would keep him warm through the coldest weather, and he wished he had more. He had too much maple. The sugar in it made it burn fast and its heat rushed up and out instead of lingering and wrapping around the cabin. He burned maple just to get rid of it. He couldn't count on it in the winter.

Tired, Pete went to bed at ten, but at eleven he was wide awake. He got up and turned on the TV. The lousy reception didn't make the smug news anchor any easier to watch. She worked out of

Campbell—population maybe fifty thousand—but she acted as if she were Dan Rather all serious. If Barbara had been sitting next to him watching, she would have skewered her. Barbara was no bullshit, but she could spot it in others a million miles away.

He'd written Barbara last week, congratulating himself on being mature enough to let her know where he was. She wrote right back. He turned off the TV and looked at the letter again, Barbara's once fluid handwriting now edges and scrawls and hard to decipher. She was angry at him, that much was clear, scratchy writing and all.

Though I hate you for slinking away, I thank God every morning that I don't have to wake to your selfish face. Your cousin called looking for you yesterday and she said it's probably all your mother's fault you ran off because she spoiled you rotten, you being an only child. I told her that no amount of explaining or excusing could convince me that we are not each responsible for exactly what we do, you included, even if she thinks your shit don't stink. She hung up on me, thank God again. I need no Flattes in my life.

It just didn't seem to him they'd been together long enough for her to hate him so. And besides, if she were right, it only seemed fair to let him explain, to turn on a light so that everyone could see why he'd done what he'd done. He tried to think of all the reasons he could give Barbara or her sisters or anybody else who wondered why he left, but all he could remember of those months right before and after she got sick was how hard it was to look at her. Nothing else came easy to mind, and in the void he saw the crooked goose in the field not knowing what hit it.

He heard a noise and went to his window, looking across the road to John's, relieved that here in Mayville, somebody else caused all the ruckus. He heard John's screen door slap shut and then saw John, buck naked again, get into the pickup and back out the drive. He ran out to stop him, but John sped off before Pete even made it to the road. When he finally fell asleep an hour later, John still hadn't returned.

Pete woke early and looked out the window, worried about John and wanting to use his truck to go into town for breakfast. He saw the pickup, dent-free from a distance—a good sign. He had a cup of instant coffee and then walked across the road. He knocked and hollered for a few seconds and then walked in on tiptoe, holding his breath, not sure what he'd see, but knowing what he'd rather not. He breathed easy when he saw John swaddled in a blanket, stretched full out on the living room floor. Knowing the late night he'd had, Pete didn't try to wake him, but took the truck and left a note saying he'd be back soon.

When he walked into the Egg and Tuna, Francine, the morning waitress, and all the customers got real quiet. After Pete ordered his eggs over hard and skirt steak rare, a uniformed state cop pulled up a chair to his table.

"Morning, sir." The officer took off his hat and set it on top of the *Mayville Weekly* that Pete read.

"Morning, officer." Pete thought fast about what he'd done wrong lately and relaxed when he came up blank.

"What's your name?"

"Pete Flatte, and yours?"

The man ignored his question, "You've been in Mayville a couple of months I hear?"

"That's right. Nice town."

"You drive that red Chevy truck outside?"

"It's my neighbor's, but he's old and I take it and do his errands and such for him. My truck died."

"You know the geese along Route 52 are dying too. Left and right."

"I heard that. I even went to see them yesterday."

"You know what's killing them?"

"Can't say I do. Probably toxic waste from that nuclear plant up in North Haven. Kind of makes you wonder what it's doing to us, doesn't it?"

"Normally, it might. But you see I've been in those fields and I'll tell you something funny, they're full of cornflakes. And when I swept up a bunch of those flakes and sent them on to the lab in Littleton, they tell me those flakes are full of arsenic."

"No kidding? Well, I guess funny is one word for it."

"And then, Mr. Flatte, this morning I get a call from a Mrs. Mary Louise Urnich and she says that she's driving by the fields late last night and she sees a red Chevy pickup parked along the side. She slows down to see if it's somebody who needs help, but the truck is empty so she just keeps on, but then she started to wonder about the geese, so she called me this morning."

"Really? Did she get a license plate number so you could trace it?"

"Well, that's funny, too, because she noticed that the plate was covered with mud, just like it is on the red truck outside. That's a violation, you know."

"I'll have to wipe that off. There's a lot of muddy red Chevys on the roads out here—I wouldn't want anybody thinking my neighbor's truck was the cause of any trouble. I'll fix that right after my breakfast. That about all you wanted, officer?"

"For now. But you be careful. I'll be watching you."

"Well, that's a real comfort. I'll make sure I look my best."

Pete leafed through the paper, not seeing a word, as he finished eating his breakfast. Keen to get back and talk to John, he chewed each bite ten times, not wanting to give anyone the satisfaction of seeing him hurry. After he'd paid the bill and left fifteen percent and an instant lottery ticket for Francine, he walked out to the truck and using the newspaper he'd just pretended to read, wiped the back plate clean. He glanced in the truck bed, before he bent down to do this, realizing he was a cornflake away from being arrested, but it was swept clean. Driving home, he cursed the Flatte luck that had brought him a crazy, naked, goose-killing neighbor. He shifted smoothly into fifth, opening the Chevy up as he cruised along the Green Arrow. He sure had a nice truck, though.

When Pete pulled up in front of his cabin, John was sitting on the front steps with a woman. She was about forty, Pete figured, though it was hard to tell for sure as all her features sank into excess flesh that enveloped any wear and tear. The woman stood up, no easy feat. "I'm Julie Gerlach, John's daughter from over in Campbell. I see you've got my father's truck."

"Well, yes. I use it once in a while to run errands and such. You know, to help John out. Hey, I'm really pleased to meet you, by the way. I didn't know John had a daughter. My name's Pete Flatte."

"So, what errands did you run for my father this morning?"

Her eyes may have narrowed as she spoke, but Pete wasn't sure, they were already so small compared to the rest of her face. "Well, actually, I didn't do much *this* morning. John didn't need anything. Listen, your dad is a great guy. I really like having him for a neighbor. He's kind of strange sometimes, but I deal with that."

"He's not *strange*, Mr. Flatte. He's senile."

"Call me Pete, please. I didn't know for sure, though I supposed it was something like that. Should I put on coffee?"

John, off to the side, counting the logs in Pete's half cord of cherry wood, hollered yes while Julie shook her head no, her flesh following the movement a beat late, as if it had a mind of its own.

"No, I don't have time. Actually, I came to meet you because my father mentioned you a few times, and I want to ask a favor."

"Anything I can do, I will."

"He's been driving the truck at night. He'll show up at my house at three in the morning. He shouldn't be out at that time. And I'm worried about his driving."

"Plenty to worry about there."

"Anyway, I figured if you're handy with cars . . . ?"

"I am," Pete nodded.

". . . that you could do something to the truck—something simple so it won't start when he tries to leave."

Pete thought for a minute, watching John at the woodpile. John's tie was straight, and the pants of his seersucker suit were sealed against his shins in the wind, which had a bite to it. He shouldn't still be in seersucker in October. He'd have to check John's closet for warmer clothes.

"That doesn't seem right to me, Miss Gerlach. I don't want to play tricks on your father, even if he is senile. If you have something to tell him, it should be flat out to his face."

"It's only for a few weeks. My daughter is moving back from Gainesville, and she and her husband are planning to buy the truck when they get here."

John walked away from the woodpile, and as he came up behind Julie, he stopped and pointed at her rear, "Look at the boot on that woman. How's she fit that boot in a chair?"

Pete took Julie's cue and pretended not to hear, though he had to choke back a laugh. "Now that's another problem. See, John wanted to give the truck to me, but I knew I couldn't let him do that, so we made a deal. I'm buying it from him."

Julie turned to her father, "Is that so, Dad? You know Pammy wants that truck. You said you'd give her a good deal on it. Did you tell him he could buy it too?"

John smiled and nodded, "Oh yes, there are too many things these days. Too many. Can't keep track of them all. Too many. I remember when we used to go fishing."

Julie turned back to Pete, "Listen, I'm sorry about what he may have told you, but as you can see he doesn't know what he's saying half the time."

"Well, he said it during the other half."

"I'm his legal guardian, Mr. Flatte."

"Then you should be taking better care of him. I can't be with him all the time. I didn't even know he had a family for sure— you should be coming by more often. Seems to me you just abandoned him. And now all you want is the damn truck."

"You're the one who's been driving the damn truck all over the damn town—don't think I haven't heard about it. And don't presume to judge. If you're taking such good care of him, why is he living on cereal and coffee cake?" She turned back to John before

Pete could answer. "Come on, Dad, I'm going to make you a healthy lunch before I go home."

John followed her across the road and Pete heard him all the way. "That's one big boot for a woman. Biggest boot I've ever seen." Pete laughed.

After that, Pete vowed to watch John more carefully. When John's light went on after midnight the next night, Pete ran over and climbed into the bed of the truck. He stayed down flat so John wouldn't notice him if he came out for a drive. Sure enough, he did, starting the truck with a lurch.

He paid attention to the turns, though he figured John was heading toward his own private killing fields on Route 52—Pete lay next to a shovel, a five-gallon paint bucket marked POISON, and a half dozen boxes of cornflakes. He looked up at the sky as John drove, the stars staying constant as the truck hurtled along the Green Arrow.

It would be the same clean backdrop for stars that he and Barbara had looked at together on the night of their wedding party. She'd invited everybody who came into the farm stand. Pete hadn't wanted a party at all. They'd gone to the county JP in Littleton to take care of the legal part—no muss, no fuss—just I do, I do. But Barbara had shushed him when it came to the celebration, "You got your way about not having a church wedding. Now I get mine. After all, I'm never going to be able to do this again, am I?" She'd wiggled her slender fingers, the diamond chip that she'd picked out from the Service Merchandise catalog lost in a weak stream of light from the sun. Five months later, Barbara's cousin Ginny, who owned a jewelry store, finally forgave Pete for not ordering the wedding ring from her, and came over with her jeweler's tools to cut the ring off Barbara's twisted, swollen finger.

But the day of their wedding party, Barbara's long, limber fingers wrapped around a cold beer as Pete stood next to her, one arm around her shoulders, the other stretched wide in a mine-this-is-all-mine pose as he pointed out the boundaries of the farm to his second cousin Billy. The band began to play "In-A-Gadda-Da-Vida" just then, and Pete swooped Barbara over to the plywood dance floor they'd pieced together in front of the barn that morning. They held each other tight, hips locked and swaying, for all seventeen minutes of the song.

When the guests left that night, he and Barbara walked out to the south hay field and, lying on their backs, looked up at the sky. They'd made love in the field—Barbara laughing, saying how lucky he was, how most women expected the honeymoon suite— Barbara as nice and easy in bed or a hay field as she was careful and hardworking out of it. But it was after the sex, when they looked up together, that Pete felt closer to her than ever before. He thought the night sky held everything good.

He could tell Barbara felt it, too, because she was quiet and calm and held his hand lightly as if it were something that could be hurt if she touched it even a little too hard. Neither said a thing for a long time. They had been happy together then. He missed that.

The truck jolted to a stop. He'd lost track of where they were, thinking about Barbara. Pete sat up slowly, not looking forward to seeing the dead geese again, holding his breath against the smell. But when he turned to face the front of the truck, it teetered on a forty-foot bluff of piled-high sand, and Lake Michigan stretched out before him.

They'd probably sink before they'd fly off, but Pete got the willies, climbed out carefully, and ran to the driver's side window. John raised his hand in greeting and said, as if they'd been having a conversation all along, "Hey son, I've been thinking. Your mother needs a vacation. I'm going to take her to Cuba next week."

Pete urged John out of the truck and sat down next to him on the bluff. And then sick of dancing around everything, just wanting to clean up the mess, he asked John directly, "You've been poisoning those geese, haven't you, John?"

"Too many. Can't keep track."

"Jesus, John, this is big. Senile or not, you could get in a lot of trouble."

"The mark of a real man, son, is that he means what he does."

Pete turned and put his hands on John's shoulders, "John, listen to me."

"Or maybe I'll take your mother somewhere quiet. She deserves some peace of mind."

"John, they're just birds. What did they ever do to you?"

"The trick is to feel the rhythm of the water and the air. If you listen closely, your fly will skitter to the fish."

"John, the geese?" Pete willed clarity on him. And in that moment, he saw a sliver of understanding in John's eyes, but it passed almost instantly, leaving no mark but sadness. When John began to cry, Pete let him alone at first. But after a minute, he took John's hand and put his arm around his shoulder.

They drove off a while later after talking some more and looking out at the lake and up at the stars. John wasn't making any sense, but his ramblings were nice and easy that night, all about the tropics and fishing. Pete took the wheel when they left, and John, his face worn out with crying, fell asleep even as Pete gunned it and backed away from the bluff.

He stopped the truck slowly, after driving only a few miles, hoping that the change in motion wouldn't wake John. He got out and took the shovel and bucket of poison from the truck bed. He left the cornflakes, no need to waste good cereal. He walked twenty feet into the woods on the side of the road. Tree roots fought his shovel all the way as he dug, but he didn't stop until he'd buried the poison three feet under.

He skipped the turnoff for the Green Arrow on the way home and drove by the geese fields on Route 52 instead. The sun, just rising, shone on a long length of green satin ribbon—an addition to the sheriff's makeshift barrier. Pete watched as the ribbon wafted in the breeze, softly brushing the neck of the goose beneath it, too late to comfort.

PATCH

Sarah removed her gloves and leaned against the tin wall of the ice rink at Heilmann Park, watching from the top row of bleachers as her daughter, Janey, glided out to her patch. Toe pick jutting, Janey etched a crosshatch four times in the ice, north-south-east-west, readying her small circle for the movements—inside edges to out, outside to in, open mohawks, pivots, three-turns right and left—that she'd repeat for the next hour. Janey didn't look up and wave, but then she'd barely said a word to Sarah on the way over, instead staring out the car window, shoulders hunched. Sarah hadn't pushed for conversation. Things were easier when Janey ignored her.

It was only seven in the morning, and already a half dozen skaters were on the ice engraving their temporary marks in the Zambonied sheen. Janey often complained that she hated Patch, during which each skater moved only within an assigned circle, ten feet in diameter, practicing figures and edges over and over, always alone, never gathering speed. The slowness, the precision—the point.

Sarah wasn't fond of it either, especially on Monday mornings when Patch started another week with a chill. She'd been dutifully carting Janey to Patch since Sam died four months ago. She wasn't a morning person. It was a trip Sam had always made, which was just another entry on the long list of ways life was less without him. He had embraced the morning. That he was with Janey made it even better, he'd said. They'd always spent plenty of time together. He hadn't been an uninvolved father. He hadn't needed a deathbed conversion to appreciate their daughter.

The arena was quiet though more than a dozen young girls, all members of the Fast Track advanced skating club, and their coaches, speckled the ice. Murmurs of muted instruction, the scrape of a blade's edge, the girls' intermittent diligent sighs were the sounds of Patch. Earliness aside, Sarah liked the careful fit of sound to figure. It anesthetized her.

After school, this same group of skaters would return to swirl and glide and jump through freestyle practice, charging the air with whoops and determination as, skirts fluttering and taut legs extended, they stroked hard to pick up backward speed in an effort to leap high enough to land solid and to spin with such tight control it would be mistaken for abandon. All these grand gestures were built on the monotonous foundation of Patch.

Sarah's cold hands were numb to the lukewarm watery coffee from the vending machine in the lobby. She didn't reach for her gloves though, this being part of her ritual penance for all the wrongs she'd done Sam—the expected ones that come of living with someone for fifteen years—and the bigger one that came as he died.

Another mother waved from below. Sarah pretended not to see, but the woman climbed toward her anyway, breath short on arrival. "Morning Sarah." Sarah raised her hand, barely. The woman, undaunted, continued, "We're organizing a bake sale to help the rink raise money for a new sound system. Could you bring cookies or brownies next Saturday?" Sarah stared at the line of the

woman's bangs, which inclined slightly over her right eyebrow.
"Sarah?"

"I'm sorry. What did you say?"

"The bake sale. Next Saturday. Will you contribute something?"

"Uh. I'm awfully busy at the store. I'll have to see."

"If you decide you can, just drop something off in the lobby
here by nine in the morning." She sidestepped down a row and
then turned back. "Do you have anything special planned for Janey
today?"

"Special?"

"Dinner out? A movie? Megan," the woman pointed to a blue
lycra leotard on the ice, "said Janey didn't want a party this year,
which I understand with her dad and all. How could you top that
scavenger hunt Sam put together for the kids last year?"

"You couldn't." Sarah struggled to pin down the date and settled on March twenty-fourth, which meant it was Janey's ninth
birthday. She'd meant to remember. Had seen the day coming a
week ago as she paid bills, staring at columns of numbers in her
checkbook and trying to find a mistake in her math that would
amount to something positive. But she'd forgotten after all, which
at least explained Janey's burrow of silence that morning. She
looked down at the woman again. "We're keeping things quiet this
year."

The woman reached up and laid a hand on Sarah's arm, "I
understand. Megan bought Janey a gift anyway. If you ever need
to talk . . ." Sarah stared at the hand, willing it away until, finally,
the woman turned and navigated the stretch of bleachers back to
the other mothers, all of them clustered in groups of three or four,
each pretending not to watch her own daughter—extravagantly
praising the precise, glimmering lines of the other girls, while secretly preferring those chiseled by her own.

From the first time she'd accompanied Janey to Patch, Sarah
had sat apart. At first, she pretended the others stayed away, didn't

approve of her. Because her hair was too gray to be so long and straight. Because she wore T-shirts and workboots. Because she made her living collecting and selling junk. Because she and Sam had never married, had just been partners in business and life and Janey.

Truth was, she didn't want to sit with them. Most of them were too young to look so matronly. Sitting together in the bleachers, carefully groomed in soft-colored shirts and socks that matched, chattering about minutiae, they looked like eggs at Easter, pastel-colored and bottom heavy. Sarah didn't want their gossipy friendship, their compliments on Janey's skating, or their curiosity and condolences about Sam's cancer and death. She'd sit near Angeline in the afternoon at freestyle, but Angeline wasn't a mother, and, despite her age, she was really more Janey's friend than Sarah's.

When Patch ended that morning, Janey skittered off the ice and wobbled to the locker room while Sarah edged down to talk to her coach. "Mark, do you have a minute?"

"Sure. Janey's doing great, Sarah. She's been very focused. It's a big improvement. Next session we'll work on landing her doubles consistently. That starts Wednesday, you know. I saved a spot for Janey, but you need to sign the consent form and write a check today or tomorrow."

"I'm not enrolling her in the next session."

"You're kidding. Doesn't she want to skate?"

"No, it's not that. She loves it. We . . . I can't afford it."

"Sarah, I'm not making any promises, but Janey is special. She's strong, she works hard, and best of all, she's fearless—lots of girls look good out there, but they're scared when they jump and that only gets worse as they get older. Janey's a little reckless. She doesn't worry about mistakes. That's good. We want to cultivate that. You couldn't have picked a worse time to stop."

"Could we work out some kind of payment plan?" Sarah looked over his shoulder at a red glove that somebody had dropped at center ice.

"If it were up to me, that would be fine. But I don't make the rules here, and Fast Track has a waiting list a yard long. Maybe you can reprioritize your finances. This is important to Janey."

"I made twenty-three dollars last weekend. There's nothing to reprioritize." Sarah dug her hands into her pockets. "Why am I telling you this? This is none of your business."

"I'm sorry, Sarah. I just don't want to lose Janey."

Janey walked up behind him then, lugging her skating bag, pink and yellow striped and almost as big as she was, the main zipper only half shut, a purple skate guard sticking up out of it and jabbing her arm with every step, a skate lace trailing from a side pocket. Sarah grabbed her mittened hand, "Close up your bag honey, before everything falls out. And let's get going before you're late for school again."

Once in the truck, Sarah turned to Janey, "So, how does it feel to be nine?"

"Who told you?" Janey dug through the pockets of her skating bag while she spoke, still not looking at Sarah.

Sarah didn't pretend. "Megan's mom. Honey, I'm sorry. I'll make it up to you. We'll do something special. Just the two of us."

"It's always just the two of us, Mom."

"Well, invite somebody along."

"Where would we go?"

"I don't know. Maybe we could have a picnic at Belle Isle on Saturday. You could ask Angeline."

"She's working weekends now—she's saving for a car."

"Well, ask somebody else, Janey."

"It's too cold for a picnic."

Sarah pulled up in front of Janey's school. "I'm sorry about your birthday. We'll celebrate tonight, after skating."

Janey jumped out and left the truck door open wide behind her. Sarah strained a muscle reaching over to pull it shut.

The junk store was closed on Mondays, so after she dropped off Janey, Sarah picked the alleys on the east side of Detroit searching for trash-buried treasure. This had always been her favorite part of the job. Sam had liked it too, but he was equally drawn to the warmth of the trade—talking to customers, rearranging stock, swapping stories with other dealers about the garage sale finds they'd made. He'd owned the store at 7 Mile and Kelly for a year when Sarah met him there, and for her thirtieth birthday, when they'd been together for five years, he changed the name from Sammy's Fine Finds to Sammy and Sarah's. When businesses around them began to close up and relocate in Sterling Heights and Southfield, Sam and Sarah decided together to stay, to hold on to their little patch of Detroit for whatever it was worth.

They weren't thinking money—they knew it was worth little of that. It was more the idea of committing to the place where they'd both grown up, a place most people didn't see much value in. Detroit had become a city you leave. It would have been easy enough to abandon it for suburbs north or west, for Chicago, for someplace warmer, for almost anywhere else. But it meant something to them both to stay.

That decision made, they found pleasure in their neighborhood in spite of the changes and then because of them. They watched as old neighbors, retired white folks who'd raised families there twenty, thirty, forty years ago, moved out in part because they didn't see that the Blacks and Arabs who'd become their neighbors just wanted to do the same. They watched as younger families moved in, hopeful and glad to be there, their frame of reference completely different from that of the people they replaced, so that house-by-house the atmosphere changed. And Sarah and Sam felt lucky to have stayed put.

On a practical level too, all that moving in and out was good for Sammy and Sarah's. People lost perspective when they moved. Tired of packing and lifting and cleaning and hauling, they left behind perfectly fine chairs and lamps and books and utensils. And when they did, Sarah and Sam were there to gather up their mistakes.

From the start, they'd both been attracted to the landscape of junk. Not everyone is. They weren't in the business for the money, though they always made as much of that as they needed, and a little more. Their satisfaction came in seeing the tableau that people cobbled together to announce their presence in the world. With Sam at her side, Sarah saw the things people owned, then discarded, as little bits of hope on display, and she felt glad for them as she collected their proof of change made. Alone, she read it another way, seeing them as blind and mistaken, blaming the things in their homes for the holes in their lives.

With Sam gone, she split her time between stocking and selling, doing neither as well as she needed to, relying more and more on the suppliers who pulled up in the alley behind the store, truck beds teetering with towers of rust-stained appliances straining against yards of twine that held them in place, or shopping carts piled high with stuff that even she couldn't envision as anything other than junk.

And though she told herself to be patient, told herself that this was still transition time since Sam's death, Sarah worried more each day about the spareness of her life. Every month she let something else go—fresh flowers in January, dinner out in February, now skating. They were trickling down to poor, edging closer to desperate. Without Sam, she couldn't make it work.

She pulled up next to a row of Dumpsters behind a line of nondescript, 1960s, blond brick apartment buildings on Whittier. The backside of the apartments had wrought iron gates painted white and guarding second-floor doors that were just for display, not opening to any balcony, a decoration to augment the view from the alley. A pile of discarded furnishings and battered boxes leaned against the brick wall of one building. Sarah lifted a full-length mirror, the backing ripped and the plastic frame cracked, onto the truck bed. She could get a couple of dollars for it. She threw in a dish drainer that might bring fifty cents. She dug through a box of tangled costume jewelry and broken baubles, and found a keychain that made her think of Angeline. It was a miniature convertible with a woman at the wheel, glamorous in sunglasses and scarf, the plastic and paint only slightly chipped. She put it in her pocket.

She moved on to the Dumpster then, shoving aside a half-dozen surface trash bags, swearing because she'd forgotten her gloves. She took infrequent shallow breaths to keep the stink out of her lungs. She dug toward a swatch of bright green, and was rewarded for the effort when she extracted a Flags of the World collection in its original box. It was clean and almost complete. Each flag, rolled tight around its staff, was about the size of a paperback when unfurled and had its country's name stamped on it in gold. And though the red in Italy had faded in streaks, Greece was tattered around its sky blue edges, and Canada and Pakistan were missing, it would do just fine as a birthday gift for Janey.

Sarah drove on down the alley. She needed to keep at it all day. But by noon, with the truck bed only a quarter full, she crept home to bake a cake for Janey. Instead, she fell asleep in the rocking chair and woke a few hours later, shivering for the afghan that had slipped from her shoulders. She rushed out the door with just enough time to pick up Janey from school and deliver her to the rink again.

Angeline arrived about fifteen minutes into freestyle and climbed toward Sarah. They'd known each other for almost a year. They'd met just days before Sam was officially diagnosed, though by that time, Sarah and Sam knew it was something serious, knew the doctor was closing in on naming the thing that had tired him for months. Sam came home from an appointment that afternoon and said the doctor had only one more test to go. He put on the tea kettle for himself, opened a beer for Sarah, and then he laid it out plain.

"Doctor Miller wants to do a biopsy."

"Of what? What does she think is wrong?"

"My liver. She sees a mass on the MRI. It could just be a cyst, blocking a bile duct, which is serious. Or it could be worse. Cancer, maybe."

Sarah took a long swallow of beer and stepped back, realizing that if Sam were sick, she'd always remember this as the moment her buoyant force began to fail her—the weight she displaced in the world no longer equal to that she needed to keep afloat. Then, scared by his news and even more by her dispassion, she went to him and led him to the rocking chair where she rubbed his shoulders until the tea kettle squealed for relief and woke them to the fact that they'd forgotten about Janey.

Sarah, needing to move, rushed to the rink while Sam waited at home by the phone in case Janey called. When Sarah arrived, she found Janey sitting in the lobby with Angeline, drinking soda and laughing.

Sarah ran to her, "Honey, I'm so sorry. Your dad and I got mixed up." Angeline hung back, head down, while Sarah hugged her daughter.

Sarah held on to Janey, even though she started to squirm, while trying to judge Angeline's intentions by her appearance. She looked to be twenty or so. Wand thin, she wore a bright green parka and dark blue plastic boots with fake fur trim. An orange headband hung around her neck and red mittens were stuffed in her pocket. She looked like a kindergarten kid, all her colors in competition. Her stringy blond hair was pulled back tightly, exposing plump ropey veins on her temples, the only thing about her that carried any weight.

She looked familiar and Sarah realized she'd seen her just the week before, from a distance. She'd stood alone at the short end of the oval of ice, where no parents perched, her face pressed to the Plexiglas rink guard, her features marred by the hockey-scratched barrier. Some of the parents had complained about her to the rink manager. About how she watched the girls too closely. About how there must be something wrong with someone who had nothing better to do. Sam had told Sarah all this just a few days before and added that he thought her harmless. But at such close range, Sarah needed to be sure. "Are you okay, Janey?" Angeline looked up then, nervously,

Sarah thought, and she pulled Janey closer, "Janey, tell me the truth—are you okay?"

"I'm fine, Mom. This is Angeline. She watched me skate and then she bought me a 7-Up."

Sarah extended her hand over Janey's shoulder, "I'm Sarah Luman. I think I've seen you here before. Do you skate?" Angeline stepped closer. She smelled of butterscotch and Sarah smiled, though she meant to look stern.

"Oh, I only wish I could. I work next door. I just watch. Janey's a good jumper."

Right from the start, their relationship, restricted to the ice arena, didn't demand close examination. Angeline shared confidences, not asking for any in return, and seemed compelled to fill empty space with talk, no matter if Sarah listened. She lived with her mother, whom she described as very religious, devout, a good woman. She also believed in God, Angeline confessed to Sarah, just not so much. She confessed other things, too, wondering out loud if her life would have been different if she could have been a skater, or one of those beauty pageant girls. But there had been no money for skating, she wasn't pretty, and, at Janey's age, she'd even been fat. "Can you imagine?" she'd asked Sarah, who looked at her fleshless face and couldn't. She'd gone to work at the Flavor Factory right next to the ice rink the day after she graduated from high school because she wasn't smart. She hated Mondays when they made strawberry. Liked Wednesday when they brewed butterscotch. She was saving her money to buy a car—a brand-new one—hoping her life would change once she got off the bus. "I want to buy a Saab. Maybe a convertible. Do you think the name is too sad?"

The day Angeline asked her this, Sarah stopped, mid-laugh, seeing she was serious, and then she felt disheartened at the thought of Angeline envying nine-year-olds and putting her faith in a car. Such meager dreams. "Saabs are awfully expensive, Angeline. Why don't you make do with a good used car. That way you could get off the bus right away. Maybe do some traveling or something exciting with the money you'd save."

"You don't understand. I don't want to just make do."

A few months after they'd met, during the beginning of the worst of Sam's illness, while Sarah struggled to keep life on track for Janey, Angeline stood at the arena door every Monday, Wednesday, and Friday at 3:30, reliable and waiting, and offering to stay with Janey during practice and bring her home on the bus afterward. Sarah never had to ask. And though she meant to, she never told Angeline how grateful she was.

Once during that time, Sarah stopped by the rink, unannounced. She'd gone to fill a prescription for Sam and the pharmacist said it would take an hour. When she entered the lobby of the rink, Sarah couldn't find Janey. Dozens of girls, readying themselves for freestyle, stretched and shouted and wedged feet into skates. She glimpsed orange and green in one corner then and moved closer to it, but still kept her distance off to the side, only watching.

Angeline knelt at Janey's feet, tightening Janey's laces, rocking her meager weight right to left as she wove the skate lace from eyelet to eyelet and then wrapped it around each hook to the top of the stiff tongue of the boot. Janey leaned forward, hands resting on Angeline's shoulders, whispering something in her ear, and then Angeline looked up and they both laughed. Once done with the laces, Angeline heaved Janey's skating bag over her shoulder and held out a hand to Janey, who pitched to a stand. Sarah studied them as they walked to the ice—Janey, an arm around Angeline's waist, rocking on her blades, and Angeline swaying with the weight of the bag. It wasn't clear who leaned on whom, but either way, Sarah noticed their complete, unsteady sync. She left that day without interrupting it.

After Sam died, Sarah went back to her old routine and stayed at the rink during afterschool freestyle. There was one change though—Angeline sat with her. Sarah didn't mind. Angeline never asked any questions about Sam's death. She never offered any heart-felt sympathy. She never suggested that Sarah cry on her shoulder or unload her sorrow. In the cold rink, there was no danger of failing Angeline. She asked for nothing, which was the only thing Sarah *could* give.

When Angeline finally arrived at the top row of bleachers and sat next to her that Monday afternoon, Janey's birthday, Sarah gave her the keychain she'd found that morning. For the next ten minutes Angeline barely watched as Janey nailed a waltz jump/toe loop combination that had given her trouble for months, intent instead on prying her keys off her old chain and moving them onto the new.

She talked while she did this. "Guess what? I picked up Saturdays at the factory. It's double time. I'm going to start looking for my car."

They both stood as Janey fell hard directly in front of them, her leg bent unnaturally to the side. But she got up quickly, stroking off before they could embarrass her with concern.

"She's such a good kid, Sarah. I hope I have a kid like Janey someday."

"You won't see her much in the next few months. I have to pull her out of skating."

"Pull her out?"

"Fast Track costs a fortune. I can't afford it. Business is lousy. But it shouldn't be for long. Summer will be here soon enough—that's always been a good season for the store."

"How does Janey feel about it?"

"I haven't told her. Not yet. I mentioned it to her coach this morning and he lectured me about my finances. He's clueless. I have to tell her tonight. Before he breaks the news tomorrow. I dread it."

"Tonight?" Angeline pointed at a loaf-shaped package wrapped in purple tissue and sticking out of her canvas bag. "But I got her a skating skirt. It's her birthday."

"You know, I'm really tired of hearing that from everyone. I think I know my own kid's birthday." Sarah heard how defensive she sounded.

"Poor Janey. She loves her skating."

"Well, it'll make her tougher. That's a good thing. She needs to learn you can't have everything you love . . ." Sarah's voice faltered, not believing a word she said, and she left Angeline to state the obvious.

"I think she already learned that."

Sarah gave Janey the Flags of the World before dinner and received lukewarm thanks. She gave her the news about skating after, and received a much more visceral response. Janey wailed—a sound more animal than human. Listening to it, before going to comfort her, Sarah envied her daughter's organic reaction. Not that she was surprised. All through Sam's illness, Janey's feelings had been consistently uncomplicated.

The day Sam was taken to the hospital, Janey stood with Sarah as the paramedics maneuvered him onto a collapsible gurney and carried him down the stairs, through the front door, and into the waiting ambulance. Janey, crying, grabbed the side of the gurney and begged them not to take her father away. Sarah pried her away with difficulty, feeling unbalanced by the agony all around her— Janey fighting her, hysterical with fear, Sam too depleted to protest.

Sam had wanted to die at home. If it didn't get too bad for her, he'd told Sarah at the start. If she could manage it, he asked in the beginning. But it did. And she couldn't. So at the end, he lay in a coma at St. John's Hospital, while she held his cold hand, trying to snake her warmth through the plastic tubes and beeping machines whose lights flashed in a medical Morse code that Sarah understood enough to read as hopeless.

She hadn't meant to fail him, but she'd lost faith in her ability to comfort him daily. In the beginning, she'd straightened his bed and read to him. Months later, as death pressed, she fed him ice chips, bathed him, and injected morphine. But all these acts were just too small to stand against death that finally hovered. She couldn't let it land in their home. She thought if Sam died in the place they'd always lived in together, she'd be left with no surface unstained by the sadness. But the sadness just seeped deeper and was sealed by her regret.

He'd deserved better. She'd never been easy to live with and love. She knew this. She guarded against big disappointments in a way that warded off good things too. But for fifteen years, Sam had loved her. He hadn't asked for more than she wanted to give, just more than she was able. At least she admitted it—she consoled herself with that whenever she had trouble keeping on. She consoled herself every day. She walked weighted.

Janey didn't. Heartbroken, angry, scared, missing Sam—she felt it, showed it, and recovered from it. Sometimes so quickly Sarah felt disappointed. But on her birthday, an hour after Sarah broke the news about skating, Janey refused comfort and, crying still, went up to her room, warning Sarah to leave her alone. When Sarah checked on her late that night, Janey sat hunched at her desk, her back to the door, duct-taping tongue depressors that she'd pilfered months ago from the hospital clinic to each of the flags in her collection so they appeared at half-mast. Her hands under the desk lamp cast deep black spots on the wall, weaving small and silent litanies of grief.

When she came down for breakfast the next morning, Janey set her skating bag like a centerpiece on the table. Flags of the world, all at half-mast, stuck like porcupine quills out of every pocket and pouch. "You were up awfully late with that." Sarah nodded toward the bag, "Janey, about skating . . ."

Janey, opening a 7-Up, cut her off, "I don't want to talk to you about that."

"What kind of breakfast is that?"

"The kind I have every day, as if you care."

"Where did you get it?"

"I bought it at the rink last night."

"Eat something else. You need fruit or cereal or something healthy in the morning, especially before you skate."

"No, I don't." Janey drained her soda with a slurp, and then plucked America from a side pocket in her bag. Walking backward, watching Sarah watch her, she ceremoniously bowed and planted the flag in the garbage pail under the sink. She dumped China in the recycling bin outside the garage as they walked to the truck, and deposited Israel in the trash can by the main door of the rink when they arrived for her last day of Fast Track. Sarah, too tired to protest, merely followed the trail her daughter left in all the foulest places.

Once inside the rink, Mark stroked right over and hockey-stopped at their feet, "Good news, ladies. You," he reached out and tweaked Janey's nose, "have been given a reprieve. Nobody wants to lose you from Fast Track, so you've been awarded the arena scholarship. You can be part of the next session."

Janey looked down at her skates, her lips pressed tight together, and when she looked up at Sarah, her eyes narrowed, as if daring her mother to inflict another lash. "Go ahead, honey. Warm up. We'll talk later."

Mark began to swizzle back, but Sarah reached for his sleeve, and drew him to her. "Not so fast. What's this all about?"

"It's great, isn't it?"

"Are you crazy? Telling me this in front of Janey? How the hell am I supposed to tell her we can't accept this."

"You're not supposed to tell her *that*."

"Where did the money come from? There's no scholarship fund here. You told me yourself there was nothing you could do."

"Anonymous donor just started it."

"Who anonymous? How did you decide so quickly that Janey gets the money? We can't be the only struggling family around here."

"Sarah, the money is for Janey. Only Janey."

"Who paid for this, Mark? Oh christ, this is insane. I know it was Angeline. Nobody else even knew. And if they did, they'd be glad to see me go." Mark dug his hands deeper into his pockets while Sarah pressed, "It was her, wasn't it?"

He swizzled backward, successfully this time, "You didn't hear that from me."

Angeline didn't show at Janey's afternoon practice. Janey hadn't said a word about the scholarship and continued, Gretel-like, to mark her trail. She dropped Poland, Turkey, and South Africa, one by one, in a Dumpster next to the schoolyard as Sarah pulled up to take her to the rink. She aimed New Zealand and Norway like missiles at a curbside trashcan while they idled at a red light. She ran ahead of Sarah when they got to the rink.

Sarah, in no great hurry to absorb more hostility, dawdled and came in ten minutes later. As she sidestepped up the bleachers, the scratchy P.A. system crackled an announcement, "Janey Luman to center ice for solo. All skaters clear for Janey Luman on center ice." It was Janey's turn to practice her three-minute program, another thing Sarah should have remembered.

Janey glided to focal point and held still waiting for the opening bars of "Winter" from Vivaldi's *Four Seasons*, music Sarah had heard almost every day for the past six months as Janey practiced the movement of her program in the confines of the house, knitting the memory of motion into muscle. It was music Sarah had gone from hating to barely hearing at high volume, even as it hung like crepe in their home.

She leaned forward in the bleachers with the first shiver of strings from the violin, and watched as Janey raised her arms to shoulder height and bent her right leg, her left extended behind, dragging on ice, until she raised it too, and began to stroke while the cello joined in, creating a dirge of sound, rain on window. And then, met by wind and cold, music and Janey were off, stroking hard, Janey's ponytail flying parallel to the ice. She two-footed the landing on her first jump, a simple waltz, to the beat of insistent cold, but, programmed to smile, this gave her no pause. Her next jump, a double lutz, something she rarely held up to, knocked her to ice while violins warned of storm. A simple single toe loop sent her sprawling, and she got up quickly, more grim than smiling now, but still stroking hard, arms extended, each finger pointing toward metal ribs of rafters, small hands open to whatever might fall.

Sarah watched, helpless, as this girl, her daughter, too young for baroque winds and sorrowful cellos of rain, fell on her last jump, too, then got up quickly, trying again but falling still, then one more attempt, and finally, successful, an axel, one-and-a-half revolutions, that ended in a layback spin whose velocity left Sarah dizzy. And as Janey bowed to the last note of music killed by the cavern of the rink, Sarah shook her head and looked away, wondering how she did it, how, alone, on ice, her daughter could rise.

Sarah used the pay phone in the lobby before they left the rink, calling directory assistance for Angeline's address. Back in the car, she and Janey drove west down 7 Mile toward Hoover and then turned south a few blocks before Mt. Olivet Cemetery, searching for Linnhurst. She wasn't sure what she'd say to Angeline when they arrived, but she was disturbed enough by her unsolicited generosity to be sure the right words would boil up. She drove slowly, looking for the street, addresses and street signs dissolving in the dropping dusk.

The box-shaped bungalows in Angeline's neighborhood were so close together, you could lean out a window and touch the neighbors' walls. Cyclone fences outlined some of the front yards, small squares of sparse lawns that didn't tempt trespassers. Janey ran ahead when they got out of the car and by the time Sarah came up the front walk, Angeline was hugging her hello. "What a surprise. Is everything okay?"

"You weren't at practice today." Sarah's statement came out an accusation and she added, "Janey was worried about you."

"No, I wasn't." Janey dropped Thailand in a pile of advertising circulars on the front porch and then walked past Angeline, though they hadn't been invited in.

They entered directly into the living room, the house demanding that all who enter get right down to business. The room, which was smaller than the front yard, was equally overprotected, with plastic covering the sofa, chairs, and lampshades. Hyper-colored crocheted covers, pink heated with orange, green muddied by brown, protected other objects—a basket full of *People* magazines, a set of coasters, a half-dozen throw pillows. The walls were decorated with religious pictures and, Sarah counted quickly, seven crucifixes. The television, housed in a casket-sized console, took up half the space in the room. A dozen plastic framed photos littered its top.

"Nice place," Sarah lied. The plastic screaked as she sat on the sofa.

Angeline pointed to a stack of brochures on top of the TV. "I was car shopping. That's why I missed skating."

"Really? Did you find your Saab?"

"Not exactly. You were right. I'll probably buy something more economical. I saw a used Ford Escort that was very nice."

"So you're giving up on the car of your dreams?" Sarah turned as she heard a noise, "Honey, don't touch those," calling Janey away from a shelf full of saltshaker-sized figurines in the dining room. Janey pulled Ireland from her bag, dropped it on the floor, and stepped on it.

Angeline shrugged, "It's just a car. It's not a dream." She turned to Janey, "It's okay. You can play with those." Janey ignored her, too, and walked to the back of the house, out of their sight.

"I thought the car was more important than that to you."

"Well it's not."

"Listen, Angeline, I know what you did, but I can't accept your gift. Even if I were inclined to, you need that money for your car."

"What gift? I didn't give you a gift."

"Don't play dumb. I know you paid for Janey's skating."

"What if I did?"

"That's not a decision for you to make."

"So you're the only one who can make a decision? Maybe I don't think your decisions are so good."

"What do you know of the decisions I've made?" Sarah, expecting indictment, moved her hands to her chest.

But Angeline only shrugged, refusing to help hurt her, "Nothing."

Sarah rose from the couch, nervous, the small room seeming even smaller, the back of her thighs sweating. She walked over to the photos on the TV console. Most of them were black-and-white and showed groups of grinning women standing in front of religious statues and dots of light from votive candles. Angeline came up behind her and pointed to the only one in color. In it, a short, old, chubby woman smiled and waved from the base of what must have been a large crucifix, since Jesus's nailed and bleeding feet rested on her head like a hat.

"That's my mother. She goes on shrine tours. She's on one now. That's the largest crucifix in the world—it's like fifty or a hundred feet tall. I don't know why she's smiling like that, after all Jesus is dead as a doornail." She stopped as Sarah breathed in deeply. "Sarah, I'm sorry, I shouldn't have said that. With Sam and all . . ." She reached for Sarah's hand.

Sarah waved her away, but she felt her weight shift to her stomach, and blood rush to her head, and then she stumbled back a bit. She picked up the photo, needing to steady herself, willing herself away from an undertow of sorrow. She stared at the picture and saw Sam instead. Saw him the way he looked before she sent him away to the hospital. His illness laying bare all that was left of him—pain and bones.

She sat on the sofa, her legs stretched out straight in front of her, all she'd lost suddenly more than she could stand. "I forgot Janey's birthday. Then I gave her a bunch of tattered flags. She hates me. I don't blame her."

Sarah closed her eyes, not wanting to look anymore, aching at the constant smallness to which she'd sentenced herself. The weight of all the wrong she'd done was displacing all the good she'd lost.

"Sarah?" Angeline sounded scared.

"Please, just leave me alone, Angeline. I can't talk now."

"I'll go make coffee. You'll be fine. Or maybe a glass of water."

Sarah closed her eyes and sat clenched, head pounding, face hot, hands cold. A minute later, she felt a sigh of air on her face and she leaned to its touch. When she felt it again, she opened her eyes to Janey who stood before her waving India with care. "Are you okay, Mom?"

Sarah shed a bit of truth. "I miss your dad so much. I just can't do anything right because of it. I'm not even taking care of you."

Janey placed India in her pocket and took Sarah's hand in both of hers, absorbing its chill. "I know."

Sarah and Janey arrived early at the rink the next morning, the first day of the new session of Patch. Sarah sidestepped to the farthest corner of the top row of bleachers and leaned back. When she heard someone approaching from a distance, she closed her eyes, feigning sleep to fend off greeting, but then changed her mind and looked up.

"Angeline? What are you doing here? Why aren't you at work?"

"I have ten minutes before I punch in. You left last night without saying good-bye."

"I was embarrassed and tired."

"It was wrong to pay for Janey without talking to you first. I'm sorry I did it."

Janey glided onto ice then, and they watched together as she began the required series of movements around her patch, some graceful, some awkward, many lovely in how simple they were, each insignificant on its own, but essential to the grand gestures she'd attempt later that day.

HERE IN CAR CITY

My family was not exactly thrilled when I bought an abandoned eight-unit studio apartment building in the middle of the city, just north of Wayne State University, and opened it as the Pensione Detroit—an inexpensive European-style hotel for students and travelers.

Even my boss Ray, the owner of the Gold Lantern Diner where I'd been working for the past year, said I was crazy. "CeAnn, let me tell you, it's not easy running a business." But Ray spent most of the day drinking and eating with friends at table 38, so I ignored him. I'd hatched the idea right there at the Gold Lantern, listening to WSU students who tied up my tables for hours skipping classes, drinking coffee, chattering about grades and sex and music, and describing the cheap, beautiful places they'd stayed in Italy, Spain, and France during their junior years abroad. That's what Detroit needs, I thought—some economical, cozy places to stay. After all, not everybody could afford the Book-Cadillac Hotel. Then I remembered, even if they could, it had gone out of business a few years ago.

I didn't tell my mother or brother what I was doing until I'd closed on the building. And I avoided telling my father at all. He was in rehab in Brighton about ninety miles away, but if he ever came back to Detroit and needed a place to stay, I didn't want him to think of me as his personal Holiday Inn.

After I wrote her about the Pensione, my mother called from Nashville where she'd moved the year before, "What the hell is a pensione?" she asked, pronouncing it like a retirement fund. "And how can you even think of buying property in Detroit? And in *that* neighborhood? Are you crazy? Even GM is moving out of there."

"They are not, Ma."

"Why yes they are. Saturn's headquarters is right up the road from me here in Nashville."

"Saturn's a cult, not a company. It doesn't count."

My brother, Dennis, who'd fled to L.A. ten years ago, was also skeptical. "Europeans purposely visiting Detroit? Well, that's a concept." But he sent me a fully equipped toolbox as a hotelwarming gift and promised to stay at the Pensione for a night when he visited at Christmas.

My mother's comment aside, I *was* living in GM country, though the wrong side of its tracks. GM headquarters squatted square on West Grand Boulevard up Woodward a quarter mile, while the Poletown Hamtramck Assembly Plant stretched out on ten acres only a couple of miles away. The Pensione Detroit, on Piquette just east of Woodward and a few blocks south of the Boulevard, had only been empty for nine months. A small, solid apartment building, it was cheap by any standard. I had some savings and I qualified for special loans and incentives for being a first-time owner in a blighted neighborhood. Buying the Pensione was not a *financial* stretch at all, but more a leap toward another way of life—any other way of life.

My block of Piquette consisted of three recent burnouts that were still standing and needed razing or at least a good board-up service, five lots where the buildings had been abandoned long enough so that grass was growing between the remains of windows and walls, two decrepit frame three-flats that seemed to house about a dozen families each, and the Pensione Detroit.

The oddest thing about Piquette? The quiet. Except for blips of activity during the day as the kids from the three-flats went to and from school, I found the neighborhood strangely still. Though I wouldn't admit it to my mother, I had been plenty worried about living in this area, but it seemed even the drug dealers and gang-bangers had given up on Piquette. Initially, I appreciated the quiet. I likened it to northern Michigan, where the lakes and dunes and birch trees created a natural serenity that settled me whenever I visited there. But it wasn't long before the quiet here in the middle of the city, its source being the rotting timber and crumbling brick of abandoned homes, made me uneasy.

One of the burned out, abandoned buildings next to the Pensione became my personal cross to bear. I was sure I'd seen rats running in and out of it. And afternoons, when I'd sit in my living room window seat to read or rest, its west wall, rubbly decaying brick, six feet from my reach, gradually blocked the good light making its way across the sky, enveloping me in a shadow that depressed me every time, though I knew it was coming, was in fact drawn to it as if my body craved a dose of daily gloom just as surely as it needed fruits and vegetables.

When I bought the Pensione, I had thought I'd be busy with interesting travelers right from the start, so I was not prepared when no one came to stay, and without the cover of a job I had to go to, I could no longer ignore how lonely I was. I called Ray after the first vacant month had passed and signed back up for work at the Gold Lantern on a limited basis—the breakfast shift on Monday, Wednesday, and Friday. This would leave me plenty of time to run the Pensione, assuming I ever had a guest.

I'd been in business two long, quiet months before my first tenant, Lodzia Szczotka, showed up on a Wednesday evening in mid-September. She screeched to the curb in a bile green '77 Monte

Carlo with a piece of red plastic tubing hanging out the back window on the driver's side.

She didn't even get out of the car. She just rolled down the front window and shouted to me where I sat on the porch. "You have rooms, I hear?" Her thick accent brought me back to my childhood when I'd struggled to make sense of my grandparents' Polish.

"Yes, yes, for only ten dollars a night."

"I need one for maybe a month. How about two hundred dollars?"

"Well, it's not really the sort of thing I can bargain on."

"Oh, you have people coming and a full house?"

I had come off the porch and stood next to her car and I moved a bit right, then left, trying to block her gaze of my quiet, vacant building. "Well, it's really just that . . ."

"Listen, lady, I'm a bird you've trapped, why beat your bushes?"

When I tried to register her moments later, Lodzia didn't have a passport or a driver's license or anything with her name printed on it except a Big Boy's Frequent Diner card. But she gave me ten rumpled twenty dollar bills that she brushed from the bottom of her purse like crumbs, and she offered me half of a stick of Juicy Fruit that had fallen out with the money.

I helped her unload her car—three large, hard-cased, Samsonite suitcases, a milk crate, and an aquarium that rested on the back floorboard, with half the water slopped out, and three garden variety goldfish flipping around in it. The red rubber tube hanging out the car window was anchored in a ceramic fish castle at the bottom of the tank. "What's this for, Lodzia?"

"I was keeping the water bubbled for my fishes. So they would stay alive until I plugged them in again. I had to drive fast on the highway—87 miles an hour—to keep the water okay."

I knocked on Lodzia's door about an hour after I'd helped her carry her things in, just to give her towels and to explain the rules of the Pensione Detroit, which I'd printed up in a large quantity on lime-green paper my first week on the job. She called for me to come in and when I did she was sitting on the floor, leaning against the bed, a drink in one hand, a picture frame in the other.

"See, my daughters," she held the picture out to me and smiled.

I saw two girls, blond like their mother, about eight and ten, sitting in a rocking chair, their dresses all stiff lace and bows, their hair tightly braided and wound round their heads like chains. They sat in front of a Sears-like backdrop of trees in autumn. "They're beautiful. Where are they?"

"In Poland, with my mother. I came here to make money to bring them over. It's better here. Too hard in Poland. I was a doctor there, but my license is no good here, they say. Here I have to take classes at the university to get licensed. So I do that and I work and soon I'll send for them all."

"It must be hard to be away from them."

"They're good girls. They understand." She shrugged.

"Well, here are your towels. I'll give you new ones at the beginning of each week. There's a pay phone down the hall for your calls. Right now you're the only guest, but later when there are more, I'll ask that you limit time on the phone to five minutes, just to be fair. Anyway, the rules are all here." I handed her the paper and turned to go.

"Wait, have a drink." Lodzia held up a bottle and began pouring before I could say no.

I looked around the room more carefully then and saw that she had not so much unpacked as set up shop. Each of the three suitcases was opened to display an array of merchandise. One held three boxes of Sweet'n Low and a couple dozen pairs of athletic socks, another, four pairs of Rollerblades and a stack of stapled copies of a report titled "Freedom Silver Fund Prospectus." In the other I saw dozens of copies of an audio cassette of the Carpenters' greatest hits and a display of brightly colored plastic funnels. It was an odd mix and match of items—like a private dollar store.

The dresser top held her aquarium and a heap of appliances— blow dryer, curling iron, electric rollers, makeup mirror, boom box, hot plate, iron, and a blender. The tangle of cords from all these stretched like a web to the surge protector she had placed on the floor. She'd covered the bed with a tangerine colored chenille spread that was worn through in spots. A bottle of Popov vodka and a shot glass rested on the nightstand.

"So, do you like my things?" She saw me looking around.

"It's an unusual collection."

"If you need anything, just let me know."

"Well, thanks, but I don't really need much."

"I mean for the Pensione. I can get all kinds of things for less money and then I can sell to you for less money too. So you just let me know."

"I'll do that."

"So, you are very busy here all day?"

"Oh yes, it takes a lot of work to keep the place running," I lied, ashamed of all the time I had on my hands compared to her full load—absent mother, student doctor.

"So, you are always stuck being here—every day, all day?" She looked at me as if my answer really mattered, and I instinctively edged closer to the truth.

"No, not *all* day. I have other commitments too."

"Yes?" She was tapping her foot and I hurried my answer.

"Monday, Wednesday, and Friday mornings I work at the Gold Lantern over on Cass. And Thursday is visiting day at the place where my father is." This was true, though I'd never gone to see him.

"So you're out at those times."

"Usually, why?" Her cross-examination bothered me.

"I'm just trying to have an idea of when you won't be around in case of a problem with something."

"Well, there shouldn't be any problems. Just follow those rules," I pointed to the green paper that Lodzia folded into a smaller and smaller square, "the Pensione is in really good shape."

An hour later, I left Lodzia's room with a copy of the Freedom Silver fund prospectus that I promised to read, a pair of Roller-blades that I traded for another week's stay, and a handshake agreement that I'd let her shill for the Pensione Detroit, giving her ten percent of all the business she brought in.

When I got out of bed at eight the next morning, Lodzia was already gone—I'd heard her creep out an hour earlier. She must have an early class, though how she'd managed with all I'd seen her drink the night before I didn't know. I wondered about the drinking. My radar for drinking problems was alternately right on target and completely out of whack. I'd have to wait and continue to watch Lodzia. She'd show her true colors eventually.

When my father went to the Brighton Clinic three months ago to dry out after drinking for forty years, I had not seen him in a while. Before that, I was an active part of his life—an essential enabler they call it—I'd even lived with him for a while, a few years back. But I finally came to understand that my emotional well-being hinged on being apart from him. Distance was absolutely key.

He would be released from Brighton soon. And then he'd settle in a small apartment near there so he could continue with the therapist he'd become attached to and the AA group and sponsor on whom he'd come to rely. My mother and brother told me all this, mentioning that he was doing well and deserved our support and encouragement. But my mother divorced him three years ago and moved to Nashville a year after that. She and my brother were thousands of miles away. It would be so easy to be supportive and understanding over a phone line. Or maybe not. I'd called him once when he was in the hospital, but when he said hello, I hung up the phone, afraid I'd get caught in his current dry spell, not ready to talk to him until I was sure I could decide not to.

A few months before he went to Brighton, really the last time I saw him, we had a fight. I'd bought a new car, a new *used* car—a Toyota Tercel—and he was angry with my choice, mad that I hadn't bought American. Even pissed off, he stood as he always did around me, shoulders sloped and knees slightly bent, so that the cuffs of his pants skimmed the ground. He only stood tall in public, at the gas station, the bank, or the liquor store, saving his good posture for people he thought he could still fool.

He was drunk that day, and he slopped bourbon—Kentucky brewed, he pointed out proudly—from his glass onto his shirt as he babbled about how much he hated the Japanese, how people like me were the reason people like him had lost their jobs. When he finally started crying and asked me how I could have done it, I told him that I bought the car because I was disgusted with everything American, especially him. And I was.

After Lodzia left that first morning, I tried out my Rollerblades and fell three times before I realized I would never be able to glide along easily—I needed to feel the ground underfoot. I took a walk instead, something I rarely did. Lodzia's energy was infectious, I guess.

My brother had sent me a magazine article along with the toolbox—a long think piece about urban blight. When it mentioned Detroit, it said things were very hopeful because the land's original growth—squibby trees and flowers and mosses, the forest floor—was actually reclaiming parts of the city that had been long abandoned. As I walked I could see this was so. A few blocks away, on Hastings, a row of four empty lots could have been the launching pad for the northern forest. It was host to phlox and violets and creeping, berry-tipped shrubs and bushes. I even thought I saw a pheasant. It was a beautiful patch of land, unsullied by drug dealers and gang members who preferred the husks of abandoned buildings where they could hide behind a rotten timber, sitting in a shadow and escaping notice when needed—buildings that were near impossible to get the city to tear down.

I knew this last part from personal experience. Since I'd bought the Pensione Detroit, I'd been working to get the burnout next door demolished and I'd been told on and off record that it would take five to ten years. Looking at the Hastings land, I thought how nice it would be to sit in my window seat and look out at flowers and butterflies and birds instead of a crumbling brick wall.

I called the Department of Housing when I got home that day and spent most of the time on hold. When I finally got through, I told the operator I'd seen rats running out of the abandoned house next door and he told me that if that was the case, I'd have to talk to Rodent Patrol in the Department of Sanitation. Each time I graduated from Muzak to a real live person and mentioned a particular problem with the building—it was a hazard for the neighborhood kids, it was a firetrap, it could become a gang hangout—the operator connected me to another department where I was banished to Muzak again. Lodzia came to my door that afternoon while I was on hold with Streets and San, and I don't think it was my imagination that she looked annoyed. "Hi, Lodzia. I'll be tied up here for a while. Do you need something?"

"No, but why are you here? I thought you visited your father on Thursday."

"Oh, well I didn't go today. Maybe next week."

"In Poland, we live with our parents and take care of them until they die."

"Is that so? I'm on hold with the city here. I'm trying to get somebody to tear down that building next door."

She made a dismissive gesture and sound, "In Poland, we'd just do it ourselves."

"Really? Well, welcome to America." She left then, not bothering to go up to her room. At the time, I never thought to wonder why she'd come home in the first place. After an hour on hold with various departments, I gave up and took a nap.

The first of Lodzia's tenant referrals rang the doorbell and woke me half an hour later. When I came to the door, his back was to me and my heart hiccuped as I saw him standing slouched, loose and defeated, just like my father. But then he turned around and he said his name was Pete and I breathed easy again. His face was windburned and his hands shook a little as he filled out the rental information card, but he gave me cash and took room six for one month. He wasn't European or a student, and this monthly rental trend wasn't what I had planned, but I felt a gratifying sense of proprietorship as I showed him his room and gave him towels.

Pete was followed the next morning by Ella and a woman whose name I couldn't understand but it sounded like Gusha. They were Polish—Ella, who spoke a little English, said they were engineers in Poland, but were forced to be cleaning ladies here. Gusha, a plate-faced woman with a wool cap sealed to her head, smiled and nodded but kept her eyes to the ground. Two days later Richard, Larry, and Judith checked in so that by week's end all seven of the Pensione Detroit's available rooms were full of paying customers who paced nervously, chain smoked, and had been sent by Lodzia.

Lodzia was happy with her cut, "See, I knew I could do for you. I'll send some of this to my girls. The rest I can save, for my school and to buy a home." I'd often see her in the tenants' rooms showing them some new goods she was selling—sunglasses or coffee mugs or screwdrivers—or pointing to a chart in the silver fund prospectus and explaining the ratio of return on investment. Then, when I was changing the sheets in Lodzia's room during the third week of the Pensione's full occupancy, I came across a two-inch thick wad of cash and a pile of SSI checks signed over to her and stuck between the mattress and the box spring, and I came to understand just how well Lodzia was doing. She was a hustler, but who wouldn't hustle with distant daughters at stake?

It didn't take long to realize that I had a house full of alcoholics. The constant cigarette smoking, the twelve-step books that were stacked on everybody's nightstand (Lodzia had a suitcase full that she had no doubt sold to them at cost), the SSI checks, the quirky way they all walked as if they were about to be jumped from behind. I asked Lodzia where she'd met these people and she confirmed my suspicions by telling me she'd recruited them by waiting outside in the hallway at AA meetings. Except she called them "alcohol meetings." Though all of Lodzia's referrals seemed to be in various stages of recovery, I still sometimes felt as if the collective unconscious that emanated from the Pensione Detroit must wobble alarmingly, shaking its foundation.

Even full, the Pensione really ran itself. I spent an hour every morning cleaning the hallways and two bathrooms using such vast quantities of bleach that the color leached from my hands. When I pushed my hair out of my eyes, the scent made me swoon. I cleaned my guests' rooms once a week (except Lodzia's—she supplied towels for me at deep discount and in return I cleaned her room every other day) and changed their sheets on Saturdays. Otherwise time was like an empty hammock swaying invitingly, while I wondered how to fill it.

In the first week or so, I actually worried about what the neighbors would say. It was, after all, almost as if I were running a halfway house. But apparently the few people left in my downtrodden neighborhood were not inclined to worry about other people's problems.

I hadn't formally met any neighbors, but I did have a nodding acquaintance with some of them. I took a walk almost every afternoon at about three as the kids came home from school. I waved and said hello to everybody and though they looked at me suspiciously the first few times, after a while they waved back, the palms of their hands flat open, inviting me to follow the lines and read the story of their lives.

As I walked, I saw more and more lots that were being taken over by the forest floor. Just over the railroad tracks on Baltimore a few blocks from the Pensione, the whole north side of the street stood empty. The buildings were not only abandoned but had also been razed, and by now nature had taken firm hold. I waded through those fields one afternoon, thinking it would be like walking through another era—a simpler, cleaner time. But the walk wasn't easy—I tripped every other step I took. It turns out that on close inspection, the shrubs and roots only covered up empty beer cans, jagged edges of broken liquor bottles, disposable diapers, and other trash. And even under that layer of discard, the remains of long-gone homes—old foundations and rotting two by fours—jutted up amidst the growing brush.

It was only when I kept my distance that the cycle of this land from forest floor to modest working-class community, to fraying neighborhood, to abandoned slum, and then back to forest, seemed balanced and hopeful, like something I should be part of. Up close, it was not to be trusted.

A month later, when the first snow came, just the thinnest dusting on the first of November, I dug deep into the front hall closet, searching for my winter jacket. I did this impatiently, throwing things aside, frustrated after being on hold with the city's tax assessment department, trying to trace the ownership of the building next door. While on my knees, looking, I saw the toolbox my brother had sent me in August.

I dragged it out and opened it up. It was loaded. My brother, Dennis, who managed other people's money well enough to make plenty of his own, believed in buying the best and this was obviously no amateur's box. Everything in it was heavy with purpose. It was a shame he had wasted it on me. He should have given it to somebody who would have put it to use or at least sold it to the highest bidder, somebody like Lodzia. Remembering how she'd scoffed when I'd mentioned my troubles with the city, I lugged the toolbox over to the building next door and heaved it through the rotting front door.

The wood gave a satisfying splinter and then broke off in jagged spikes. Inspired, I picked through the toolbox and then walked to the side of the house that was responsible for my afternoon gloom. Hammer and chisel in hand, I began chipping away at the crumbling mortar of the worn down face brick. Lodzia came home about an hour later and invited me to Big Boy's for dinner, her treat, in honor of my finally taking things in my own hands and making a start.

After that, I went to the house and worked on it whenever I had a free hour or two. While I worked, my abandoned neighborhood came to its version of life—its faint pulse increasing a beat as the kids rode by on their bikes and stopped to watch and the few cars that usually sped past slowed down, drivers honking their horns and waving. In the beginning, before it got too cold, some people came out and sat around smoking cigarettes and drinking beers and giving advice or offering to help. And though I was warmed by these offers, I turned them down. I wanted to do this alone.

But as it got colder, more and more often, it was just Lodzia and me. Usually it was late afternoon and as dusk settled, Lodzia would join me on her way in from her day. She'd perch on an overturned milk crate, vodka bottle and glass in hand, and sometimes she'd build a fire from the scraps of wood I'd torn down. She kept me company, telling me stories of the Polish countryside and her mother's farm there.

"My mother is so good. I'd like to be her. She works hard. And she's smart. Before I married my husband, she told me not to."

"Why?"

"He was no good. He drank too much. He fought. He was very lazy. She saw this. I pretended not to."

"So where is he now?"

"He had a growth. He died when my girls were just babies."

"I'm sorry."

She shrugged, "Like my mother said, he was no good. His dying was not too sad. But he gave me my girls, so I have to like that. I had to leave them to help them. You know what I mean, CeAnn." And I always assured her I did, because I did.

Sometimes she'd bring out her boom box and a Carpenters' cassette and she'd sing along as Karen crooned about the birds and played her sad guitar. She'd pass me a glass of vodka while I worked. I never drank it, but she'd smile as I poured it on the ground, returning the fermented potatoes to the earth. By that time, I had no illusions about Lodzia's drinking problem, but it was not something *I* would ever be able to fix. My struggles with my alcoholic father had taught me this, a lesson I'd learned late.

I never shared any of my stories with her—she never asked. I never told her how when I was a girl, my father worked in the skilled trades at Plant 37, Tool & Die, Cadillac Assembly and that we drove a Coup de Ville—a new one every other year. He was proud of that. He lost that job, because of drinking I found out later, though at the time my mother only said there had been layoffs industry-wide. After that he worked for Ford and then Chrysler and finally AMC, and then for a number of small independent bump shops where he did body work. Every time he'd lose a job, we'd get a smaller, older, less reliable car. And when I was fifteen and we were down to a rusty Duster that wouldn't start on rainy days, my mother and brother and I finally faced the fact of my father's problem.

I rushed through my chores one morning a few weeks after I'd started on the house, eager to get back to it and continue the demolition. But I lingered a little in Lodzia's room. It was always hard not to—she could stock a flea market stall with all her stuff. That morning I studied some new pictures of her daughters. They were posed more casually than the first picture she'd showed me. In one, they laughed while sitting on a floral slipcovered couch. In another, they sat on swings in a yard that was enclosed by a Cyclone fence. They looked happy—the only clue that their lives in Poland were any different than they would be in America was the absence of Lodzia.

After I'd picked through the new boxes of goods Lodzia had collected since I'd last cleaned—a gross of Days Inn ashtrays, a dozen T-shirts advertising a local hardware store, a case of Cremora, six boxes of Avon lavender sachets—I tried to dust her dresser top between the tangle of appliance cords and I gave her fish two shakes of food as I often did though she'd never asked me to. I shivered a little as I stood over the fish tank. It was cold in her room—the Pensione needed new storm windows.

I looked through her closet, wondering if she'd stored anything new in there, but as usual Lodzia had everything out in the open, on display. The closet was empty except for three dresses, two everyday polyester, and one thick white satin elaborately puckered and gathered like the inside of a coffin. I was also looking for clues that her medical studies were progressing, that she was what she said, but I never found any—no anatomy textbooks, calculators, notepads, or tuition bills from WSU. And though I was pretty sure Lodzia lied about being a doctor, I had to admit she didn't seem to hide anything else.

Her door stood open for everyone in the Pensione. Just the night before I'd come up past eleven to drop a load of clean towels in the linen closet and there was Gusha, just home from work, sitting on the edge of Lodzia's bed, wool cap on, her feet soaking in a pot. I heard Lodzia before I saw her. She was speaking in Polish and Gusha, always before quiet, laughed, answered back, and peeled the hat off her head. Then Lodzia moved into the picture framed by the doorway and hummed as she brushed Gusha's hat-flattened hair and then scribed it into small patches with the tip of a comb, winding each around aqua-colored, squiggly, foam rollers. When Gusha left the house early the next morning, she walked slowly, and though it was cold outside, her head was uncovered, and her hair billowed around her shy, wide face.

Maybe the unlimited access she gave me and the others to her room gave Lodzia leave to think she had the same right. When I came home two hours earlier than usual from the Gold Lantern one morning a few days later, she was in my apartment, talking on the phone, though I'd never given her a key or permission to do so. As I came in, she quickly hung up and turned to me accusingly, "What are you doing here?"

"There was no business and I have a terrible headache, so Ray let me come home." I answered before remembering that I should be the one asking questions. Before I could say more, she mumbled that she was looking for a safety pin and then she muttered something in Polish and looked annoyed. I could smell booze on her breath as she pushed past me and ran upstairs.

Just seconds after she left, the phone rang. When I picked it up, the man on the other end began threatening me. "Listen, lady, quit calling here. I mean it. My mother does not want to buy into your silver fund. I've put a stop payment on the check she sent you. If I hear from you again, I'm calling the police."

I protested as soon as I could get a word in, "Who is this? What are you talking about? You must have a wrong number."

"I have caller ID, lady. I know you just called. And I know you've been harassing my mother for the past two weeks."

"I have not."

"Well, if it's not you, it's your Polack partner. All I know is one of you scammed my mother on this Freedom Fund bullshit and talked her into sending a check for five thousand dollars. I've looked into that pyramid scheme enough to know it's illegal."

I sat down, stricken by this confirmation of my suspicions about Lodzia, but still not wanting to believe it. "My Polish partner?"

"Lusta or Lofta or something. My mother is ninety-two—she doesn't remember the exact name or even how much money she's sent so far. For god's sake have some decency and leave an old woman alone."

"Are you sure there's no mistake? Where did you say you're calling from?"

"Playing dumb is not going to help."

I reached for the Ameritech bill that had been lying on my desk unopened for a few days, just noticing how unusually thick it was. The first thing I saw was the total—$827.85. And then I saw the fifteen pages of long distance numbers—all calls made in the morning, probably on Monday or Wednesday or Friday when I was at the Gold Lantern. "Sir, I'm sorry about this. I'll have to get back to you."

"You don't get it, lady. I'm saying you better *never* call back."
He hung up, and as I examined the phone bill further to get a
handle on what Lodzia had been doing, I heard her on the stairs
and then the front door slammed and when I looked out the window she was getting in her car.

I ran out to my car and followed her. I wanted to confront her
now, in the heat of the moment, so I wouldn't back down. She
drove as if she had a tankful of fish in the back seat, but I kept up.
She got on I-75 from the Boulevard, and exited right away on
Holbrook and then we were in Hamtramck.

Staying well back, I watched as Lodzia parked and walked up
to the front door of a neat, trim house on Lumpkin. A woman in
a bright green sweatsuit answered and after they argued for a few
minutes she let Lodzia in, but even from a distance, I could see
she didn't want to. She flattened her shoulders against the door
and turned her head as she let Lodzia pass.

I sat in the car for half an hour before I got bored enough to
leave, but just as I was about to pull away, the door opened again
and I saw Lodzia walk out followed by two little girls and the
woman in the sweatsuit. Lodzia knelt down and hugged the girls,
squishing them together as if they were made of Play-Doh and
burying her head in the taller one's shoulder. The girls weren't
dressed up as they were in the pictures dotting Lodzia's room at
the Pensione Detroit, but it was clear that these were her daughters
who were supposed to be in Poland. I wondered if she knew that
despite the Juicy Fruit (my father had used Listerine), the girls
would know she'd been drinking. I wondered if the woman was a
legal foster mother or a good friend or just a distant relative. But
really, what did that matter? She wasn't their mother. When I
drove off after Lodzia, the girls were turning cartwheels on the
front lawn, and the woman in green sat on the porch watching
them, laughing and clapping at every successful revolution.

Lodzia turned right onto Campau, and parked in the middle
of the main shopping strip a few blocks down. Then she reached
into the backseat and carried a corrugated cardboard box into

Srodek's Sausage shop. Ten minutes later she came out carrying a half-dozen flat parcels wrapped in white butcher paper and string. She put them in the backseat and took out another box that she carried into a bar, three doors down the street.

I waited for a while, and then I went into the New Palace Bakery and bought myself a cup of coffee and a sweet roll. I also bought a thick slice of poppyseed cake, rich and dense and heavy as a paperweight, and placed it on the front seat of Lodzia's car, in a desperate hope that she'd eat it and miraculously sober up before she got behind the wheel again.

I wondered what excuses Lodzia used. Perhaps she told herself she drank because her girls had been placed just out of her reach. Or maybe her drinking had placed them there and she drank even more because she couldn't accept the truth that she was the instrument of her greatest sorrow. Either way, she had to go. I felt my face flush at the thought of the cake I'd left in her car—such a futile, even childish, gesture, and one she didn't deserve. Driving home, I lectured myself not to be naïve and forgiving. I rehearsed what I would say when I told her to leave the Pensione.

I worked on the house next door that afternoon. I figured I'd get a lot done, and my anger at Lodzia did fuel my chisel. But I quit after an hour, bored without Lodzia around to tell me stories. Coming in, I saw the phone bill on the hall table and angry as I was, I laughed a little at the thought of Lodzia talking Ameritech into taking payment in athletic socks, audio cassettes, or ground beef.

That evening, as I washed the dinner dishes, I heard a screech and felt a crash so close it shook the foundation of the Pensione Detroit. I ran to the front of the house and was met there by my tenants, who looked shakier than usual, as if the noise had upset some precarious inner ear balance they'd just recently achieved. We went out to the front porch together and when we saw Lodzia getting out of her Monte Carlo, which was half embedded in the building next door, we exhaled in unison as if we'd each been punctured.

She walked unsteadily toward us, her arms full of the butcher packages she'd extracted from the car, and came through the opening we made for her. As she passed me, she stopped, "That's how you knock down a wall. Boom," she clapped her hands, dropping all but a few of her packages, "it's done." She didn't bother to pick anything up and as I watched her walk into the house and up the front stairs, I saw the poppyseed cake I'd placed on the seat of her car, smashed flat on the rear of her fake fur coat.

When I went upstairs a few minutes later, she was wrapped in the chenille bedspread, warming her hands over her hot plate, and staring at the aquarium. "Have a drink?" she raised a glass as I approached.

"No thanks." She took a sip, spilling a little on her dress. Seeing her like that, all drunk and clumsy, disgusted me. "Lodzia, some guy from St. Louis called. And my phone bill came. You can't stay here any more. Did you think I wouldn't notice that you're using my phone?"

"I meant to mention it. I just forgot."

"You *forgot* that you're stealing from me? Did you forget that you're always drinking too? Look at you. You're a mess."

"Get out of here, CeAnn. You know nothing about anything."

"I know your daughters are in Hamtramck, not Poland."

She looked surprised, but then she shrugged, "Poland, Hamtramck—what's the difference? They're not with me."

"Because you're a drunk."

"No, because I have a drink once in a while. At home, everybody does. Here in car city, you're so sensitive. I worked hard and provided for them and still they say I'm no good for my own daughters. Don't look at me like you're better. I wouldn't want to be like you. I'm not afraid of anything. I get things done." She pointed her finger as she spoke. "Just leave, CeAnn. I'll move out tomorrow morning. I'll pay your phone bill then too. I could pay you right now, but I can't count the money." She raised her glass to her temple, "I have this turmoil in my head."

I backed out of the room, tripping on one of the butcher packages she'd left on the floor and knocking over a picture of her daughters, and as I caught myself, she yelled at me in Polish, loud, thick-edged words the meaning of which was clear.

I woke at two that morning to the sound of the smoke detectors blaring and the cries of tenants above. At first I didn't know where I was—the Pensione Detroit smelled like a short order grill, the rich, sizzling scent of frying bacon wafting through its halls.

When I rushed up to Lodzia's room, sure the problem was there, Larry was already helping her out and Pete, who poured the contents of the aquarium on a towel that was on fire and then smothered the flames that flickered up from a frying pan, hollered that he'd already called 911. Lodzia was only half-conscious, but she sobbed how sorry she was. When we got downstairs, the fire department had just arrived, bringing along paramedics who sat Lodzia down on a stretcher. I told them how drunk she was and on cue, she slumped down, passed out.

Pete and Larry had caught the fire just in time, but there was still a lot of damage. Lodzia had been frying bacon on her hotplate and fallen asleep. Everything in her room and the upstairs hallway was covered with a thick layer of sooty grease. The paramedics asked if Lodzia had health insurance and when I said I doubted it, they told me they'd take her to Detroit Receiving. Did I know her next of kin? No, she's alone here, I lied. When they asked if I wanted to come along, I said maybe I'd visit later.

I didn't think I would. I tallied her traits in my head—thinking of the good, but also bad she'd done since she'd arrived a few months ago. Lies and stealing and now this? Why on earth should I visit her? But when I turned around to go back inside, I saw the Monte Carlo sticking out of the house next door, crumbling bricks piled on its front end, moonlight shining on its silver fenders and bouncing unobstructed into my living room window seat, and I closed my eyes against the glare.

The insurance adjuster came out early the next morning and mentioned what to me seemed an unbelievably large amount of money. After he left, some of the tenants offered to help me clean up and by late afternoon we'd made good progress in the hallways—only Lodzia's room was really trashed.

I started to pick my way through it the next day, but when I came upon a charred copy of the silver prospectus, I lost heart for the job and offered Ella and Gusha and Pete a free month's rent if they'd scrub and paint the room. When I went upstairs a few hours later to see how they were doing, I crouched to pick up a grease-streaked, water-stained picture of Lodzia's girls and found myself staring at Pete's raggedy pant cuffs. My pulse froze hot for a second again, but this time I stood and took Pete by the shoulders and told him to straighten up for Christ sake. And though that had never worked with my father, when Pete came to me later that day asking for Lodzia's keys, offering to move the Monte Carlo, his posture was perfect. I turned him down anyway.

Two days later I forced myself to go to Detroit Receiving. As far as I knew Lodzia was all alone and that seemed too sad, even for a drunk. She was watching *The Price Is Right* when I came into the room she shared with three others on the psych ward. She didn't look at me, but she lowered the volume.

"So, how are you feeling, Lodzia?" She shrugged her shoulders, but I could see her trembling. Her hair, usually defiant in its heat-inspired curls, now lay collapsed against her head. It had been almost seventy-two hours since she'd had a drink, but the nurse on duty told me she'd blown 2.3 upon admittance—enough so that she should have been dead. Lodzia finally spoke, but she still didn't look at me, "I hope the Pensione is okay."

"It's fine. Just smoke damage. The insurance adjuster came out. I think I'll actually make some money."

"Good."

"If I only get half of what he said, the settlement will be huge—I'll be able to buy out your whole stock of lavender sachets." I heard a skittering chuckle—it came from me.

She looked out the window, "*Zielona gapa*," she muttered, and then she looked over at me. "Do you know what that means? It means don't be a green dumb sapling, CeAnn. I'm not asking for your help. Why are you here anyway?"

"I'm worried about you."

"Don't be. What do you know of it? Worry about yourself. You have many more problems than me."

"Maybe, but I know plenty about it. My father drank for forty years. He's in rehab now." In this first story I shared with her, I didn't tell her about all the other times my father had stopped.

"I can stop whenever I want to. I don't have a problem like your father. It's too late anyway."

And then I remembered I'd brought her something, and I pulled out the picture of her girls from my bag. It was the only one that hadn't been completely ruined in the fire. The background and the girls' dresses were water-stained and gritty, but their faces were shining.

Lodzia looked at it for a second and then put it in the wastebasket next to her bed.

"What are you doing that for?"

"Why shouldn't I? It's no good, CeAnn. I think that woman has made my girls afraid of me. I don't want them to see me like this. They'll hate me. They won't ever forgive me." She looked straight at me then, begging to be contradicted.

I told her the whole truth flat out, though I felt sorry for her girls as I did. "That's not so. Children always forgive."

"I don't know. I'm so tired. In many ways, it was much easier in Poland. Here I have to work so hard for so much."

Then we watched TV, not speaking for a while, but during a commercial for a local surgicenter, I turned to her again. "Tell me the truth now, Lodzia. You weren't really a doctor in Poland, were you?"

At that she drew herself up under the covers and turned to me haughtily, "Really, CeAnn, you insult me."

We talked more about her daughters then. She was eager to hear what I had to say. I told her how happy they'd be to see her sober. How they would be naturally understanding because they were too young to be distrustful of her sudden conversion, except I didn't put it that way.

She stopped me as I gathered my things to leave, "CeAnn?"
"Yes?"

"I really want to see them. Do you think my girls could come here tomorrow?"

She picked at the sheet while she asked, and I hesitated. But I knew what she wanted to hear, so I said, yes, sure, that's a fine idea, smiling encouragement. I knew it was just a matter of time before she'd be drunk again.

She reached into the wastebasket and drew out the photo. "They're such good girls, my girls." She looked at the picture for a long time, and when I turned again to leave, she held it out to me. "Keep it for me. This is no place for them."

I started the Monte Carlo when I got home, backed it up and rammed it into the wall once and then again and then one more time, finishing the job Lodzia started. Then I got out of the car and began to shovel up the broken bits of brick.

LUCKY

It had been a long time since Trudger Rhodes expected anything but drugs from his doctor, who often said, "Let's try *this* new combination of psychotropic medications and see if it helps you, Michael." Nobody at Macomb County Bureau of Community Health Services remembered he answered better to Trudger, and they probably thought it was just another sign of his illness—called paranoid schizophrenia fifteen years back, cyclothymic personality disorder about six years ago, and schizoaffective disorder these days—when he didn't respond. Whatever they called his sickness didn't matter much to Trudger. He just took the prescriptions they gave him to Perry's Drugs and got them filled for free with his Medicaid card.

And then he waited to see if the new drug they prescribed for him did anything but constipate him and make his hands shake. He was thirty-six years old, and he wondered why they thought that after twenty years of being sick, he could simply take a pill and change his nature. Because his nature was powerful, even on his bad days when he looked up at the sky and saw it crack into pieces. Maybe especially on his bad days.

He had one of those days late in February, the day he lost his job sweeping at Oakland Mall. It hadn't started out bad. He slept until noon and then he watched *One Life to Live* and *General Hospital*. He left his apartment in Sterling Heights at 2:45, so he'd have time to stop at Perry's and refill a prescription, and still punch in for work by 3:30. It wasn't a bad plan.

He came out of Perry's feeling fine, holding a white paper bag of meds in one hand and swinging his key chain around his right index finger in a loop, admiring the centrifugal force it created. He swung it faster, and the chain crept closer to the tip of his finger. And then he watched while his keychain vaulted up and off and sailed through the air, landing twenty feet away, which would not have been a big deal if a garbage truck lowering a Dumpster from the side of Subway hadn't also been twenty feet away, its rot-filled mouth wide open to the gift of his keys. Surprised to stillness by such bad luck, Trudger watched the truck rumble away around the back side of Subway and Perry's and Kroger. By the time he ran after it, it was too late, it had turned on to Big Beaver Road, heading west toward more garbage.

Trudger walked back to his car, and slid into the driver's seat wondering what to do. It wasn't much of a car—sixteen years old, an '82 Chevy Citation, light blue. Trudger wasn't too good at maintenance so some spots on the left side were rusted right through and the right headlight didn't work. When he drove at night, a short in the dashboard lights made them flicker off and on like roadside neon.

The car had been his mother's until she died three years ago. Before that she'd understood him better than anyone, loved him in spite of it, and said many times before she died, "Now Trudger, don't you be dreaming about me when I'm gone."

The first time Trudger took the car out was the night of his mother's funeral when he'd left the gathering at his father's house because too many people were staring at him, whispering about what was to become of him now that his mother was gone. The whispers didn't do much to disguise their satisfaction at his predicament—Trudger heard the pleased tones, all of them thinking that now it was settled, now Trudger would take his rightful place somewhere with visiting hours, breakfast, lunch, and dinner in a cafeteria, a Ping-Pong table in a rec room, and a high fence around the grounds. When he looked up from the corner where he sat, all of his mother's mourners stood separate and tall and planted like iron spikes, caging him. So, holding his breath, Trudger stood and maneuvered through them, turning his shoulders left, then right, ducking and sidling, eyes to the ground, slipping away from their smiles that might be fake or might be real, but better to keep moving, just in case.

And when he finally made it to the back door, he left and drove his mother's car the ten or fifteen miles from Madison Heights into Detroit, not planning to, just following a car in front of him on the road. The car exited at Brush, near the interchange where the Chrysler met the Ford, and he followed it until it sped through a yellow light that turned red before Trudger reached it. Not knowing where to go, or what to do, Trudger parked on the overpass and got out of the car and stared down at the traffic whizzing underneath him, white lights approaching, red lights retreating. Standing there watching, he wanted to be part of that skein of light spun by speed, connected by the movement.

From then on, Trudger drove wherever he could, whenever he could, merging into the flow of traffic, staking his claim. The motion softened the edges of his days. At times he was so comfortable driving that the car drifted across lines white or yellow.

The parking lot at Perry's was busy the day that Trudger tossed his keys, and as he sat in the Citation wondering what to do, other cars idled, waiting for his spot, finally beeping and holding up their hands in question. Three times Trudger waved them away with a finger, but the cars still made him sweat. His boss had yelled at him five times in the past three weeks for being just two minutes late, including three days ago when he'd said one more time and

Trudger would be fired. His boss regularly made fun of Trudger, calling him crazy boy right to his face and then sending him off to sweep alone in the farthest corner of the mall where Sears was and hardly anybody shopped. Trudger could see ahead to how he'd have to meet his father at McDonald's for lunch and tell him about this latest job he'd lost. He could imagine his father slugging him on the arm and telling him to buckle down, even as Trudger would explain that he hadn't meant to be late. Just like he'd explained that he hadn't meant to get in a fight at the last job he'd had. Or to scare the sixteen-year-old girl at the cash register when he stared too long at a spot on the wall near her head at the job before that.

Before the job sweeping at Oakland Mall, Trudger had been out of work for six months, and he'd sat home alone, thinking too much. Without a job, he'd have no place to drive to, and he needed one. Trudger knew that much about himself.

With only twenty-five minutes left before he had to punch in, Trudger got out of the car and kicked a tire and then a headlight and then the front fender and then the driver's side door and then he took his hands out of his pockets and pounded everywhere he could reach with a fist. And when his feet and his hands hurt too much to go on, he leaned on the hood and cried. A security guard, a big, young guy in a brown jacket, came up behind him and told him he better get a move on.

"I can't get a move on. I threw my keys in the garbage." Trudger snorted up tears as he spoke.

The guard didn't back off, or squawk into his walkie-talkie for help, instead he reached into his pocket and handed Trudger a Kleenex. "Wipe the snot off your face. Do you have a screwdriver?"

Trudger rummaged through the backseat where he kept all kinds of stuff, tools, newspapers, McDonald's bags, shoes, clothes, and two Frisbees. He found a Phillips head, but the guard said that wouldn't do, so he dug some more and found a plain old screwdriver. The guard took it and slid into the driver's seat. He ducked under the dashboard and did something Trudger couldn't see. Within ten seconds, the Citation gunned to life, and the guard got out of the car and showed Trudger the trick.

The guard stood next to him then, outside the open door, and Trudger, following his instructions, inserted the screwdriver and turned off the ignition. When he tried starting the car himself, he got it on his second try. He turned to thank the guard, and then hugged him hard, right around the waist, crying into his belt. "Thank you. Thank you, man. You saved my life."

"Nah, I just started your car."

Trudger jammed the screwdriver in his back pocket so hard his jeans ripped, and he hurt his thigh. He still had time to get to work though, so a bruised thigh and a ripped pocket didn't seem too big a price. He inched out of the parking lot driveway, waiting for a break in traffic, gripping the steering wheel hard so his hands wouldn't shake.

A van blocked his view to the left so he didn't see the Jeep Cherokee barreling his way. Trudger stomped the brakes and so did the driver of the Jeep, and nobody was going too fast, but still it ended up with a crumple in the glistening, white, front panel of the Jeep and the left headlight on the Citation popped and shattered on impact, so it matched the right.

It could have stayed a little accident if the lady who climbed down from the Jeep hadn't screamed at him and cried that he could have hurt the baby that squalled in the backseat. Trudger barely heard her over the sound of the baby, so he held his hands to his ears and said, "Hey lady, you want to shut that kid up." He laughed as he said it to show he was kidding, even though he wasn't really. The woman moved in front of the door closest to the baby and set her legs in a stance. Then she pulled out her cell phone, walked over to the front of the Jeep, and called the police, which was a waste of money because they were already on the way. Trudger heard sirens.

The baby squalled still. Its cries crashed against Trudger's forehead. The baby didn't see a thing—Trudger could tell from its unfocused eyes. Its noodley neck wasn't strong enough to hold up the head that made so much noise. Shut up. Shut up. Shut up. Trudger whispered instruction to the baby, not realizing he inched closer to it until the woman screamed and put her arm to his chest, waking him to his movement. Trudger looked left, right, up, down, trying to find something to latch on to, something he could see that would put this baby and lady into motion so he could feel them moving away. He needed them to get away.

He looked at his watch, trying to hold his left wrist steady with his right hand, but by now both shook, so it didn't do much good. It was just shy of impossible that he'd be on time for work if he left that second. And between the baby crying, the lady yelling, the sirens whapping, and the time clock unforgiving, Trudger got in his car, jammed the screwdriver into the steering column under the dash, and backed away. He drove fast through the parking lot and out the other side of Perry's, heading east on Big Beaver, doing sixty in a forty mile per hour zone so he wouldn't be late for work.

The cops drove seventy. They pulled him over at Dequindre Road, just half a mile past Perry's. Both cops got out of the car and kept hands on guns as they approached the Citation from opposite sides. Trudger looked left and then right and then he looked at his own face in the sideview mirror. It was bloated from medication and shiny because he needed a shower. His ragged hair came down past his ears except for a patch on top where he was going bald. Even to himself he looked like a loser. He put his hands over his ears and he bowed his head to the steering wheel, stunned by the sudden stillness. Mad at being stopped.

When the cop said, "What's your problem, Buddy," Trudger laughed. And as the one cop pulled him out saying maybe he'd had a little too much to drink, the other one walked over with Trudger's bag of meds from Perry's and said, "Hey Frank, maybe that's not the problem here." They punched in Trudger's license number, and, sure enough, they found two other moving violations and a note that he was medicated and before Trudger knew it, instead of leaning on the handle of his four-foot-long dust mop at

Oakland Mall and counting how many different colors the T-shirts came in at the Gap, he was sitting in jail.

They left his car right on the side of Big Beaver, and one of the cops took the screwdriver from his back pocket. When he got out of lockup the next morning, they gave him back his wallet and his screwdriver and his drugs, and they issued him a ticket, but they held on to his license, and gave him a court date to try and get it back, saying a guy taking so much medication shouldn't be steering a ton of steel. If he drove on that ticket, they told him, they'd lock him up for good, which Trudger believed because it wasn't as if he could afford a lawyer to get him going again. Trudger handed back the screwdriver, "Then you might as well keep this, too."

The desk cop didn't look up, just waved a hand, "I'm not a pawn shop, buddy." So Trudger slipped the screwdriver back through the hole in his pocket and started the long walk home.

He hadn't walked anywhere in a long time. He'd gotten his name from walking when he was nine. His mom and dad only had one car back then and his dad used it every day for work. His mom did all her errands on foot. She didn't mind. She said the walking gave her time to think. "About what?" Trudger used to ask her. "About you, honey," she'd say. But then she slipped on the icy back-porch steps—steps he hadn't shoveled one morning when his dad told him to—and she broke her leg.

All that winter, with his mom in a cast from toe to thigh, Trudger ran errands for her. She'd send him places after school—to the A&P or the Laundromat or the fruit stand or Cunningham's drugstore. She wanted him to take her shopping cart for the heavy errands, but he wouldn't. Only ladies pulled shopping carts. Instead, he swung a cloth bag over his shoulder and onto his back and walked home, head down, stooped like their eighty-year-old neighbor Mrs. Bobb. People got used to seeing him that winter, walking home on snowy sidewalks, shoulders bent under a ten-pound sack of potatoes or Del Monte green beans, eight cans for a dollar, or two whole fryers that his mother whacked with a cleaver, the sound of the splintering backbone killing Trudger's appetite for the day.

Walking home alone back then, with a sack on his back, Trudger had understood what his mother meant about thinking, because staring at the snowy sidewalk underfoot he knew that if he never looked up, he could probably walk on forever, with just his own thoughts for company. Maybe it was the mailman who first said, "Look at the little trudger," or maybe it was Mrs. Bobb, or maybe it was the cashier at the A&P. But whoever it was, the name stuck. And though Trudger hardly ever carried anything on his back after his mother's cast came off that spring, almost everybody called him Trudger from then on.

As he walked home from the police station, Trudger thought about his mom for a while, so at first it wasn't too bad. But then his thoughts turned to how losing his license and his car was probably the beginning of a new round of bad luck. And he knew that bad luck once started hardly ever stopped. He was living proof of that. He was crazy. He was a trudger.

After he'd walked a couple of miles, he came to the Citation on the side of Big Beaver. Two tickets flapped like flags from its side window. Trudger kicked the left front tire and glass tinkled from the smashed headlight. He still had four more miles before he'd get home. Without a car in Sterling Heights, it would be impossible to pretend to fit in with everybody else.

He opened the car door and slid behind the wheel, the screwdriver digging into his thigh. He remembered the baby screaming and crying the day before. But being in his car blunted the edge of the memory and tempted him to drive on. Then he thought of what the desk sergeant said. He didn't want to be locked up so he couldn't move at all. Truth was, without his job, he didn't have anywhere to be anyway. He got out of the car and walked on before he could change his mind.

A few miles later, Trudger stopped in the middle of an overpass that crossed the Clinton River. He reached into his back pocket and took out his screwdriver. If he was going to play by the rules, he'd better get rid of the temptation. He threw the screwdriver as far as he could, which was pretty far because whatever was messed up in his head, there was nothing wrong with his arm.

And as he watched the tool tumble shank over tip in the sun and then splish into the river twenty yards out from the overpass, he wondered what was to become of him. He had nowhere to go, no car to get there, and nobody to talk to. And though he'd kept it together through times without one or two of those things, he knew he wasn't lucky enough to make it through without any of them at all.

Three days later, Trudger left his apartment for the first time since getting out of jail and walked over to McDonald's half a mile away early in the morning when he could lie and get a cup of coffee for a quarter just by saying it was for his grandma who was too old to get out of the car and get it herself. He sat in the parking lot drinking his coffee, watching the cars coming and going. At ten miles an hour, they didn't do much to ease his mind, but at least they moved. He was staring at a silver Saturn inching toward the drive-through window when he heard somebody call his name. "Hey, Trudger, is that you? It is you." Trudger looked up to see his cousin Jerry approaching, a car seat with a baby in it, swinging on his arm like a purse.

He hadn't seen Jerry since the last family party maybe a year ago, some second cousin's first holy communion, but Trudger had heard from his father that Jerry had been fired from his nursing job at Sinai hospital. His father didn't know exactly what happened, but he said he guessed that Jerry deserved what he got.

Jerry's wife worked at Social Security downtown, and Jerry stayed home with their three-month-old baby, which meant, Trudger's father told him, Jerry dropped the baby off at his mother-in-law's house most mornings while he sat in a bar and made calls to his bookie. Trudger knew that *could* be true because a few years ago he and Jerry used to run into each other in the afternoon at Fat Jack's Saloon when they both lived on the east side of Detroit. The first few times he saw Jerry at Jack's, his cousin was in his nurse's uniform, white pants and shirt, drinking at the bar before his shift, just one beer, sometimes two. But after a while, Jerry showed up in jeans and a Michigan State sweatshirt and complained he'd lost his job because he wasn't a woman.

That morning at McDonald's, Jerry's baby, bundled in a fuzzy yellow snowsuit, sat slumped like a sack of rice in the car seat, which had a green ruffle around its edge. Trudger, being polite, patted the air around the baby's feet.

"Hey, Jerry. What are you doing here? This is a girl, right?"

"I had to go to Handy Andy next door. No, it's a boy. Jerry junior. Named for me." Jerry unhooked the car seat handle from his arm. "You want to hold him?"

Trudger stepped back quickly, bumping into an old lady who swore as she slopped coffee on her shoe. "No. No. No way. The drugs I take, they make me constipated. But this is my third cup of coffee and now I have to go the bathroom."

Jerry sat hunched over the *Daily Racing Form* when Trudger returned. Jerry junior slept in his car seat, on top of the table like a centerpiece. "Hey Trudge, sit down. What were you doing in the parking lot?"

"Just looking. I lost my job and my car. How about you?"

"I'm taking care of my boy. I'm looking for work. But you know, the mistake I've made in the past is I settle for something. And I'm not going to do that anymore. It's been eight months since I got screwed out of Sinai, and I'm still working to get my mind straight about it all."

"The mind, Jerry, it does funny things. You know what I mean?" Trudger reached for the salt shaker as he spoke, and Jerry senior grabbed his arm, nodding and looking hard at Trudger, like he'd said something important.

"If you've got some time on your hands, Trudge, I'm building a survival shelter in my backyard. I could sure use your help."

· · ·

Trudger climbed in the front seat of the car when he saw Jerry putting the baby in the back. "How come you've got this baby with you? I heard your mother-in-law watched him."

"She did, for three weeks. But she goes to the casino in Windsor on Wednesdays. And Tuesdays she goes to Meijers for senior citizen's discount day. Plus, she gave me too much grief. She says if I don't have a job, I should take care of my kid. I don't need grief from her. You know what I mean?"

"Oh, I do." Trudger held his breath as little Jerry squawked, then let it out slowly as the baby shut up.

"My supervisor at Sinai was giving me grief even before she fired me. She was out to get me. She was a fucking lunatic bitch. Crazy. Not as crazy as you, but still." Trudger looked over and met his cousin's glance. "No offense meant, Trudge." Trudger waved the comment away, and Jerry went on, "I mean I have to get the only nurse supervisor in the Detroit metropolitan area who doesn't want to face the truth of how fucked up doctors are.

"Listen to this story. This patient admits on my shift, complaining about stomach pains. I do the history. It's obviously an ulcer or some run-of-the-mill gastro thing. I get him comfortable and take care of him from 3:30 to 11:00, and then I leave him for the night and day shifts. All standard procedure here—the guy needs some tests. Sure, maybe he'll be unlucky and have stomach cancer, but probably not. He's a nice guy. Not too old. Could be you. Could be me."

Jerry looked in the mirror again, as little Jerry started to fuss. "Hey Trudge, stick that pacifier in his mouth, will you? So anyway, I come back to work the next afternoon. I'm early, so I poke my head in the guy's room to say hello. And he looks awful. He's a black guy, but I swear he's so pale he could pass for white. He's sleeping, but barely. Moaning. In pain. And I'm thinking, what's going on here? He should at least be on pain meds by now. Then I see it. They've cut off his fucking leg. A thirty-year-old guy comes in with a stomachache and we cut off his leg. That's how we handled *that* problem. I said so at the shift change meeting and then again to the prick doctor who did it. Motherfuckers. And that kind of stuff happens all the time. I tell the truth about it so I get fired. And it's probably just as well that I did because, I'm telling you Trudge, I couldn't take it anymore."

Trudger stared at his legs. "I guess I'll never go to Sinai." He looked out the window and counted up all the hospitals he'd been in.

"Doesn't matter. Sinai, Beaumont, Henry Ford, St. John's, Harper, Detroit Receiving—they're all the same. Truth is, if you're sick, you're screwed."

Ten minutes later, Jerry turned the wheel sharply to the left and screech-stopped in the driveway of a beige brick ranch house with a bent gutter drooping over the front door. "Here we are. We'll be working in the garage. Come on, let's go build that shelter."

Trudger thought they should keep the baby in the house while they worked, but Jerry said no, he couldn't leave him alone that long and he had a space heater in the garage so it would be warm enough. Then he went in the house and came back out a minute later with two bottles of Stroh's and one of formula. He handed a beer to Trudger who wouldn't take it. "I don't do that anymore. The drink, for me, it's evil."

Jerry held out the baby bottle, "Then do me a favor and feed him while I have a beer."

Trudger wouldn't take that bottle either. "If it's all the same to you, you're going to have to do that yourself."

The baby sucked hard the instant Jerry jammed the nipple between his lips, but then he made a snarfy, gurgly sound and Trudger jerked away, scared the boy would choke to death. But Jerry senior wiggled the nipple, gently this time, and then he sat on a milk crate in front of the space heater and rocked back and forth while the baby sucked and Trudger, following his cousin's instructions, unrolled a blueprint and laid it on the floor.

"The idea with this shelter, Trudge, is to have a place to go in time of trouble."

"What kind of trouble?"

"Any kind. A government invasion, a hurricane, a riot, a nuclear attack."

"There aren't any hurricanes in Michigan."

"That's not the point. The point is I have to keep my family safe."

Trudger looked at little Jerry. The baby's cheeks bellowed in and out, and his eyes were wide open, staring up at his father's forehead. "Yeah, I guess you do."

"It's the Rule of Three's."

"The what?"

"The Rule of Three's. I read about it in *American Survival Guide*. I memorized it." Jerry stared at little Jerry while he recited, " 'A person can live for three seconds without thinking; three minutes without air; three hours without shelter; three days without water; three weeks without food; three months without hope.' So I'll store food and water in this shelter I'm building. It has air vents, of course. And I'm always thinking. So if a disaster happens, we'll be fine."

"What about hope?"

"That part is bullshit."

By noon, Jerry senior had drunk three twelve-ounce beers, the baby had sucked up two six-ounce bottles of formula, and Trudger had taken his scheduled ten milligrams of olanzapine.

"So, Trudge, what's the deal with you and all those pills, anyway. Do they help? Do you hear voices?"

"I hear everything."

Little Jerry spit up on Trudger's shoulder when Jerry senior thrust the baby at him so he could go out to the car and unload the wood. It left a pasty spot on Trudger's jacket that smelled rusty, like nails. The space heater gave off waves of warmth that cooked the drops of gas and oil on the cement slab floor and made Trudger feel happy dopey. After an hour, he went outside for fresh air, just in case, and Jerry senior told him to take the boy, too. Trudger took him by the handle of the car seat, and watched the boy smile in his sleep with the first slant of sunshine on his face. So they passed the morning with little Jerry sleeping and eating, content in his car seat next to the space heater whose orange glowing rods gave off heat that looked liquid, while Trudger and Jerry worked on trimming lumber from a heap of scraps that Jerry got cheap at Handy Andy.

They all went inside to eat lunch, which Trudger fetched from the Taco Bell just a half mile away. Jerry threw him the car keys and ten bucks to go get it, but Trudger threw back the keys, saying, no, he wasn't allowed, and he'd rather walk anyway. After lunch, which was two beers and six Taco Supremes for Jerry, Burrito Grande and Nachos for Trudger, and six ounces of Similac with iron for little Jerry, they stayed inside and napped.

At least the Jerrys did. Trudger couldn't sleep in strange places, so instead he stretched out on the living room carpet and listened to little Jerry in his carseat in the corner making wet breathy sounds every few minutes, and to his cousin on the couch, snoring, his hands folded on his chest like a saint. The sun came in the uncurtained windows with the full force of noon, which was not much force at all in February, but it fell over them all the same, not one of them getting more or less of the warmth and light it offered, and Trudger thought how that didn't happen too often, and he felt lucky, and that didn't happen too often either.

Back outside, after the nap, little Jerry started to cry. Jerry senior tickled him under the chin and then he picked him up and rocked him, but still the boy cried. Trudger held his breath as Jerry pulled back the elastic waist of the baby's pajamas and peered down the tunnel of his little butt, but it was clean and then Jerry checked in front, too, but he shook his head no, the boy was dry. Trudger handed his cousin a half-full bottle of formula from the workbench. "Maybe this will keep him quiet."

"I don't think he's hungry." Little Jerry refused the nipple, holding his slippery lips tight together, but crying still, so Jerry senior put him back in his car seat. Trudger stared at his watch, willing the baby quiet. But little Jerry's cries grew more shrill, his face raging redder.

"No, this is colic." Jerry senior rocked the car seat with his foot. "It usually happens at night, but babies, who can tell anything with them. There's nothing you can do about it. You just have to ignore it. Come on, let's just finish up here." Jerry picked up a rusty hacksaw and braced a short piece of lumber against the workbench, while Trudger backed into a corner as far from little Jerry as possible. The baby's cries were like the crack of gravel on a windshield, hitting him in the chest, ricocheting to his ears. He wondered how thin his eardrum was, if cries like this could pummel through leaving nothing but a ragged hole of permanent silence behind. Trudger sat on the milk crate and covered his ears, rocking back and forth, until he heard another sound through his fingers.

"Goddamn. Son of a bitch." Trudger looked up to see Jerry holding his hands tight together as if he were reciting a prayer, blood leaking out of his clasp. The baby shrieked louder as Jerry stomped the cement floor and then came to Trudger in the corner and opened his hands to him, offering a deep and ragged flap of skin that traveled down his thumb to the meat of his palm, oozing red the whole way. "Jesus Christ. Look at this. This looks bad."

"Then don't look." Trudger moved his hands to his eyes.

Jerry held his hand up and wrapped a dirty rag around it. "I've got to do something for this. It's deep. Maybe stitches and a tetanus shot too, I bet. Stay here with little Jerry for me. I can't take him with me when he's all worked up like this. Beaumont Hospital is just up on 21 Mile Road. It won't take long."

"Don't go. They'll cut off your legs."

"Trudge, you've got to stay here and help me out with little Jerry, okay?" Trudger shook his head no as his cousin walked to the car and drove away.

Little Jerry cried still. Trudger got off his milk crate and stood over him, looking down. The baby's body vibrated with the pitch of each shriek, like he was a drum skin being beat. And not knowing what to do, but knowing he couldn't listen to that anymore, Trudger picked up the little boy and held him close to his chest, hoping the beat of his own heart would let him know everything was okay.

But Trudger's own heart beat too fast and his hands shook so the baby probably knew better. Everything wasn't okay at all. Trudger walked into the house, thinking maybe the baby was cold. By that time, the boy had been crying for twenty minutes straight and his face was red. Sometimes the cries were so high they made no sound at all and lasted for a long while without a break for breath. Trudger tried to remember Jerry's rule for how long you could live without air, scared that the boy would suffocate himself or break some cord in his throat that would mute him for life. So he held him tighter, then looser, and he rocked, then stood still, then paced between the living room and kitchen, but it didn't seem to matter to the boy, who was answering something inside him that wouldn't stop.

Trudger wondered if babies crying at him was to be the newest torment in his life. His hands shook and he felt like he'd better do something, anything. He kicked his jacket off the couch and onto the floor and shoved it to the part of the room where the sun shone in. Then he placed little Jerry in the middle of it and tried to fluff up the down around him, hoping the boy would feel the ease that came of lying in the sun just like they'd all felt together before.

And then Trudger stood in the doorway and watched and listened. He wasn't hopeful. Something had started that had too much momentum to stop. He'd known such things before. Knew nothing good came of them, whether they started out good or bad. Remembered how when he was seventeen, he'd gotten suspended from school because one morning he'd skipped his classes and walked up and down the mausoleumlike hallways instead, kicking lockers on either side, just listening to the metal vibrate. Remembered how he'd taken up running the year after that, running for hours every morning, not stopping even when he'd lost so much weight his mother cried. Remembered when he was twenty, he ate only hot dogs for eight months. Chewing. Laughing at his mother as she begged him to eat something else. Knew that he'd fight his father again. Hitting. Slamming. Though now his mother wouldn't be watching. Pleading. Sobbing. Trudger was the reason things started and didn't stop, that much was clear to him. He left the house. Left little Jerry alone there. He couldn't be there anymore. His head hurt too much. Pinching. Goading. The boy couldn't stop. Wailing.

Once outside, Trudger moved along the side of the house to the living room window and looked in. The sun had moved on to slash another strip of the room in light, so Jerry junior lay in shadow and cold, curled and tense in the swaddle of Trudger's jacket. He cried still, an awful wail, though the piercing note of it had dwindled, as if he'd been beaten badly and had only enough strength left to whimper. Without his jacket, Trudger was cold. The sun had shifted west to settle on others, the room he looked in on was dim except for the one strip of sunlight away from little Jerry.

Trudger stood still at the window, breathing hard, waiting to feel the relief of his escape from the little boy. But it wasn't right. His heart still beat too fast and his head hurt. He needed to move. He reached in his pocket for keys that weren't there, looked at the driveway wishing for his car, but seeing only an oil spot seeped deep into concrete and glistening on the surface. He had no means to leave with the speed he needed. He had to stay still.

He walked back into the house slowly and pulled his jacket full of little Jerry across the carpet to the only slash of sunlight left in the room. The baby rolled onto his stomach along the way, and Trudger kept him that way as he arranged him in the sunlight. Then he rubbed the baby's back and stared at the side of his face, which was squished red like a stewed tomato and misshapen from his long bout of unspoken terror. Little Jerry hiccupped now between cries. Watching him, Trudger thought how his cousin Jerry sure wasn't perfect, but he could be a lot worse. Jerry was just a little luckier than Trudger. His father was probably luckier than them both. And between cancer and having him for a son, his mother hadn't been so lucky at all. Trudger wasn't sure about little Jerry's luck. That would take more time to tell.

If he could have gotten in his car and driven away from the little boy, he would have. But instead, Trudger stayed still in the shadows, giving the sunlight to little Jerry, and making quiet, coin-sized circles on the baby's tiny back.

Though thirteen-year-old Joey Waterson had been living in Chicago with his father and his father's wife, Louise, for just three months, he already knew life with them would be another version of not-so-good, even if the sheets were cleaner and the dishes matched.

But the wind's chill blasted all those thoughts from mind when he came home from school one snowy Monday in late February and realized he'd lost his house key. His father and Louise wouldn't be home from work for another two hours at least. He stood on the porch, looking at the snow, which had subsided to flurries. Jacket open, hands rooted in his pockets (he'd lost his mittens too), he shifted his weight in his canvas sneakers.

He found a half-eaten granola bar in his backpack and nibbled it slowly, remembering all the survival movies he'd seen. A minute later the granola bar was gone, eaten in two distracted gulps, his attention diverted by the flyer for Quicky's Oil Lube Shoppe that he pulled out of the mail slot and by the erection, his second that day, that pressed against his jeans. He ran up and down the driveway then, hoping the movement would warm his feet and maybe soften his dick.

As he ran, the curtains in the window of the house directly across the street moved, and he saw the old lady who lived there watching him. His father had helped her with some heavy boxes just the week before. He said that she was in her late seventies and her husband had died about six months ago and she was lonely and confused because of it. When Joey asked how so, his father said she seemed forgetful sometimes. That she liked to listen to show tunes and sometimes just stared into space in the middle of a sentence. None of that sounded too bad to Joey, so when he saw her at the window that cold day, he figured maybe he could go over there and stay at her house for an hour or two.

He rang her doorbell four times, then began to doubt that he'd seen her at all. He stepped off the porch, looked at the window again, and there she was staring right at him. When he waved, she backed away. Seconds later, the door opened a few inches, and he saw a slice of her face bisected by the chain lock. "Yes?"

Joey stepped back and took his hands out of his pockets, "Umm, yeah, hi. I'm Joey Waterson. I live over there. I lost my house key and my dad and his wife won't be home for a couple of hours. I thought maybe I could wait here. It's cold out today."

She looked suspicious. "Oh really? You think I'm some old fool? How do I know you're who you say you are? What's your father's name?"

"Mark Waterson. He's a lawyer." Joey thought his father's job might lend legitimacy to his cause.

"And his wife?"

"Louise Patchel."

"And what kind of cars do they drive?"

"They only have one—a green Volvo." He saw her abandon an "aha" she'd planned on that one, and she looked so disappointed, he almost wished he had criminal intent. "Listen, just forget it. Maybe my father will come home early today."

She looked at his wet shoes. "Your father never mentioned a son."

"I was with my mom in Detroit before."

"How old are you?"

"Thirteen."

"Hmmmm. Why did you show up now?"

"I lost my key."

"No, no. I mean why are you with your father and not your mother?"

"She had to leave."

"I suppose you caused some sort of trouble?"

Joey jammed his toe into a crack in the porch, "I don't know. Maybe."

"Well at least you've enough sense not to deny it. Come in. Sorry for the third degree, but you can't be too careful these days. Boys your age always seem to be attacking old ladies on the ten o'clock news. You can wait here. My name is Helen Hupp, by the way." Joey walked in as she opened the door wide. "Hold on just a minute now. Take off your shoes."

He stamped his feet to get rid of the snow clinging to his high-tops. Helen put her hand on his shoulder and frowned, "Please. You're shaking the rafters." She walked away as Joey slipped off his coat, then returned a moment later holding a pair of brown leather slippers. "Here, put these on—they're my husband Walt's." Joey looked at his wet socks. "Don't worry. He won't mind. He's dead."

Once in the slippers and the house, Joey turned suspicious, the heavy stillness of the place was unsettling to him. He looked at Helen again, more carefully. Delicate blue veins patterned her temples like a china plate design. She wore her graying red hair swept up loosely on her head. He'd never seen anybody so old who was so pretty. Taller than most women, she moved like a slow flow of water, arriving all of a piece, instead of limb-by-limb like almost everybody else. She moved like his mother he thought, remembering how she used to glide into his room at night, brushing his cheek with her fingers and wishing him sweet dreams.

Helen motioned him to follow her to the kitchen and at her urging he ate two large pieces of Sara Lee crumb cake that she proudly and repeatedly told him she'd bought at a ten percent senior's discount at the outlet store. After he finished, Joey sat uncomfortably and watched Helen hum a song and rap her knuckles in time on the table. She stared out the window. The clock on the wall ticked slowly—creeping toward four. Had he really been that cold outside?

"Say, Mrs. Hupp, how about I shovel your driveway? It's a mess."

Helen looked at him annoyed, "That's the last thing you should be doing. You know the doctor said to take it easy."

"What?"

"Deny, deny, deny—that's all you do these days, Walt. You have to accept it. You have to slow down."

"Umm, Mrs. Hupp, I'm Joey Waterson, your neighbor. I'm not Walt. I can easily do the driveway. I'm skinny, but strong." Joey thumped his chest like Tarzan.

She looked at him, still annoyed. "Call me Helen. I know you're not Walt—don't be foolish. But I can't afford to pay you, and I'm perfectly capable of shoveling my own snow. I might even wait for a thaw. I have nothing to be on time for."

"You don't have to pay me. I'll do it for free. It's a return favor for letting me in."

"Oh, well then, that's different. Let's do it together."

Helen lent Joey a pair of Walt's fur-lined, brown leather gloves, and she arranged a pair of red fuzzy earmuffs on her own head, carefully covering her ears, without flattening the upswept wave of her hair. Once outside, Joey and Helen worked out a system to clear the driveway. Arms straining as he pushed, barely equal to the task of lifting the heavy snow once he got to the edge of the driveway, Joey cut the first wide swath through the almost foot-high accumulation. Helen followed behind, gleaning the spillover he left on either side of his wide shovel, her own shovel narrower, her own arms trembling equally, though her load was much lighter.

An hour later, the front walk and the driveway cleared, Helen invited him back in. She poured them both a cup of black coffee, telling him only a child would drink it any other way. Joey, cold enough to obey, winced with each hot dark swallow.

They sat like this until Helen got up suddenly and began searching the counter behind her. She came back to the table with a pill bottle in hand. "These are for high blood pressure. I'm in remarkably good condition for a woman my age, but I'm not supposed to drink coffee anymore. If my daughter knew, she'd kill me." Joey watched as she put a small white disk in her mouth, took a swallow of coffee, and threw back her head. "If you ever meet Joanne—that's my daughter—don't tell her I did that."

Joey looked at the clock again. "How about we play a game or something?"

"No. I hate games. When Joanne brings out Trivial Pursuit at Christmas, it's enough to make me wish I were alone in a nursing home drunk on eggnog."

"Not that kind of game. I'm thinking of this thing these kids at school play. Not that I play it with them. Nobody includes me, which is fine. Anyway I listen in during lunch while they play this game. It's called The Worst. You take turns telling one of the worst things that ever happened to you or that you did to someone else and the other person has to guess if you're lying."

"That sounds awful."

"Well, maybe, but it's fun. I'll show you. See I had a sister, well half-sister, Allison—my mom never even married her dad—and she died. She had a brain tumor. But that's not what I care if you believe. Here's the worst. Two years ago, she killed my dog, Wigs. She purposely left open the gate and Wigs ran away and got hit by a car."

Helen studied his face. "That's a horrible story. I don't believe any of it."

Joey laughed and gave himself a point while Helen protested,

"Wait a minute. How do I know you're telling the truth about telling the truth?"

"You just do. If you lie, something bad will probably happen. This girl, in my class, Katie Mullins? She lied and said her parents were getting divorced and she sprained her ankle in gym that afternoon. Come on, you go now."

"But I want to hear more about your poor sister the dog killer."

"That's not the game. You just tell stuff—not why."

"That's a shame. But then, it is your game." Helen closed her eyes. After a minute, Joey cleared his throat, thinking she'd fallen asleep. She spoke then, "I never go visit my husband's gravesite."

"You lie." Joey grabbed his turn again, not waiting for Helen to admit the truth. "My mother took off and left me alone after my sister died."

Helen looked at him and took another swallow of coffee before she spoke. "I suppose that could be true, but then you seem nice enough, and what kind of a mother would abandon her child? No, you're lying. And even if you're not, I'm sure there's much more to it than that."

"One more point for me." Joey, gleeful, punched his fist high in the air, his troubles good for something after all. But when he told Helen to take her turn, she looked puzzled, got up from the table slowly, and said she didn't know what he was talking about and what was he doing in her house? At first Joey was confused— the sudden change was creepy—but then he remembered what his dad had said about her, and he became more curious than scared.

Joey stayed in the kitchen and watched as Helen went to the stereo in the living room and started the album on the turntable and then sat in a chair looking out the front window. When he realized she might sit there for a while, he went into the living room, picked up the album cover from the coffee table, and followed along with the lyrics to *South Pacific*. Ten minutes later, while Helen hummed and Joey read lyrics for a song titled "I'm Gonna Wash That Man Right Outta My Hair," Joey saw the Volvo turn into the driveway across the street. He gathered his backpack, slipped into his soggy sneakers and, pretty sure that Helen didn't notice his thanks or departure, ran to his father's house.

Louise only pretended to be furious when Joey told her he'd lost his key. He could tell she was secretly glad he'd screwed up again. He tried to play by her rules, but no matter how he placed the dishes in the dishwasher or made his bed, he never did things to her liking.

He'd only met her three or four times at most before he moved in, though she'd been married to his father for almost five years. His dad and mom had divorced before he could say the words to question why, and his father hadn't lived close enough to visit often. Though he knew why they'd married in the first place— he'd been born four months after their wedding—his parents gave conflicting reasons for their divorce. His mother insisted it had truly been a case of love—opposites attracting, she said—but they'd never figured out how to swim through the mess of differences they found. His father never mentioned love. Instead, he mentioned that they'd each been twenty when they married. He only said they had been much too young.

His father and Louise had moved from Detroit to Chicago soon after they married, and Joey saw less of him, his always infrequent visits becoming even rarer. For the two years that Allison was sick, he'd visited only on Joey's birthday. Joey didn't understand how his father could get it so backward, moving farther away when he needed him most. His mother tried to console him by pointing out that Allison had never even met *her* father. That at least his father sent a monthly support check. But Allison and Joey had decided long ago that her father must be dead or a priest or in prison, so this gave little comfort.

When Joey finally called him, after his mother left, his father asked him three times to search the apartment for a note with a number where his mother could be reached. After picking him up in Detroit and while driving to Chicago, his father assured Joey

things would be different living with him and Louise. But he
switched lanes to avoid a tailgating semi as he spoke, and though
he might have meant to comfort, his voice got tight and the words
came out as a warning.

The first week, Louise approached him like a camp counselor,
chirping directions on how to clean the bathtub and make his bed.
Now, three months later, she acted more like a secret service agent,
quietly superior, barely raising her voice, just nodding and pointing. She was pretty enough to have made Joey shy the first time
he'd met her. He'd only been seven at that time—his father had
picked him up from his mother's to take him out for dinner and
brought along Louise, his new girlfriend. Joey remembered how
he'd been unable to look up at her directly for how much her sky-
colored eyes and gleaming black hair made him smile. Now, six
years later, living with Louise and his father, Joey found her pret-
tiness was overshadowed by other things about her that he didn't
like so much. He was sure she really believed she was better than
everybody else. And she had good reason. Everything she did, she
did well. She sewed, played tennis and golf, cooked, swam, vol-
unteered for everything. She even cut her own hair—and it had
layers and bangs—and she sprayed it so that it looked just as good
when she came home at the end of the day as it had when she left
in the morning.

Louise worked as a librarian in a law firm while she went to
law school part-time. Joey could tell she couldn't wait to do better
than his father, who had a small private practice, but he also knew
she couldn't have picked a less interested opponent. His father
rarely took up a challenge. When Louise wanted to leave early to
be sure to be on time for a party that would probably start late,
his father turned off the TV and got ready to go, no matter that
it was fourth quarter, game tied. When she said they needed to get
outside and start cleaning the gutters, Joey watched his father put
aside the Sunday paper without even a sigh, his coffee still steam-
ing, and follow her agenda.

Joey noticed these things right away because he was good at reading people. He'd always been able to predict his mother's behavior—knowing just how much attention he could steal before she'd turn back to Allison, just how much heartache she could endure before she'd crack, just how best to comfort her when she did. He'd thought he knew her inside out.

But maybe he'd lost his touch. Maybe getting it all wrong was going to be a new phase of his life. It certainly seemed that way in Chicago, because the week after Joey lost his house key, he misread things again. He should have noticed the reluctant way his father came to the dinner table, like Judas at the last supper. Louise passed a plate to Joey. "Joe, it seems to me that since you moved in with us, you haven't pulled your weight around the house. I know it's been an adjustment, but we thought maybe it would make things easier for all of us if we worked out some basic ground rules. We've drawn up a contract . . ." She pulled out a batch of papers from under her placemat as she spoke. Joey looked quickly at his father, who buttered a dinner roll, and then swiveled his attention back to Louise. ". . . It outlines the duties and responsibilities you have as a member of this household. I think you'll find it fair and reasonable. We've suggested a signing deadline of one week. That gives you plenty of time to look the contract over. To make sure you understand it. To let us know if there's anything you want to negotiate."

Louise handed Joey the contract and then took a tissue from her sleeve and sopped the drops of water condensing on the side of her glass. He read the first sentence, *This contract is being entered into on the date set forth below by the parties Joseph Waterson (hereinafter referred to as JW) and Mark Waterson and Louise Patchel (hereinafter collectively referred to as MW-LP).* She must be kidding—Joey laughed.

Louise placed a platter of chicken on the table and then stood behind his father. "It's no joke, Joe. You need to learn to be responsible, and your father and I want to help you. I know you've had a lot of changes lately and your mother wasn't ever a good role model, but you can't carry that around as an excuse all your life."

Joey looked at his father, who nodded, barely. "It's just Louise's way," he said. "It's nothing personal." Louise's hand clamped his shoulder. "Just read it and sign it," he said, self-consciously. "It's not so bad. You'll see. We really aren't asking for anything out of the ordinary. It's just some chores and common courtesy." Joey folded the contract into his shirt pocket. He looked at Louise looking at him and he coughed, making a point not to cover his mouth, while he stood and reached across the length of the table for the chicken.

He was mad at himself. He should have seen that trying would never be good enough with Louise. He shouldn't have counted on his father to reel her in when she went too far. From the day he moved in, that had been clear. His father had shown him his room and then left him alone to unpack. He stayed alone for a few hours, trying not to think of his mother, wishing someone would come and talk to him.

When he finally went downstairs that day, he found Louise mopping the kitchen floor. She looked up when he came into the room. She'd tied a white bandana around her head and her hands seemed enlarged by the yellow rubber gloves she wore, but Joey remembered thinking, even then, that she was awfully pretty. She leaned on the mop and waited for him to speak. He'd hoped she'd say something nice to him, but she'd just stood there, looking at him, leaning on the mop as if his arrival that day had weakened her. He'd asked for his father because he didn't know what else to say. He's working out, Louise said, and pointed to the basement door. Joey clomped downstairs, buoyed at the thought of a home gym, but except for the furnace, washer and dryer, and workbench, the large unfinished room was empty.

His father looked up and waved as Joey entered the room, but he kept walking the perimeter, arms pumping, counting the short laps as he came round full circle. He didn't say anything until Joey broke the path of his stride. "Hi son. Move a little out of my way there, please. I'm almost done here. Only twenty-five more laps to go."

"What are you doing, Dad?"

"Speed-walking. It's too small to jog down here."

"Why don't you run outside? It's not that cold."

"I usually do, but Louise is nervous right now. Some guy mugged somebody at gunpoint just two blocks from us last week. The police think it's an aberration—this is a really good neighborhood—but they warned us all to be on the lookout. So I told Louise that when it's dark outside, I'd speed-walk inside instead of going for a run. That's what she wanted. You'd be surprised at how good a workout this is."

Joey nodded, just to be polite. His mother had always been matter-of-fact about being on the streets of Detroit at night. Lots of times she took the bus to work because their old car was always breaking down. Work was always some factory job or other that Joey knew she was too smart and pretty to hold. When he was ten and Allison was eight, their mother had been a cutter at Sunway Corrugated Cardboard Factory right off Mt. Elliot near the GM Cadillac Assembly plant she was trying to get into so that she could have a union job with good insurance and a grievance procedure for when her foreman kept asking her out or the guy working next to her made two dollars more an hour. She never did.

But two years ago, just a few months before the doctors found Allison's brain tumor, their mom got a job at Champion Spark Plug near 8 Mile and Gratiot. It was a lot farther from home, and it wasn't a union shop either, but the hourly was good and they gave her Blue Cross. When Allison got sick his mother swore at God and then thanked him for the timing. Just six months earlier, she told Joey, and she would have had the cheap insurance she'd bought on her own and Allison probably would have been herded into some lousy osteopathic hospital instead of Children's Hospital of Michigan, the best there was, and close to their apartment too. In the end, none of that made a difference.

Joey tried to imagine Louise taking the bus to a factory job. He could see her setting down a newspaper before she'd sit on the seat, or placing a tissue around the pole before she'd hold on to it, because somebody raggedy had gripped it tightly the moment before. Louise would only travel in daylight, he was sure of that. His mother used to walk home from the bus stop late at night, depending on her job at the time. Joey asked her once to be careful, and she told him not to be afraid for her. "Joey, I've only got mace and a bus transfer on me when I'm out there. There's no payoff in mugging me."

"They don't know that. Or what if they just want to hurt you?"

"I'm fast and strong and I can scream. Nobody is going to bother me. I have to get where I have to go, don't I? I don't really have a choice, do I? Come on," she hugged Joey, "don't worry so much. I'll be fine. Really. You worry too much."

Watching his father's long strides around the perimeter of the basement, Joey wanted to tell him this story. He would have, too, if only he understood why his mother had left him without so much as a good-bye. How courageous was that? Maybe his parents had more in common than they thought.

In his room after dinner the night Louise gave him the contract, Joey sat at the window, lights off, radio tuned to his favorite station, trying to think of nothing, staring into Helen's house. Her window shades were rolled up and the lights were blazing. He'd stopped by to see her almost every day since he'd lost his key the week before. He had nothing else to do and she was easy to talk to, though he wasn't too sure she heard everything he said. He'd have to remind her to pull down the shades at night—she shouldn't expose herself that way. He turned away from the window to change the station as a song he hated blared.

As he settled on WBEE, he heard the DJ announce that the fourteenth caller would win tickets for a weekend concert at the Rosemont Horizon. He didn't hear the name of the band, but he pushed the preprogrammed Killer Bee speed-dial button on the telephone and waited for an answer, and wasn't too surprised when he won. The DJs at most of the stations he listened to knew him because he called and won things so often. He was lucky that way.

When he turned back to the window, cheered by his good fortune, he saw Helen in her living room. She wore a frayed pink bathrobe that clung to her in damp spots like Saran Wrap on Jell-O. She must have just come out of the tub. Her breasts stuck to the thin fabric in two damp circles. Looking at them and at the slices of her thigh that flashed where her robe gaped, Joey felt himself get hard again.

A few months ago, he thought he'd go crazy trying to stop these erections that came on out of nowhere, like more bad news. There didn't seem to be any connection between what he saw or thought and what happened to his penis. A math problem, a girl, a dead squirrel in the road—he'd gotten hard at all of these.

At his old school, before he'd moved in with his father, the health teacher had talked about sex in a careful, roundabout way that made it seem like everything connected to that world was soaked with regret. When she'd finished, she seemed so shaken that Joey wanted to do something to comfort her, but he had no idea what that would be. He left class with all the other boys, half of them making smart-ass comments, the other half looking scared. He'd know what to tell that teacher now. That sex or death or life or whatever, she better learn to care a lot less.

He sat at the window watching Helen a little while longer, and then went to bed, where he didn't sleep well, dreaming of small tight spaces where arguments take place.

Joey woke early even for a school day, but hearing somebody already in the bathroom, he didn't get out of bed right away. He picked up the contract from his nightstand and read a paragraph. *JW shall be entitled to use of bathroom and kitchen when MW-LP is not in need of said facilities. JW agrees to wipe faucets with sponge*

3223322222322

after each use to avoid water spots. JW will wipe up all kitchen spills immediately to avoid marks on floors just scrubbed. Tea bags and loose tea are to be dumped into trash can immediately to avoid sink stains.

What was Louise thinking? He didn't even drink tea. And why had his father agreed to be part of this? He must realize that since moving into their home, Joey had been careful of everything he did. He had nowhere else to go, so he was on his best behavior.

On the very first night he'd arrived, Joey had overheard his father and Louise talking about him. She said she wanted to hire a private detective to track down his mother. His father wasn't so sure. He lobbied for patience. "Her daughter just died. I don't want to make her feel hunted. I think she'll come back on her own. She's probably in shock. But he's her son, Louise. She won't stay away forever. We should wait. Give her time. She loves Joey."

"She left him. What kind of love is that? I don't care how shocked she is by her daughter's death. What if she never comes back? How long do we wait, Mark? How patient do we have to be?"

"Well, he's also my son. I have a duty to him."

"You've always sent child support. On time, too."

"True."

"And you were three hundred miles away."

"But nothing should have kept me from him, should it?"

"No, of course not—not in a perfect world—but we had a life, a home, responsibilities. Your practice takes up so much time and energy. You always sent money. I don't think you've been negligent."

"I bet he does."

"No. She abandoned him. You picked him up. He'll remember that." Her voice trembled, "He's a teenager. Think of the trouble he could get into. I don't know how I'm going to handle this, Mark. It came on so suddenly. I know it's not his fault, but I'm not good with surprises."

"You'll do fine, Louise. You always do. It won't be for long.

And don't worry. He won't get in trouble. She'll come back for him. I'm sure of it. He seems like a decent kid."

Joey crept upstairs after that, the uncertainty in his father's voice reinforcing all the fears he'd ignored during the three increasingly desperate nights he'd spent waiting for his mother to come back. The first night wasn't so bad because, worn out, he slept through her departure. They'd spent the day clearing Allison's things from her room. She died just four days before, but his mother wanted to do it right away, before she lost her nerve, she said. In the beginning, she stared at each item before she put it in the "throw away" or "give away" pile. She swore she couldn't keep a thing. But after an hour, she started a third "to keep" pile, and Joey watched it grow biggest of all.

Late in the afternoon, when they'd finally finished, his mother had called Goodwill and scheduled a pick-up of Allison's white wicker bed frame and dresser, for the first available opening, which was the following week. Then she went into her room and cried, alternately curled up in bed like a discarded ribbon or hunched over her open dresser drawer, looking at a tea-colored lock of hair that she'd clipped from Allison's head and wrapped in wax paper two years earlier, right before they'd shaved it for her first operation. Joey remembered the warm powdery smell, soft like clothes from the dryer, that rose from the drawer whenever he opened it. For two years while Allison had operations, chemotherapy, radiation, remissions, and relapses, her lock of hair lay beside his mother's lipstick and a tiny sewing kit from the Ramada Inn. After Allison died, his mother added a holy card to the waxed paper packet. It listed Allison's birth and death dates along with a prayer for peace from St. Francis of Assisi.

Joey paced the apartment as his mother cried that evening. He was tired. He'd carried boxes of Allison's things down to the Dumpster at his mother's instruction. He'd packed books and clothes in other boxes that she wanted for Goodwill. He'd moved furniture aside so she could sweep up dust and doodled scraps from Allison's notebooks and stretched out hair scrunchies. He worked as fast and hard as he could, trying to save his mother from the task. He saw how her misery and anguish had come between them like a shield, blocking him off from her, and he knew he couldn't pierce it now. He could only care for her and wait until she was able to see through to him again.

He hovered in her bedroom doorway that evening. Every now and then he'd ask her please to eat the soup and sandwich he'd made for dinner, but he was afraid to get too close and give her a chance to push him away. He went for a walk after he ate some soup. He thought maybe fresh air would help him think of what to do, of how to somehow save his mother from this grief that had downed her.

Once outside, he walked fast, squinting through a light rain that dissolved into the dusk and gave the street a pewter cast. When he got to Mt. Elliot, he turned left and slowed down. He looked around as he walked—it wasn't a safe place to be alone at night. The block was lined with board-ups. Only a few places—a tattoo parlor, a bar, a *taquería*—still did business in the rubble of his neighborhood. Joey stopped and looked through a plate-glass window on which LEW'S TATTOOS was spelled out in neon. He saw an old man sitting at a table, watching a portable TV that rested just inches from his face. When the man looked up, Joey waved on instinct. The old man didn't wave back, he just stared at Joey for a while and then looked down at his TV. Not knowing what else to do, Joey headed home to watch his mother cry some more. He fell asleep late that night oddly comforted by her sobs, which were at least proof of her presence. When he woke to silence the next morning, he sensed her absence and he stayed in bed awake for an hour before he finally overcame his fear, got up, and proved himself right.

The second night was worse, because he knew she'd really left him, maybe even for good, and he dreamed it as well. In his dream, his mother lay on a hill next to him and Allison, a gun in her hand, shooting out the stars, which exploded into each other every time she aimed and pulled the trigger. With only one bullet left, she handed the gun to Allison, who turned and rested the barrel against Joey's temple. He begged her not to shoot him, and distracted her by pointing to the only star remaining in the sky, the North Star. He told her he'd do anything for her, give her anything she wanted, if only she could hit it.

Allison moved the gun from his head, aimed at the sky, and pulled the trigger. The shattered star streaked toward them, a streamer of fire and sparks that exploded as it landed on her. She crumpled and burned, like paper on an open flame, bits of her floating past Joey and his mother, delicate pieces of ash that hovered around them, before being torn to dust by the breeze. His mother turned to Joey, her face a shroud.

He waited alone in the apartment for one more long day and night, during which he kept the TV blaring and slept spasmodically on the couch in front of it. The sound of soap operas, talk shows, game shows, sitcoms, and late night TV rescued him from dreams. The next morning, he finally called his father after he looked in his mother's dresser drawer. The waxed paper packet was gone, the powdery smell already musty.

Now, three months later and in Chicago still with his father and Louise, he hadn't lost hope that his mother would return, but he was no longer certain he'd run into her arms when she did.

Joey carried the contract in his pocket all week long, rereading it before, during, and after classes. *MW-LP agrees to provide JW with three meals per day plus snacks provided JW helps with grocery shopping every week, only buying those items that MW-LP has specifically noted on a detailed list. JW also agrees to use a glass to drink milk or orange juice and to rinse and place said glass in dishwasher when finished with it.* She had him there, Joey thought, wondering when she'd snuck up and seen him gulping straight from the carton.

By the time the final bell rang on Louise's deadline day for signing, he knew the contract by heart, but he didn't know why Louise had to ask so coldly. Did she think it was his fault that his mother had left? That he could have said or done something to

make her stay? He slammed his locker shut on his finger and set
his lips tight, trying not to cry.

He'd had chances after all. A few days before Allison died, when
the doctors said they couldn't do anything more, Joey had kept
vigil with his mother at the hospital. Allison looked better than
she had in months, as if she understood that soon she wouldn't
have to worry about any of this anymore. His mother, on the other
hand, looked terrible—her skin was gray from exhaustion and her
hands trembled through hourly cups of vending machine coffee.

Joey tried to tell her they'd be all right. But she must have
known better. They both knew they never would be. Still, she
roused herself that night, right before sending him home to get
some sleep, she held him hard and told him she'd always love him
no matter what. Yet she'd left.

In the contract, Louise agreed to do his laundry, providing he
paid her for it with two hours of errand running per week. Joey
saw the advantage of this forthright exchange versus the uncon-
ditional love his mother swore to, then abandoned. But what kind
of father would agree to something like this? How had he come to
have two such parents? Helen hadn't believed him when he'd told
her about the contract one afternoon while they played The Worst,
she was sure he was lying. He brought the contract over the next
day to prove he wasn't. She sat at the table reading it and Joey
watched her expression change from skeptical to angry to concerned. When she finished reading, she hesitated and then, choosing her words carefully, said that if this is how they wanted it, then
he'd better negotiate firmly, adding that it was an awfully peculiar
thing for a father to do.

After school, on the contract deadline day, Joey walked home
up Lincoln, the sun shining in his eyes, blinding him to details.
When he reached his block he went to Helen's, hauling her empty
trash cans up the driveway. She wouldn't admit it, but she really
needed his help. Maybe she was the answer to his problem. Maybe
he could move in with her.

If he could talk Helen into letting him live with her, he could

take care of her, making sure she took her pills on time and gradually switching her to decaf—smoothly, secretly, so that she
wouldn't even notice. They could continue to play The Worst,
and each time Joey would relinquish another bit of his true story.
He could watch his father come and go as scripted by Louise. They
wouldn't lose touch. And he'd be able to watch out the window
for his mother—he wouldn't risk missing her when she came to
get him. It would be good for everybody. Helen would see that.
He'd have to bring it up carefully though. It was a serious favor.
He'd wait for just the right moment to ask.

After he put the trash cans in the garage, he went to the front
door and rang the bell repeatedly. Loud music seeped out the
door—he knew she was home. Finally, hearing Robert Goulet
singing "If Ever I Would Leave You," he gave up trying to get
Helen to answer and he turned and opened his arms to the street
as if it were filled with his audience, and then he began singing
the song, which he'd memorized at Helen's urging just the other
day. Caught up in the lyrics, Joey didn't notice when Helen finally
opened the door. It wasn't until he'd sunk to one knee, with his
hand on his chest, and bowed his head wishing he were in Camelot
that Joey heard Helen clapping.

"Bravo, Joey, that's wonderful. Come in."

"Oh, hi Helen. Thanks." Joey got up and faced her, "I just
stopped by to see if you're okay or if you need help with anything
or anything."

"No, I'm fine. Don't need any help. But come in anyway. No
sense staying out in the cold. I heard you on the radio this morning."

"You did?" Joey stamped his feet as he entered the house.

"Mmm hmmm. You were taking that quiz about basketball. I
knew it was you even before I heard your name. You came through
clear as a bell."

Joey crossed his arms over his chest, embarrassed, but wanting
to preserve his pleasure at her praise. "I won a Sony Walkman. I
already have two. You can have it if you want it."

"No, no. You keep it or give it to somebody else. Headphones ruin my hairdo. Besides, I only have records."

"So, do you have any work or anything you want me to do?"

"Work?"

"Yeah, you know, cleaning up stuff or moving stuff or whatever?"

"Why the sudden interest in work? Sit down. I'll make coffee. I've got day-old donuts too. And I thought of another game we can play. I think we need a break from The Worst. Forgive me, but it's too depressing. This new game—my mother used to play it with me and my brothers and sisters when we were little. It came to me last night. I'll go set it up now. You stay here."

Minutes later, Helen called him to the kitchen. She sat at the table, her face lit by a candle—a rough stub of paraffin a half inch high. She motioned him to sit in the chair across from her, in front of another lit candle. Though the sun pierced the sheer curtained windows, the burning candles gave the kitchen a sacred air, and Joey sat down, feeling calmer and more settled than he had in months. He asked Helen what they were doing, but she only told him to be quiet and watch his candle.

They sat like this for a few minutes, until Helen spoke again, "Your candle is burning faster than mine."

"So?"

"You have to watch it closely for as long as it burns. The one whose flame goes out first will die before the year is over."

"What? I thought you said this wasn't depressing."

"I know. It sounds crazy. But then we're not doing it completely right. As a girl, we *only* did this on New Year's Eve. That's the proper timing. I often lost and I'm still around—so there's no *real* need to worry. Still, it spooks you doesn't it?"

"Well, yeah. This was your mom's idea? She *let* you play with fire? What kind of mother was she?" Joey remembered the favor he'd come to ask, and changed his tone, "I'm sure she meant well."

"Well, it's not as if she left us alone—she watched us while we did it. She was superstitious and this was an old custom. She may have mixed it up a bit. Or maybe I did. Mothers were different then. They didn't worry so much about everything. My younger sister and I thought it was a wonderful game, though I remember my older brother Tony got quite upset one year and knocked over all the candles before they burned out. The oil cloth started to melt, and my mother had to pour a pitcher of water on the table. I think Tony took it too seriously. He just didn't want to die. Not that I wasn't scared whenever my flame went out first, but I realized soon enough it didn't have to mean the end. During the year, I only thought back to it when miserable about something, and then it seemed like it might not be so bad if I *did* die."

While she talked, Joey's candle burned down lower until it was just a puddle of wax with a wick—a faint floating flame. Helen's candle still held a hint of its shape and burned steadily.

"Helen?"

"Yes?"

"Maybe I should come and live with you. I mean you could probably use the company and I could help out around the house—shovel the snow and stuff like that. I wouldn't be any trouble. I would only be a help, you know."

Helen stared at her candle flame while Joey spoke. He wasn't sure she even heard him. Seconds later, he saw a thin trail of smoke coming from her candle, and its wick glowed orange, branding the air around it. Helen looked up at him, "No Joey, that won't work. I can't start expecting help now. I like being alone right now, anyway. Your father will come to understand how much he wants you with him. Your mother will, too. Besides, look," she pointed at her candle, "I'm going to die soon. Where would you be then?" She smiled as she spoke, but a quiver in her voice made him think every word a lie.

He couldn't get her attention after that. She stared into space. He snuffed his candle and went into the living room—angry at Helen for refusing him and at himself for asking her in the first place. He looked at the pictures of Helen and Walt and their daughter scattered all over the room. In most of them, Helen stood to the side, or behind the other two. Her husband always stared straight ahead, and when he smiled, his eyes weren't in it.

Helen came up behind him and pointed at Walt's right eye in one picture, "It's glass. That's why he looks so odd."

Joey was still mad, but his curiosity ruled. "Cool. How did it happen?"

"Childhood accident. Nothing dramatic. A stick or something—he used to lie and say it happened in the war. I think he lied about a lot of things."

"How long were you married?"

"Fifty-five years, but it seemed like a hundred. The man was no saint, let me tell you. I think I hated him for one reason or another most of the time we were married."

"Why do you have all these pictures then?"

"I don't know—habit, decoration. And anyway hate is not a simple thing. It gets complicated."

"Not for me. People screw you—they're history." Joey snapped his fingers as he said this and made a slashing motion through the air, knocking down a picture of Walt that stood on the coffee table.

Helen looked up at him as she stooped to retrieve it, "Now Joey, I know for sure that's a lie."

Joey left when she turned to put an album on the stereo.

He didn't want to go home right away, so he turned left and walked to the tracks along Ravenswood to watch the rush hour commuter trains. He kicked patches of old snow, stubbly ground cover, dried up azaleas, and sturdy evergreen shoots as he hiked up the sloping banks leading to the tracks. Near the top, prickers scratched his hand as he pushed through a brambled patch of bushes. He stopped to watch the blood beading along the ragged line of flesh, then wiped it on his pants. Once at the top of the bank, he scaled a six-foot fence and walked to the easement between the north- and southbound tracks, waiting for a train to hurtle past.

He'd come here before, drawn by the coppery echo of the train's whistle as the engineer saw him standing close and blared a warning. But he needn't have worried. Joey wouldn't step on the tracks. His thrill came in trying to stand stone-still while the rush of metal hurtled past. Sometimes he screamed obscenities as loud as he could, but usually he just searched the blur of faces behind the passing flash of windows hoping to see somebody, anybody, he knew.

A train approached from downtown that day as he ran to position, six feet west of the northbound tracks. As it came into sight, a quarter mile down the line, he felt himself get hard again, and tired of only standing by, he put his hand in his pants and wrapped it around his dick. Then as the 5:12 sped past, destination northern suburbs, Joey stood in the noisy vacuum it created, feeling the full weight of his burdens, and in that rush of wind and noise, he cried, jerking off with his bleeding hand, wishing that just for once the train would jolt to a stop so that the blank faces at the dirt-pocked windows would be forced to see him. But it never did. They never saw a thing.

An hour later, he went home, exhausted, his hands and face streaked with tears and dirt and blood, his pants spotted. He walked like a zombie, not noticing when people stepped out of his way. Louise pulled the car up the driveway as he approached, waking him from his daze. It was Thursday—one of his father's late nights at the office. She rested her head on the steering wheel for a few seconds after she cut the engine. She must be tired too. For a moment, Joey saw how hard his being there must be on her, and he approached as he never had before—with concern, not trepidation. But when she opened the car door, before she even said hello, she asked him if he'd signed the contract, "It's deadline day, you know."

"I'm not going to sign it. It's bullshit."

"Hey, no swearing here, Joe, you know the rules." She stepped back, leaning against the car, as she looked at him. "Oh my god, you're filthy."

"You're such a bitch, Louise." Joey, who had been heading into the house, stopped and then moved toward her instead as he spoke. He heard her catch her breath. He saw fear in her eyes. He understood this better than anything she'd ever said to him, so Joey backed away and started to apologize. But then he thought of Helen sitting in her living room surrounded by pictures of a person she hated, and he ran past Louise into the house, fists clenched, taking the steps two at a time to his room. He locked the door, shouting at his father to leave him alone when he knocked an hour later and asked if he could come in and talk.

He stayed put all evening, catching up on homework he'd put off for the past week. Done with that, he looked out the window for a while, then finally fell asleep on the floor while reading *Sports Illustrated*.

When he woke after midnight, he was stiff and hungry. He walked into the hallway. He heard water running in the kitchen and crept downstairs, ready to run back up if it were Louise. The kitchen was dark except for the light over the island sink in the middle, where his father stood scouring the gleaming white enamel, a shaker of cleanser in hand, his sleeves rolled up to his elbows.

"What are you doing, Dad?"

"Nothing. I told Louise I'd clean up in here tonight and then I started watching Leno and I lost track of time. She went to bed early—before I got home even. She didn't feel well. She said she had a bad day."

"I called her a bitch."

"She mentioned it."

"I'm not signing that contract."

"I know. She doesn't blame you. You know, she really means well. She just does the wrong thing sometimes. Once you get to know her better, you'll see. Her life hasn't always been easy." Joey imagined himself in twenty years trying to explain to his son how first his father and then his mother had left him. How he knew his future by heart, reading it over and over in the dismay of everybody who heard his story. His father continued, "Joey, I wish you'd just give this some time. I mean we don't even know each other."

"Whose fault is that, Dad?"

His father, shaking cleanser, began to answer and then coughed as a cloud of powder enveloped his head. Joey, tired of waiting, turned and started back upstairs, then slipped out the front door instead without his father even noticing. He needed to be farther away for a moment.

It was warm for March. Helen's house was dark, all her shades but one drawn tight—she'd listened to his advice, but said she wouldn't give up the moonlight in her bedroom. He thought about how she listened to her old albums and stared into space, sometimes for hours. She probably was a little senile. Maybe that was her secret—checking out every now and then might be the thing that made her able to endure. But it didn't make her someone he could count on.

He sat down on the far end of the porch. The contract, in his back pocket, crackled. He recited the last paragraph in a whisper, *The parties involved agree to do their best to coexist in a healthy manner that is based on mutual respect and family ties. It is the responsibility of both MW-LP and JW to foster said ties.* He heard the dead bolt on the front door slide into place. His father, completing his nightly rounds, had just locked him out without knowing it. He saw clearly then that as long as he lived with his father and Louise, life would be a matter of endless maneuvering around matters mostly small. There wouldn't be room for anything more—no chance of change—everything would stay secured in its current proper place, while he wandered, lost, in a maze of rules.

He lay on his back on the porch looking up at the faint stars and thought of all the people he had good reason to hate: his father, Louise, his mother, even Helen. He envied Allison's escape.

He pointed his right index finger at the brightest star he could find, directly above him, squinting shut one eye and making a trigger of his thumb, cocking it and taking careful aim. He counted slowly to three and moved his finger to his temple. When he felt it resting coolly there, he pulled the trigger and made a crack of sound that splintered the quiet night. He felt a momentary sense of readiness that calmed and assured him, telling him he'd finally found a place filled only with quiet and ease.

A light went on at Helen's then, denying him that rest, illuminating the more likely landscape of his life. The one against which he'd do battle alone, struggling not to be like his father, who quietly accepted all things wrong, or like his mother either, who ran fast and strong but in the wrong direction.

He lay anchored on the cold cement for a long time, steeling himself to return to the people inside the dark house behind him who didn't know they'd locked him out, his mother who did, and the old woman across the street who was destined to die.

SETTLED

Sylvia sat on the five square feet of her Bunnert Street apartment porch hoping for an evening breeze. The beer she'd opened fifteen minutes ago was already lukewarm. Strange weather for May. Different from what she was used to. Most everything was.

She looked up and down the street. Her apartment complex faced 12 Mile Road to the north. Traffic sped by all day and thinned only late at night, so that she slept to the intermittent whoosh of tire on pavement, a suburban version of waves on the shore. It was only seven, it was hot, it was still light outside, but no kids skipped down Bunnert or 12 Mile Road. No wonder. Even now, traffic was heavy.

If she'd been sitting on the front porch of her old house on Charlevoix in Detroit, she would have been surrounded by the neighborhood kids. Charlevoix had been full of kids with stories to tell. They'd hung around her house, especially on spring and summer evenings, probably because she didn't have kids of her own to siphon attention away from them.

Charlevoix—Sylvia sighed a little thinking about it—such a

beautiful street name. Detroit had lots of others like it—Lafayette, Kercheval, Grand Boulevard. She was forty-two years old and after driving on those streets for the past twenty-six years, she couldn't get used to living on Bunnert Street in Warren, just four miles north of the Detroit city limits, and traveling up and down streets like Schoenherr, Hoover, and Groesbeck. Those street names caught like phlegm in her throat.

She'd moved to the apartment complex just six months ago when her landlord on Charlevoix had sold the house she'd rented for ten years to his niece and nephew, but her family had urged her to move for years before that. "Get the hell out of there Syl, before you get shot at or worse." She couldn't remember which of her three older sisters had put it exactly that way. It probably hadn't been the oldest one, Donna, who lived in Canada and rarely called or visited the States, as if she needed a whole other country as buffer. Her others sisters, Laurel and Anne, urged her to leave Detroit too, "Why don't you move here to Chicago . . . to Boise? Why do you live there?" Her mother and father, who had fled Detroit for the suburbs in the 1970s while Sylvia, their youngest, tried college, used to go on the same way. They'd both died a few years ago, understandable deaths, complications of old age—hearts tiring, joints wearing out. She missed them. But they had added their voices to the din, and she didn't miss that.

When the building manager had shown her the Bunnert Street apartment, only the third she'd seen one afternoon, she'd realized she was sick of looking already and she'd filled out a rental application before even checking the water pressure and the locks on the door. What did it matter? She didn't know where she wanted to live and until she decided, Bunnert Street was as good a stop as any.

Since moving, she lied to her sisters, "Oh, I like living here— I'm glad I finally moved." She didn't think they could hold the truth of how much she missed life on Charlevoix. Besides the neighborhood kids, she missed buying milk at the corner store, where it cost seventy-five cents more a half-gallon, but where she didn't have to wait in line under fluorescent lights to pay, and where the Chaldean store owner always asked about her cat, which was nice of him even though he clearly had her confused with someone else—she was allergic to cats. She missed waiting for the bus on the corner of Charlevoix and Algonquin. Missed the liquor store on the corner there, especially when the lotto jackpot went over twenty million and she could walk in and see a long line of hope on display, desperation too, all for the price of a Coke. Here in Warren, nobody waited for the bus. Instead, everybody drove everywhere as if their own right foot was created just to hit the gas pedal. The stores weren't on corners. And the people bought their lotto tickets at the gas station, cars idling a few feet away.

But until recently, she'd lied to herself about the move to Warren even more than she lied to her sisters. Her mistake hadn't been leaving Detroit. It had been staying there too long. Not because of crime or safety. Because of inertia. She'd trapped herself in the comfort of stillness on Charlevoix. And if she wasn't careful it could happen again, even in too-many-cars-and-gas-stations, not-any-kids-or-corner-stores Warren. For the time being, she was more suspended than grounded, but she wouldn't hang forever, and she knew it was distinctly possible that if she didn't make a decision about what she really wanted before she settled back down, she'd die alone of old age on Bunnert Street.

She heard the phone ring through the screen door behind her. That would be one of her sisters. Probably Laurel, just arrived, after driving in from Chicago. Donna and Anne were flying in early the next morning and going straight to Mt. Olivet Cemetery where they were all due at noon. She found the phone on the seventh ring, hidden behind a stack of boxes she'd finally started to unpack that afternoon.

"Syl? Is that you? I just got here."

"Where are you, Laurel?" Sylvia raised her voice over a car alarm that screamed outside. She shut the door seconds later, when it didn't stop.

"Not far. The Holiday Inn. In Mt. Clemens. Did you sign all the permits? Is everything ready for tomorrow?"

"It's all set. But I'm a little worried about this. What if it's a big mistake? What if it's just too sad? What if we all can't stop crying?"

"You know Mom and Dad would want this."

"They're dead. I don't know that at all."

"Sylvia, we've been through this a dozen times. They didn't want Maureen left buried alone at Mt. Olivet. Even you finally left Detroit, though I can't believe you moved to Warren of all places. That is the most god-awful suburb of Detroit."

"Rent is cheap here."

"It should be. Listen, I've only been here twenty minutes and I'm already bored. Meet me somewhere for a drink."

"Come over here. I don't feel like going out. Anyway, you should come see where I'm living now."

"No thanks. Warren depresses me more than the Holiday Inn."

"Laurel, do you want to have a drink with me? Or do you want to insult my choice of home?" Really, Sylvia thought, it was asking too much to be put in the position of defending Warren.

"You're right. I'm sorry. I'll bring over a bottle of wine. Do you have anything to eat? I'm starving."

Sylvia looked in the refrigerator and saw mayonnaise, olives, a Coke. "I'll make something."

After hanging up the phone, she went back outside to finish her beer. She looked at the nine other porches on the first floor of her building—nobody even had a doormat, much less a potted plant. Laurel was right, this place was depressing.

The Farmer Jack Grocery store sign towered across the street from her porch, on the other side of six lanes of traffic, reminding her she was hungry and Laurel expected dinner. If only Farmer Jack weren't so deceptively far away. There it was glowing like Oz, yet to get there, she had to walk a half mile west to Schoenherr so she could cross at the light. Warren, with its wide streets and extra lanes and green-arrow left turn lanes wasn't looking for foot traffic.

Of course, she could drive, but it was so close that would be ridiculous.

She looked at her watch. Laurel would be there in thirty
minutes. She'd be ridiculous. She got her purse and car keys and
went out the back door to her assigned parking space, number 8A.
It was empty. She looked at the Taurus in 9A and the Honda in
7A, thinking she might have parked a number off. Starting to
panic, she looked at spots one through seven and ten through
twenty. And then she remembered the car alarm she'd ignored
during Laurel's phone call.

Her GEO was definitely gone. She'd lived in Detroit all of her
forty-plus years and never even seen a crime committed. Six
months in supposedly safer Warren, and she was a statistic. Everything was backward here. Nothing was right. And tomorrow she'd
be party to the disinterment of her sister Maureen from her grave
in Mt. Olivet Cemetery in the middle of Detroit and its reinter-
ment to Resurrection Cemetery in the suburbs. Yet another body
deserting the city. And she'd agreed to it, had even signed the
papers that allowed it. So that was her fault too.

The headstone was already removed from the gravesite when Sylvia
and Laurel arrived at Mt. Olivet the next morning. They could see
a mound of dirt and a truck next to the open hole when they
parked. They were hungover—Laurel had arrived at the apartment
with a bottle of red and white wine and after Sylvia had reported
her stolen car to the police, both had gone down smoothly with
olives.

"Syl. I think I'm going to puke, I swear to god." It was too
warm for May, 95 degrees. Laurel's air conditioning didn't work
and a glisten of sweat condensed on her forehead, which was white
as ice. She'd dyed her chin-length, dark brown hair red a few
months earlier. As it grew out now, she looked like an ice cream
sundae—vanilla, chocolate, cherry.

"Go sit under that tree until Donna and Anne get here." Sylvia
helped her sister over to a maple generous with shade. Laurel sat

down carefully, as if she'd slop out of control if she moved too fast.

"How come you're not sick, Syl?"

"I am. I just refuse to acknowledge it. You stay here, while I go look at the grave."

This part of Mt. Olivet, the children's section, was pretty with oaks and elms and maples and evergreens. The ground swelled gently here and there so that the headstones seemed supported. It was probably small comfort to grieving parents, but small comfort is what you get most times. At Resurrection Cemetery in Clinton Township, where they'd rebury Maureen in a plot right next to their mother and father, the ground was flat and treeless and the traffic off Clinton River Road sped by, disturbing the peace.

A battered blue pickup was parked to one side of the open grave. When Sylvia walked past it, she looked in the truck bed and saw Maureen's rose-colored marble headstone, face-up. Her mother told her once that she'd paid extra for the lighter rose tiles that rimmed the edge of the stone. Sylvia reached in and brushed dirt from the chiseled inscription. "Maureen Stanton. Beloved daughter and sister. God's little angel. 1953–1962."

Maureen had been nine years old, second-oldest after Donna, when she died suddenly of congestive heart failure. Sylvia, five at the time, the youngest of the five sisters, had clean streaks of memory of how sad everybody in the family had been, but only filmy recollections of how she'd felt herself. It was as if she'd been in a tornado, could describe the wreckage—the bathtub in the tree, the chimney blown to rubble—but couldn't remember feeling even one gust of wind.

She remembered that after Maureen died, Laurel, who'd been just eleven months younger than their dead sister, didn't eat dinner for a month, that their parents, who typically would have spanked such behavior out of existence, alternately ignored her and held her tight, maybe just needing at times to hold on to another little girl, one almost the same size as the one they'd just lost. She remembered how Anne, next in line after Laurel, had thrown herself into caring for Sylvia, fed and dressed and pushed her in her stroller around and around the block. She hadn't minded that it was Anne and not her mother who took care. Sylvia, who more than any of the others looked like Maureen—had her dark brown hair, light brown eyes, and a scatter of freckles on her nose—was glad for any attention. She remembered that Donna, the oldest at eleven, had ended up alone, too stunned to cry, spending whole afternoons hanging her head over the top bunk where she slept, looking down on the bottom one where Maureen no longer did. Sylvia remembered going to Donna once, standing on the lower bunk and looking at her oldest sister who lay still on a winter afternoon. The bedroom was cold, but Donna didn't use the blanket. She remembered her oldest sister staring at her, telling her in a croaky whisper to leave her alone, waving her away, and then rolling over to face the wall.

Or maybe it hadn't been that way at all. Maybe the bathtub was in the attic, not the tree. The wall in splinters, the chimney intact. Sylvia just wasn't sure. The particulars were hazy. The resulting solitude too real. All of them, parents and sisters, had been so shy about their sadness. Or maybe they'd discovered, the girls as young as they were, their parents in shock, that this is grief's secret—that grief, undiluted, is impossible to share.

Now, almost forty years later, Sylvia thought too that all her sisters had chosen good lives as a way of making up for losing Maureen. Donna had devoted herself to study—finishing high school in three years, college and med school in seven, becoming an oncologist, marrying a neurologist. Laurel had become a social worker and therapist who ran a group home for troubled teenagers. Anne was a mom with five kids, a sense of humor, and infinite patience. Sylvia thought that maybe if she'd just remembered more, felt more, she could have moved away from Detroit, just like her sisters. She could have been successful, been a scientist or computer programmer or professor of something. Instead she'd settled for less and less until she forgot that more existed.

Her sisters had given up on urging her to go back to college and make something more of her life, though in the past they'd all done a fair amount of that. Sylvia's most recent job was at an audio transcription company that focused on the financial services sector. Her qualifications for the job were of a general, anonymous nature—she could hear; she could type. She sat in front of a computer all day long and shuttled the audio that streamed through her headphones verbatim onto the computer screen, giving the "uh's and "um's" equal billing with the "sustainable levels of growth" and the "self-perpetuating cycles of deceleration." The language was inflated to direct attention away or toward more simple truths: "Hang on, it will get better" and "Times will always end up tough." Before this job, she'd been a secretary, before that a waitress, and before that a cashier at Kroger, and no matter how hard she tried, unlike her sisters' meaningful work as doctor, social worker, and mother, she couldn't make a case for any of those connecting to Maureen's failed heart.

Sylvia jumped when she felt a hand on her shoulder that morning at Mt. Olivet Cemetery.

"Syl? Are you okay Syl?"

"Annie." Sylvia hugged her sister who had just arrived from Boise. Anne's littlest girl, just two months old, was asleep in her arms. "And you brought Jessie. Oh, I'm so glad to meet her." Sylvia wondered if she'd recognize her sister without a baby in her arms or a toddler tugging on her hand.

"Well, trust me. This is how you want to spend time with her. She's such a cranky baby." Anne leaned down and kissed her sleeping daughter.

"I don't believe that. She looks like an angel." Sylvia looked over Anne's shoulder for a second. Donna and her eight-year-old son, Adam, stood under the maple tree with Laurel. Donna's wheat-colored linen dress had already crumpled in the heat, like a piece of paper wadded for the trash. Adam was Donna's only child. She'd been forty when she'd had him. Sylvia didn't know why she'd waited so long. Maybe it had been her career or fertility problems. Or maybe Donna took a while to get her courage up, afraid that she'd be left to stare at an empty bed again. Sylvia reached out and touched Jessie's cheek, "How's Donna doing? Did you come from the airport with her?"

"We rented a car together. She's in a terrible mood. She wouldn't even stop and let me get coffee. I feel bad about it though. I think she's just hiding how upset she is. She's still very against us doing this."

"We're all upset. She doesn't corner the market on being upset."

"You seem okay, though, right?"

Anne didn't wait for an answer, but looked down again at Jessie, who squirmed in her arms. Donna walked toward them slowly, her arm around Laurel on one side, holding Adam's hand on the other. When Adam saw Sylvia, he broke away from his mother and ran around the open grave. Sylvia opened her arms wide to catch her nephew, hugging him, feeling his shoulder blades, prehistoric, birdlike, jutting from his skinny frame, which looked even smaller in the huge hockey jersey he wore.

"Hi Adam, how are you buddy?"

"Guess what, Sylvia? I was assistant captain on my hockey team this season so I have this A on my sweater." Adam puffed out his chest and pointed to a patch above his heart. "We finished eighth out of ten in the league and that's not good, but still. And look, my mom bought me a yo-yo at the airport this morning. And in school, on my last report card, my teacher, Mrs. Pavliak, she said I was very creative." Adam was all talk and motion, jerking his arm up and down, the yo-yo bouncing at the end of its string.

"That's great, Ad. I used to be pretty good with a yo-yo. I'll teach you some tricks later. I remember your mom was good at it too." Sylvia looked across the grave at her oldest sister. "Hi Donna. How was your flight?"

Before Donna could answer, a man on a tractor drove up, and then another man, walking alongside, hopped into the grave with a pick and began carving a trench around the perimeter. The hole was about three feet by four feet. Sylvia remembered Maureen as being bigger than that. She looked at Donna across the open grave. Her sister looked down, but at her feet, not the grave, her hands smoothing her dress over and over, which was obviously a lost cause. More than any of them left on earth, as the oldest, Donna's memories cast the longest darkest shadow. No wonder she didn't want this site disturbed. .

Laurel and Anne had first e-mailed Sylvia and Donna about disinterring Maureen just about the time of Sylvia's move to Warren, and Donna had been set against it. Laurel and Anne tried to convince her. They set up a conference call so they could all talk about it together. Sylvia, who really hadn't cared either way, but was inclined to vote with her friendlier sisters, weighed in. "The new cemetery will be a lot easier for me to visit from my new apartment."

"Well, how often do you visit, Syl?" Donna asked, and all of the sisters on the conference call line got quiet, waiting to hear evidence of their youngest sister's devotion.

"Oh, I'd say once a month?" Sylvia lied tepidly, hoping her good intentions to go more often counted for something.

Donna continued vigorously. "Anne and Laurel, you put that idea in Mom's head just before she died. It's maudlin and disturbing. She never would have thought of moving Maureen's grave."

"But the child should be with the mother, and the father too." Anne spoke over one of her kids, crying in the background.

But Donna had patients in the waiting room and hospital rounds that afternoon, and she had no time for such sentiment. "They're all dead for god's sake. Listen, I've looked into this. Back in those days they didn't even require that a coffin be placed in a concrete vault. And if Maureen's coffin wasn't put in a vault, then there's nothing left to move anyway. You could end up spending a couple thousand dollars to dig up and rebury a bone chip."

"Well, I'm sure Mom and Dad would be happy to rest next to their little girl's bone chip." Anne dug in. "Plus she'll be out of Detroit. It's not safe for Sylvia to go visit there. She's so spacey some times—she's probably not careful enough. It's a bad neighborhood. I heard a report recently about all the crime that goes on in cemeteries. It's terrible."

"Oh bullshit. Sylvia exaggerates. I doubt she visits even once a year. Listen, I'm not going to stop you from doing this, but it's totally unnecessary and disruptive. Hold on a second, I have to take this call."

With Donna off the line, Sylvia sighed, tired. Spacey? Exaggerates? As the youngest, she often heard this kind of thing from her sisters. She tried to decide which charge to defend herself against first. In the pause, Laurel lobbied for her position, "Sylvia, we really need your help on this. You'd have to make the calls and sign the permits and all since you're still in Detroit. It will be a good thing. Maureen should be with Mom and Dad. That's what they all would want."

When they finally all got off the line that first time, Sylvia thought they'd raised more questions than made decisions. What would their mom and dad want? Would it be too sad? Should they just leave things be? Was there a vault?

There was a concrete vault. And that morning at Mt. Olivet, preparing to unearth it, a grave digger cleared a two-inch trench on its perimeter, and then another grave digger jumped into the hole and tried to attach a braided polyurethane cable to quarter-sized iron rings embedded in the cement on each long side of the vault. But the large cable clasps couldn't fit through the small iron rings. As the worker climbed out of the grave, he left his bootprint on the top of the vault. Two other grave diggers walked up to the site, and they leaned on shovels around the open hole. None of the men looked at the sisters, and though they talked freely about the problem with the tiny vault, they lowered their voices to a murmur. The funeral director who had guided Sylvia through the permit process also arrived. It was all official and necessary, the witnessing, the papers. Sylvia inched closer to the grave diggers so she could hear.

"The clasps on the braided cable are way too big for the vault's guide rings. The chain link has smaller clasps—we could try just using it to pull up the vault, and forget the cable. It's an awfully small vault—chain link will probably hold it. It must have been a little kid. What was it? A four-year-old?" The grave digger scratched his elbow as he spoke.

The funeral director came over to Sylvia and she introduced him to her sisters. He wore khaki pants and he didn't take off his sunglasses. He explained the problem, while one of the grave diggers jumped back into the grave with a six-foot length of chain link with small clasps on each end that he successfully attached to the iron guide rings on the vault. The tractor driver maneuvered the boom arm directly over the grave then, and the man standing on Maureen's vault attached the chain link to a hook that dangled over his head on the end of the tractor boom. Then he climbed back out again.

The driver raised the boom slowly while he backed up the tractor. The chain link ceased clinking as it went taut, and the earth gave up and the little vault pulled free of the dirt that had encased it for thirty-seven years and came clean to swing in the air at the end of the chain, at the end of the boom, surprisingly pristine except for the grave digger's boot print on top. Then, for a moment, the concrete, coffin-shaped vault, no cracks or chips marring its surface, suspended, not grounded, swayed at the end of the silver-colored chain link, shining white and cool against blue sky. A bright green laminated tag, attached by a thick black braided rope to a small iron ring imbedded in the narrow end, clattered against the concrete in the breeze. It was the only sound as the sisters and Adam looked on.

"Did you see that, etched in the side of the vault?" The funeral director removed his sunglasses and broke the spell as he murmured to one of the grave diggers. "It's a Guardian. I've never even seen one. They've been out of business for years."

The tractor backed up a little then and the driver swung the boom arm around to hover over a flatbed truck that had pulled up to the site. The tractor driver lowered the vault onto the truck bed, and then all the grave diggers put their shovels or picks on their shoulders and walked away. The funeral director, sunglasses back on, came up to each of the sisters and shook her hand and patted Adam on the head and then he told them he'd meet them at Resurrection Cemetery at the new gravesite in section ten in thirty minutes. As he drove away, Sylvia heard lite FM leaking through his open window.

Sylvia didn't look into the empty grave. She looked at her sisters, one by one. Almost forty years passed, she wanted to really see them, to acknowledge every feeling about Maureen that she'd ever ignored or denied or just been too young to understand. But nobody looked back. Instead, Anne unbuttoned her blouse and began to feed Jessie, who wailed. Donna almost fell into the deserted grave lunging for Adam, who slipped while jerking his yo-yo up and down into the hole. And Laurel, sweat dripping down her face, went back to the shade of the maple, leaned her head against the trunk, and threw up, barely missing her own shoes and two-toned fringe of hair.

Laurel swore she'd puke again if she didn't sit in a car with air conditioning. She gave Sylvia her car keys and asked her to drive it to Resurrection, and then she climbed into the front of Donna's rental, reclined the seat, and closed her eyes. As Sylvia gave Donna detailed directions to Resurrection Cemetery in Clinton Township, Adam got in the front seat of Laurel's old car.

"Oh no, Ad. Get out of there. You're coming with me." Donna put Sylvia's directions in her pocket and walked over to the passenger side window where she spoke to her son.

"I want to go with Sylvia. Plus, Mom, I can't concentrate when that baby cries."

Sylvia walked over to them, "He can come with me, Donna. It's no problem."

"It's not you I'm worried about."

"You know Don, that's so unfair. You wouldn't care if he wanted to ride with Anne or Laurel." Anne, settled in Donna's rental, tooted the horn. Sylvia slipped between Donna and the car door and then nudged her sister away. "You'd better go. Laurel's hungover. She needs to move."

"Honestly Sylvia, I can't believe you guys got so drunk last night."

"*Us* guys? I'm not throwing up." Sylvia felt a vein throbbing in her left temple and her mouth felt dry and tasted metallic. It was a miracle she wasn't heaving in tandem with Laurel.

"Well, you probably have a much higher tolerance."

"For your bullshit? Yes, I guess I have to."

Laurel moaned again through the open window. "You guys, quit fighting. This is my fault. I'm really embarrassed and really sorry. Can't we just get this over with?"

Donna's cell phone rang then, but before answering it, she turned again to Sylvia. "Be really careful," and then she leaned in the window and kissed the top of Adam's head. "Listen to Sylvia, honey. Buckle your seat belt." As Sylvia drove off, she heard Donna ask the cell phone caller how high the patient's fever was.

Sylvia turned north on Van Dyke out the cemetery gates and merged easily into weekday afternoon traffic. "So Adam, tell me something about school or hockey or home."

"Well, in my room, my mom and dad gave me a TV that doesn't really work, but that's not a problem because I can play Nintendo 64 on it. And *that* suits me just fine. And my friend Peter, he came over yesterday and he almost broke my Nintendo. But he didn't, which is good, because *that* would have been a problem."

A minivan in front of Sylvia swerved to the right. Unable to see over it, Sylvia swerved a little too, just enough to run over something metal and sharp. She heard the puncture before she felt Laurel's car sinking on the left front side. She slowed down and moved over two lanes, the car clopping along the road unevenly. She didn't see a gas station, so she turned into a 7-Eleven half a block ahead, pounding her fist on the steering wheel and swearing as she parked. "God damn it."

"You sound just like my mom when she drives." Adam tried to rewind his yo-yo string.

"You ever changed a tire, Adam?"

"Nope."

"Do you want to learn how?"

"Not really."

Thirty minutes later, Sylvia finally loosened the jack and the spare from the floorboards of the trunk where they'd been bolted tight and rusting in a puddle of water from a leak. She wondered if her GEO, wherever it was, had a jack and a spare. It was only nine months old. She'd never had reason to check. Sylvia looked at her watch after she'd worked the jack free and lifted out the spare. Adam leaned against a lamppost and worked on his yo-yo skills. "We'd better call your mom. They'll all be worried about us by now." She watched her nephew's still-futile efforts to make the yo-yo perform. It was hard to believe he was coordinated enough at hockey to be assistant captain. "Hey Ad, give me that and let me show you how to do it. Then you run inside and call your mom and let her know what happened."

Sylvia loosened the slip knot and wiggled her index finger into the yo-yo string. "First, you need to roll up your sleeves. Your hockey jersey is way too big. It's getting in the way. Then, the trick is just to flick your wrist, but not too hard. Don't use your arm so much. Keep it at a steady height. See?" Sylvia heard the whir of the yo-yo as it unwound from her palm and slapped back up again. "There are lots of tricks, too. You can make it sleep." Sylvia flicked the yo-yo down and let it spin at her ankles, suspended just an inch above the blacktop, until she twitched her wrist and brought it back again. "And once you learn to let it sleep, you can go around-the-world. That's where you kind of fling it out hard in front of you, and while it's still sleeping, you swing it back around and then . . ."

The yo-yo made a circle at her side and smacked back into her

palm. Adam clapped, and Sylvia smiled, surprised it had worked—
she hadn't yo-yo'd since she was his age. She slipped the string off
her finger, and then she dug into her purse. "Okay Ad, here's some
change. You know your mom's cell phone number, right?" She
looked at her watch, "It's one now. Go inside 7-Eleven and find
the pay phone and call and tell her we'll be another half hour or
so. Tell them not to start without us. Explain what happened. Tell
her it wasn't my fault."

Once freed from the rusty trunk, the jack fit right in place on
the front undercarriage, and Sylvia clicked the handle up and
down, raising the car's frame easily. As the tire spun six inches in
the air, she thought of Maureen's vault swaying gently at the end
of silver chain link. Maureen had been just a year older than Adam
was now. She wondered if Donna saw people die every day at the
hospital, wondered how that compared to her single loss of a sister.
Who would have thought, once they'd settled Maureen safely, per-
manently at Mt. Olivet, that forty years later they'd yank the vault
cleanly from the ground and find no roots or mud clinging to it,
just a bramble of memories? Sylvia picked up the tire iron to re-
move the lug nuts, but then jacked the frame back down again—
she'd forgotten to loosen them while the tire was on solid ground.

It took a lot of leverage to move the gritty threads of the rusty
lug nuts, but finally she loosened all five. Then she notched up the
car to her knees again, and took the nuts off, one by one, the iron
smell of them seeping into her hands, which were now streaked
with oily grime and dry copper-colored swaths. She was sweating
and as she reached up to push a damp strand of hair out of her
eyes, she glanced at her watch. It was 1:25. Adam was taking too
long. She rose up from her crouch and looked over at the 7-Eleven
just as a man, wearing a baseball cap and holding a purse tucked
under his arm, ran out the door. She froze for a second and then
she dropped the tire iron to the pavement. The clang woke her to
action. She ran.

Once inside, she scanned quickly. A woman, kneeling on the
tile floor, held her hand to her cheek. She wore blue jeans and a

bra. A clerk in a green T-shirt stood next to her, holding a white blouse dripping with a foul-looking substance, orangey-pink and lumpy. Sylvia looked around again and let out a deep breath she hadn't known she was holding as she saw Adam coming out of the candy aisle. But before she could get to him or even call him, he shrugged himself out of his hockey jersey. Then, bare-chested, shoulder blades protruding like wings, Adam walked up to the woman, draped his jersey over her back, and then patted her shoulder awkwardly. When he stepped away, he crossed his skinny arms over his bare chest, but Sylvia could still count the ribs in his skeletal frame.

"Adam." Sylvia called and he ran to her. She hugged him hard, imagining what it would be like never to do so again.

He hugged back, then quickly released his hold, and began to talk fast. "The phone was broke. I couldn't call my mom. I was just looking at the candy. This guy, he poured that disgusting stuff on the back of the lady's shirt real quietly. I saw him do it. Then he went up to her and he pointed to it and acted like somebody threw up on her. Then when she was trying to look over her shoulder, he grabbed her purse. But she didn't let go, so he hit her in the face and then he ran out."

"Oh my god. Are you okay?"

"I gave her my jersey. A lady should have a shirt on."

"That was really nice of you."

"I didn't want to look at her underwear."

A police car, siren squawking, pulled up, and two cops walked into the store.

The clerk and the woman gave good descriptions of the purse snatcher, so the cops let Adam and Sylvia go. "Kids today," one cop said to Sylvia as she patted Adam on the head, "it's hard enough for them to grow up without putting them through the system even as a witness. It's brutal."

"Yeah, kids today." Sylvia grabbed Adam's hand and left before the cop changed her mind.

Back on the road to Resurrection, she looked over at Adam,

trying to reassure herself. The shoulder harness cut across his skinny chest like a punishment, lashing him to the seat. Better to keep her eyes on the road. Donna would be frantic. They'd left Mt. Olivet almost two hours ago for what should have been a twenty-minute ride. Sylvia knew it wouldn't look good—being so late. Her hands and face were filthy and Adam no longer had his jersey. She didn't even have anything to cover him with. Despite her rusty, leaky trunk, her broken air conditioning and radio, Laurel's car was uncluttered—no blanket or old jacket or dirty laundry in the back seat.

When they pulled into Resurrection, Sylvia drove slowly looking for the signs to section ten, for Donna's rental car, or for her cluster of sisters, but the cemetery was deserted. Finally, after circling for ten minutes, she rounded a curve in the road and saw an open gravesite in the distance. It had a mound of coffee-colored earth on one side of it, and a woman sitting on the grass, her shoulders sagging, her head bent to her lap, on the other. The woman looked up as Sylvia drove closer. It was Donna, crying, all alone.

She ran to the car as Sylvia pulled up, but Adam was even quicker. Unleashing himself from the seat belt, he jumped out of the car and ran toward the grave to meet his mother. She grabbed him and held him hard, looking over him at Sylvia, furious through her tears. "Where have you been? I thought you were in an accident. Why didn't you call? Anne and Laurel are out looking for you. We waited an hour and then the grave diggers had to lower the vault. They wouldn't wait any more. How could you do this?" She sputtered, crying, as she spoke. Sylvia looked at her sister's dress, which was more tightly crumpled now and dark with sweat in the dip of her chest. A grass stain made a diagonal slash near its hem.

Adam, squirming, finally twisted loose of his mother's hold. "Mom, mom. Don't cry, Mom. I'm okay. It wasn't Sylvia's fault. We got a flat. A lady got her purse stole. So I gave her my hockey jersey. And look what Sylvia taught me." Adam held out his hand to display his yo-yo. Then he flicked his wrists and hips like Elvis, and flung the yo-yo wildly toward his mother, who ducked. Again and again he tried, and failed, to make the yo-yo sleep and then swing it around-the-world. Tried both to make his mother feel better and to keep her at bay, all while Donna stood guard, crying still, getting in his way, but refusing to leave him alone, or be left that way herself.

Sylvia, streaked with rust and oil and sweat, walked away and looked down at Maureen's freshly dug grave. The concrete vault had settled straight in its new earthen hole, the fit snug, the grave digger's boot print a dusty shadow now. Over her shoulder, she heard Donna, tangled in feelings past, sobbing still. Heard Adam, caught in the moment, laughing. Sylvia, tired past feeling, knew that sadness lurked. Knew that one day this skinny little boy would lose his exuberant belief that he could somehow make it right. She turned away from Maureen's new gravesite and moved to Donna's side. To hold her ground.

IF YOU TREAT THINGS RIGHT

My sister Lily is a handsome woman. At least that's what Giles, our foreman, always says. "And you, Jenny," he'll add, winking, "you'll do in a pinch."

Summers in the GM plant that Lily and I have worked in for the past twenty years aren't so bad early in the morning, but by nine or ten o'clock the heat pushes its way through the hundreds of small square windows, painted shut, glass and all, that line the walls. The paint bothered me until I realized that if it didn't block the light, the years of dust and dirt and grease would. Sometimes when the line breaks down and we get an unscheduled break, I stare at those windows and pretend that each pane has been washed clean and sparkling. If I stare hard enough, I can see and feel and hear light and air flowing in and heat and noise blowing out.

I work the main crib in the middle of the plant—where small parts are inventoried and stored. Lily works down at the end of the line as a cushion inspector. The plant is big and we're really not allowed to leave our work station, so we don't see each other much except for lunch. We've been with GM long enough so that when news of layoffs leaks out of personnel, we don't worry too much.

We both own a home—we live around the block from each other. We live comfortable lives, nothing too fancy, although Lily says I have too many knickknacks. And we'll have pensions. Mine will be nice and fat, because except for when I was laid off during slowdowns, I've punched my time card every day for almost thirty years. And that's just so far. I'm only forty-eight. I bet I've got twenty more years of work in me yet. Lily's will be smaller because she came and went, not appreciating how lucky she was to have this good job. But she's only fifty herself, so if she keeps her head on straight and stays here at GM, what with her Social Security and pension, she'll have a decent retirement too.

This summer, like every other one, a bunch of college kids, the sons and daughters of the plant supervisors and other management people, are working at the plant. They're hired as runners for special projects, coming to the crib to gather pieces that are missing from the models and bringing them to the workers on the line. Having these kids in the plant makes normal operations shift to a different gear. It's not really slower or faster—just not the same. It's like eating a nectarine after you've been stuck on peaches for a long time—you know it's different, but it's a matter of degree.

The kids in the group this summer, mostly boys, don't look any different from all the others who've passed through the plant over the years. They generally keep to themselves, laughing and joking and eating lunch together in the cafeteria, so I'm surprised when I walk out to the car to meet Lily after work today and one of those kids is leaning against the hood talking to her. His back is to me, but Lily sees me coming and at least she has the decency to look a little embarrassed when he grabs her hand and shakes it in both of his. He runs off to his car, waving to her, just as I show up.

I think about pretending I haven't seen anything, but I know it's bound to come out anyway so I ask her flat out, "What's he want?"

"Nothing, he's just a nice kid who thinks I'm interesting."

"Oh really? His father is tool and die supervisor on the fourth floor—a real bastard. You better watch out, Lily."

"Oh, watch out yourself. Listen, the truth is he's not *just* interested in *me*. He's doing research, some kind of psychology paper for a summer course he's taking at Macomb Community College. He's interviewing women who've worked in factories for a long time. You know how I like to talk. Hell, if you'd ever stop and say anything nice to anybody, he'd probably want to interview you too."

"As if I don't have enough to do without wasting my time yapping about the good old days to somebody too young to know how lousy they were. And I don't know why he has to go to college to learn how to ask women old enough to be his mother what it's like to work."

As Lily merges onto the freeway, I pick up my needlepoint bag and bring out the seat cover I'm working on. The pattern is pretty—orchids and greens on a mauve background. I think the conversation is closed, but Lily goes on.

"You've got enough to do? You call dusting tables you dusted yesterday and vacuuming the drapes enough to do? And how many of those damn things have you needlepointed in the past five years? There aren't enough asses in China to sit on all the seat covers you've made. Come on Jenny, let's do something tonight. Let's go out to dinner or to the show." Lily swerves to avoid a car that's cutting her off from the right.

"No thank you. I have meatballs that I have to eat before they spoil. And my show is on TV tonight. And if you don't like the seat covers I made for you, you just feel free to throw them away or cover them up with newspaper—my feelings won't be hurt."

I look down at the crewel wool in my hands and the oblong cross stitch pattern I'm weaving onto the canvas in my lap, but out of the corner of my eye, I can see Lily shaking her head slowly and I hear her sigh real deep. Ten minutes later, she drops me off at my house. It's been hot enough this summer that we've been

taking her car—a brand-new 1974 Impala from Rinke Chevrolet—
every day because it has air conditioning, instead of taking turns
driving as we usually do. I give her $2.50, which is my share of
gas for the week.

Before I go inside, I stop and inspect the boulder that rests
heavy on the corner of the lawn at the foot of the driveway. I
lugged it up from a field out in the country about eight years ago
after Lily had backed up crooked and put tire tracks on my lawn.
It's painted white so she can see it even in the dark. I look it over
every few days to see if the paint needs touching up. It's still in
good shape today.

I open the front door slowly, but then make a point of being
loud. I bang the door shut, jump up and down once or twice, and
run my needlepoint bag along a row of empty hangers in the front
hall closet. If a burglar is in the house, I'd just as soon he knows
I'm home so he can get his ass out the back door with no questions
asked.

My front room is tidy. I like it that way. The crystal prisms
hanging from the lamps are gleaming and the plastic covers on the
sofa and easy arm chairs are free of dust. I've had the carpet for
fifteen years now, and it looks as good as the day it was installed.
If you treat things right, they'll hold up for you. When I go into
my nieces' homes, the mess almost makes me sick. Lily isn't as bad
as the young girls, but she doesn't really care. The corners on her
bed are sloppy, her dishes pile up in the sink during the day, and
I can't say I've ever seen her vacuum more than once a month
under the sofa.

Lily can make fun of my ways, but I learned how to do things
right a long time ago and it stuck. If Lily had stayed with our
family after our mother died, she would have learned with me.
Hell, I've never criticized her for running off way back then, so I'll
be damned if I'll apologize for ironing sheets the right way for the
past thirty-seven years.

I settle in pretty quickly for the night. *The Carol Burnett Show*
is on TV and it would take more than dinner with Lily to make

me give that up. I work on my needlepoint, but my hands are stiff and I barely finish two square inches while watching.

On Saturday morning Lily calls early—she's going to Charmaine's Beauty Shop to get her hair done, do I want to come along? She catches me off guard—I don't have a good excuse, but I say no anyway. Then five minutes later, I change my mind and walk through my backyard and out the back gate, cross the alley, and cut through my neighbor Mrs. Stanky's yard. Once I'm through her yard, I walk down Mrs. Stanky's driveway and cross the street to the foot of Lily's front walk. You see, as the crow flies and thanks to Mrs. Stanky, Lily and I are really very close.

I catch Lily just as she's leaving. We're both surprised that I'm there. My sister's hair is combed carefully, and before she backs down the driveway she outlines her lips in thick red and then, placing a tissue between them, presses her lips together. She tosses the tissue, which holds a perfect shadow of her mouth, on the seat between us, and when I open the window to throw away my chewing gum, the tissue is lifted up and out—mouthing a silent farewell as it floats away.

Lily turns and looks me up and down as she drives along. "God, Jenny, you're a sight. What did you do, sleep with your head in a mixing bowl?"

"Well I'll be goddamned if I'm going to fool with my hair when I'm going to spend money to get it done up. Don't be so nasty Lily. And anyway, why the hell are you getting your hair done? It looks fine. You were just at Charmaine's last Saturday. You're not supposed to go again until next week."

Lily's face turns pink behind her rouge and she makes an exaggerated effort to switch lanes in the almost empty street, never answering my question.

At Charmaine's, Lily and I are given large plastic drapes that wrap tight around our necks and fall over our shoulders and down to our feet. We look like pup tents with heads. Charmaine works on Lily's hair. Her assistant, Betty, tackles mine.

When Betty asks me to lean back so she can shampoo, I'm stiff and reluctant at first, but within seconds I collapse under her strong strokes on my scalp. Her fingertips rake through my hair moving in small circles that gradually widen to the nape of my neck. When she rinses with warm water, I feel as if she's washing away the weight on my shoulders. I leave the shampoo chair feeling ten years younger, but when Betty sits me down in front of the big mirror where she'll trim and set, I see I look ten years older without the fringe of salt and pepper that framed my face before she slicked it back.

Charmaine's scissors click and snip without stopping as they work through Lily's hair two seats away. I read a magazine, trying to memorize a Jell-O recipe so I can bring it to my niece's house when Lily and I go there for dinner next week, but I give up as I catch a bit of Lily's conversation, "So, he's coming by this afternoon to talk to me and to interview me for his project." I look at Lily in the mirror she faces. Her eyes are closed and she sits straight, a half smile on her lips. With her makeup on and her hair flat and wet against her head, she looks like a store window mannequin who has lost her horsehair wig.

When we're driving home an hour later, I give her a little advice, "Don't go getting yourself all worked up about this kid, Lily. He's interested in his project, not in you. If you want my opinion, you just wasted $12.95 getting your hair done when it didn't need it."

"Oh, so now his project is legitimate? Seems just yesterday you were saying the reverse. And if we're going to talk about wasting $12.95 . . ."

I admit I am curious, but I purposely don't call her on Sunday, and when she picks me up for work on Monday morning, I say hello and pretend nothing at all has happened. Lily does the same. She's wearing her new pink blouse—the one she had been saving for our niece Rose's wedding shower next month.

When we get to work, we stow our purses and lunches in our lockers and walk out into the plant. Lily's head is spinning around like a dashboard dog—I'm sure she's looking for that kid—but still I don't say anything. It's only when she walks across the yellow caution line and straight into the path of a fork lift driver that I finally speak, "Lily Marie Dusza, I don't know what's got into you, but if you don't calm down and watch where you're going, you're not going to be alive to tell me what the good news is. Now pay attention. I'll meet you in the cafeteria at eleven."

The morning passes slowly. You've heard what they say about factory work and the assembly line—the monotony, the repetition—well, believe it. It's the same, the same, the same. I make it through my shift by playing games with myself. Silly things. I try to hold my breath until the next three people walk by, and then I try to guess the exact minute my coffee will go from lukewarm to cold. I play the time game more than any other—that's one where I'll bet myself it's 10:00, even though I really expect it to be at least 10:40 when I look at my watch. Most days when I look it's only 9:45.

Lily looks better when I finally meet her for lunch on the sixth floor, but as we're walking toward an empty table with our trays, I see the college kid approaching from the right. He has his tray in hand and he's left the pack of management people that always eats together on the south side of the cafeteria. I can't believe he has the nerve to try to join us, but I'll be damned if he'll succeed. Lily is far enough in front of me to miss seeing him. I call her back to a table with only two empty seats among all its others. The kid pivots and goes back to his usual lunch partners.

The cafeteria is hot and crowded and noisy. The only difference between it and the plant below is that the windows are clear up here so that sunlight shines through. On some days this helps. On others, it only seems to spotlight the bad food and dirty cement floor. We start eating without talking. I finish my ham sandwich in six big quick bites, then take my canvas and needle out of my needlepoint bag. "Now Lily, I know something happened at that interview with that kid. Spare me the details, but tell me what the hell is going on."

Lily looks up from her bologna sandwich, "Nothing happened Jenny. It was just a nice afternoon with a nice young man. He had his tape recorder on and he asked me questions about the plant and about what the city was like then and about my life. We drank iced tea. He thinks I'm extremely sensitive under my tough exterior."

I listen with one eyebrow cocked, my fingers flying through a double cross-stitch pattern on the petal of the orchid I'm needle-pointing.

I'm hoping that's the end of it, but two days later at the end of our shift when I come out to the parking lot to meet Lily, I see the college kid sitting in the front seat next to her. It's hot—95 degrees in the shade. The rotating fan that stands in the center of the crib has blown warm dirty air into my eyes all day long. My shirt is wet on my back and my glasses slide heavy down the oily slope of my nose. I moved slowly all day, even when Giles was around telling me to hop to it. A few times, when no one was waiting for parts, I fell into a half sleep-half stupor on my stool. When I woke up my quick dreams were already floating away in a river of sweat. Now at day's end, I have no energy. But seeing that kid in the car—in my seat in front of the air conditioning vents—really burns me up.

I walk toward the car, a little faster, the sandals that I've just changed into sinking into the blacktop so that I have to curl my toes to keep from stepping out of them. The air around me looks shiny and liquid through the clear exhaust that comes out of the tailpipes of the cars gunning to go home. I am dizzy.

Lily motions me to the backseat as I come near—the college kid isn't leaving. As I open the back door on the driver's side, she starts in on me, "Jenny, where have you been? I've been waiting ten minutes already."

I move my face forward into the stream of air blowing out the vent in the middle of the dashboard until my head is hanging over the front seat between the two of them.

"I'm tired Lily. And I'm not moving too good. What's he doing here?" I bend my head toward the college kid, without looking at him.

Lily turns to him, "I don't believe you two have met. Joe Palmer, this is my sister, Jenny Palazolla," then looks back at me. "His car is in the shop. He's going to come over and ask me some more questions for his project, and then I'll drop him off at home later."

Joe reaches back to shake my hand, but he misjudges the distance and grazes my cheek with his knuckles. I don't say anything as he apologizes. I just hold my cheek in my hand and nod to him.

"So, Jenny, Lily tells me you've been at the plant for a long time."

"Uh-huh."

"You must like it there."

I think to myself that he's an asshole. What the hell is he talking about? Do I like paying my mortgage every month and buying groceries? He's been at the plant a month now—does he plan to drop out of college and join the union? But I don't say anything and he doesn't push it, which I half think is smart of him until he starts to chatter.

That's when I realize that this is what he wants to do all along—just talk about himself—not hear about me or Lily. He brags to Lily about how well he's doing in his classes, which doesn't prove a thing because Macomb Community is not exactly Harvard, and how he got high scores on all his tests to get into college and how he has to continue to get good grades to keep up some scholarship he got from some company that makes surgical bandages. And he talks so much it hardly seems possible that he ever actually listens to Lily.

Lily drives fast. I can tell she wants me out, which is fine by me. When she pulls into my driveway, I jump out of the backseat before she or Joe can say good-bye. She backs out, scraping her fender on my white boulder.

The house is stifling. I walk down to the basement to start some laundry, but when I get there I lie down instead on the old couch where I usually sit and fold sheets and towels. I reach over and put my hand on the cool wall and then touch my palm to my cheek. I fall asleep.

When I wake three hours later, the basement is dark. I walk upstairs, take a cool bath, then eat some cottage cheese and cling peaches. Outside the kitchen window I can see the dusk settling in. I feel better than I did before my nap, and when I walk out the back door to sit on the porch, I'm surprised and grateful that the air is cool.

I think about Lily and work as I sit there—seems those two things have always been important in my life. Work because it was always there. Lily because she wasn't. I remember how scared I was when I was eleven years old, what with my mother just dead, and Lily running away to live with some distant relative in New York. I was cooking and cleaning for a father and four brothers. I didn't know what I was doing, but I remember lying in bed at night, too tired to be scared anymore, but still missing my mother and my sister too. I guess Lily had to do what she had to do, lord knows I wanted to leave just like she did. But, oh, I needed her company back then. Maybe I've been holding a grudge for almost forty years without even knowing it.

Thinking back makes me want to talk to Lily—maybe tell her what I've been thinking about, or maybe just apologize for being so crabby on the way home. I walk over to her house. On the way, I stop and look at the flowers in Mrs. Stanky's yard. They're closed to the night air, but their fragrance waves back and forth in the breeze like clothes on a wash-day line. The sky is clear of clouds, but the spotlight arcing back and forth from the used car lot a few blocks away dims the light of the stars.

When I walk out front and come to the foot of Mrs. Stanky's driveway, I look across the street at Lily's front bay window. The shades are up and a light is on in the living room. I can see in clearly. Lily sits in her wing chair—leaning back on a cushion I needlepointed for her fiftieth birthday. Joe Palmer sits on a footstool at her feet. They hold white paper cartons and each has a pair of chopsticks in hand. He directs food into his mouth with ease while Lily struggles to taste a morsel without dropping it in her lap. They are laughing and talking. I watch him put down his chopsticks and paper carton and come to Lily's side. Then, with his right arm draped around her shoulders and his hand wrapped around hers, he carefully guides the chopsticks from the carton to her mouth placing a peanut on the tip of her tongue. My sister looks up and smiles shyly at him.

I head home in the dark without Lily's company again.

I hold my tongue the next morning—I don't ask Lily a single question. She wants me to ask. She's almost asking me to ask, but I've *seen* her embarrass herself, I shouldn't have to *hear* it too.

When Joe Palmer comes to the crib the first time that morning, I ignore him and let him wait until somebody else is free to help. The next time he comes by, Giles is looking over my shoulder so I have no choice but to ask Joe what he needs. He's cheerful.

"Hi Jenny, how are you today?"

"Fine. What do you need?"

"A piece of molding for the X car, right front panel."

I walk away to find the piece. When I come back, he's talking to Giles.

"You treat him good, Jenny, or his father will be on your ass." Giles claps him on the back and pats me on the rear and then walks away.

"Sorry about that, Jenny. The guy is a jerk."

I turn away, "Takes one to know one."

"What?"

"You heard me, Mr. Community College."

"But Jenny . . . I don't understand . . ."

He's cut off by the shouts of people in line behind him. "Hey shut it—move on buddy. Come on Jenny, you're going to make us late for break." Joe Palmer walks away looking over his shoulder as if there is something wrong with me.

At lunch break a few days later, Joe Palmer sits down with Lily and me—a mistake. Management doesn't eat lunch with union. And Joe Palmer is management even if he has grease under his nails and steel-toed boots on his feet. I know trouble will brew, if not now then later, when I see Giles walk by and pretend not to see us. Joe and Lily are too involved in conversation to notice that Giles is purposely *not* noticing them.

At first I try to get Lily's attention so I can warn her, but then I realize I'm glad Giles is sniffing around where it's none of his business. That means I don't have to. I want Lily to pay for her foolishness. And I want to watch while she struggles to do it. She's kidding herself. She's a factory worker. She makes fun of my needlepoint, but did she tell Mr. College she plays bingo every Thursday night?

I'll watch him make a fool of her, and then I'll be there for her, arms open wide to hold her, just like when she came running home from New York, tail between her legs and divorce under her belt, five years after she left me. And there I was, already old at sixteen, worn out from raising four brothers into good men despite the help of our drunk father. She says I don't know what it's like to take a chance and do something? She's dead wrong. I did something. I raised a goddamn family and I learned while doing it not to be a fool.

I hear Lily squealing then and when I look up she is leaning over the table and hugging Joe Palmer who looks embarrassed. Lily sits back down and turns to me. "Now Jenny, isn't that great news?"

"What? What's great news?"

"Weren't you even listening? He got an 'A.' Joe got an 'A' on the paper he wrote about me. Oh, I know," she waves Joe off as he protests, "it wasn't *only* about me. He interviewed three other girls too, but still. He's going to bring it in tomorrow so we can read it."

Joe protests again, "Lily it's no big deal—and it's not that interesting."

Lily shushes him, leaning over the table to hug him again, "Oh, I am so proud of you." I watch him carefully and it seems that now he is embarrassed *and* annoyed.

Lily has a minicooler in the front seat next to her when she picks me up the next morning. I look in it and see a quart each of rainbow sherbet, Hawaiian Punch, and 7 Up, and the small bottle of cold duck that has been in her refrigerator since she got it two years ago as a birthday present from our teenage niece Mona, and who knows where she got it in the first place because she was too young to buy alcohol back then. She still is.

"What's all this?" Lily ignores me, so I poke her arm.

"Ouch. Stop it, Jenny. If you must know, I thought we could surprise Joe and celebrate his 'A' at lunch today."

"What's this 'we' crap? I don't want anything to do with him."

She doesn't say anything. When I look at her, she is staring straight out the windshield waiting for the light to turn green and she looks sad. When she finally speaks, I know she is confessing an uncomfortable truth, "I wish you'd be nicer to him. I really like him. I know he's young, but I think he likes me too and with this paper he interviewed me for and all, well, I feel special. It's like I posed for him while he painted a picture or something. It's silly, I know. And I know nothing will come of it, but for now it's fun, like I'm a girl again." She turns and hugs me and doesn't let go until the idiot behind us starts honking. At that she releases me, looks in the rearview mirror, gives him the finger, and then screeches off.

She sees Joe as we park the car and after asking me to carry the cooler, she runs after him. I watch as they talk for a minute and he slowly reaches in his knapsack and brings out the paper.

. . .

Lily reads it during our morning break. I search and then find her in the third floor bathroom—the most brightly lit one in the plant. I can see her feet in the corner stall. She's wearing the new Hush Puppy pumps we'd found on sale the week before at Bakers. I call out to her, and she tells me to go away until she's done reading, but I stay and wait.

And it's a good thing I do, because just a few minutes later she comes out of the stall, her hands to her face. She pushes me out of the way, and I try to catch her hand, but then I let her go and instead I pick up the paper that she's left behind.

Joe Palmer has highlighted those paragraphs that refer to Lily whom he identifies only as LD. I read the first few neon yellow passages.

> LD first worked in factories in the 1940s during the War. She was a young woman and she assumed it was something she'd do temporarily until she married and had children. But now, almost thirty years later, she is still working on the line. She lives alone and she has lost all perspective. The smallest things are the most important to her. Trivia and minutiae are the guiding forces in her life, which to an objective observer seems empty. Yet she is not unhappy, probably because any finer senses she had have been dulled by years of manual labor. Her hearing is assaulted by the constant factory din; her vision is dimmed by the industrial lighting. She is a woman who makes acquaintances indiscriminately because she is cheerful and out-going and has a wonderful sense of humor, but she has no real friends . . .

I stop reading as the bell rings signaling break is over. I walk by Lily's station on my way back to the crib, but she isn't there. I ask Ginny, who works across the way, to tell Lily I'm looking for her and I'll come get her for lunch.

Oh, I feel for my sister—deeply. And I also feel some satisfaction in knowing I've been right all along. Here's Lily thinking she's

Dinah Shore to his Burt Reynolds and this kid is looking at her and seeing Grandma Whistler. That yellow highlighting is worst of all. Does he think her senses are so dulled she doesn't even know her own damn initials? Or maybe he wants to make it clear what he thinks of Lily without having to say it to her face. Either way, this is the favor he does her, for though Joe Palmer writes that Lily has been dulled by the plant, I'll bet anything she is not too dull to know she has been played for a fool.

When I go to Lily's station to get her for lunch, Ginny tells me she left early. I still have the paper in my apron pocket and I head up to the cafeteria hoping I'll find her alone there. Giles gets on the elevator with me and right off he makes a crack about how strange it is that me and Lily are sisters, her being so damn pretty and all, and does she throw me all her old boyfriends?

He points at the paper and asks what it is, and I ignore him, but he asks again and then once more, and finally as I'm getting off, he plucks it from my pocket. I turn to grab it back. The elevator doors are closing, but slowly, and I admit I don't try too hard, even though it's not Lily's fault she's so damn pretty.

Joe Palmer is sitting at a table near the elevator and I go right up to him, planning to give him a piece of my mind or to snub him, I haven't quite decided. But as I sit down across from him, he looks over my head, surprised, and when I turn around I see Lily coming toward us, smiling, laughing, and carrying a big glass bowl of rainbow sherbet punch that sloshes with each step she takes. Except she's put the sherbet in too soon and it's hot and when she sets it in front of Joe all that is left of the pretty colors is a foamy green streak that cuts through the bright red Hawaiian punch like an infection.

Lily serves up the punch and goes on and on to Joe about how great his paper is and how he knew her better than she knew herself. My sister is tough. Giles walks by as Lily is giving Joe Palmer a congratulatory hug that is not spontaneous or heartfelt or hopeful like the ones the day before, and he asks what the punch is for, but before Joe Palmer can answer, Lily and I clink glasses and say "to life" just like from the song in *Fiddler on the Roof*, which I saw four times even though it is a long movie and I am not a Jew. I am glad to help Lily with her face-saving act, pretending everything is all right, especially since I know it isn't.

Driving home that day, I try to tell Lily how sorry I am about the college paper, "He's right about you having a good sense of humor." But she holds up her hand and says, "I will not talk about this silly thing, Jenny. It is less than absolutely nothing to me." She continues on in her usual way, being snotty about how much better her life is than mine, saying, "I'm thinking of going dancing at Metro Beach this Saturday night, but I don't suppose you'd want to go—you might miss some old rerun on TV."

Except for Giles, that might have been the end of it. I never told Lily that I'd let him steal the paper, but after a few days it became clear to her that something was going on. All of the sudden, instead of being his usual grabby, flirty self with her, he's being real nice like she has cancer or something. He smiles at her and says good morning and he brings her coffee with three packs of sugar, just like she likes it, even before break has started, saving her the time of waiting in line at the vending machine.

And as nice as he is to Lily, that's how mean he is to Joe Palmer. We both see it. He keeps running him to the crib to get stuff that doesn't even exist. The other day, there's Joe Palmer mumbling that he needs a divot-lock wing nut for the steering column. And when I ask him to speak up, even though I heard him just fine, he says it louder and everyone in line laughs because there is no such thing. Joe got all red and said Giles asked for it, but nobody but me heard him over the general laughter.

Now Lily was being her usual snotty self to Giles this whole time. I mean she had turned him down for twenty dates if she had turned him down for one when he was just another guy working on the line instead of our boss. And she was truly puzzled that he keeps on being nice despite her rudeness. But it all becomes clear when he gives her back the college paper. I see him holding it out to her and patting her on the back as I come up for lunch, five minutes late because some muckety-muck in management was looking for a goddamn thumbtack in my crib and insisted I help him find it—union rules be damned.

I can't see Lily's face, she's looking down, her hand to her forehead, but Giles has this look on his face, half hopeful, half sure, like he had just uncovered two hundred-dollar boxes on an instant lottery ticket and was halfway through scratching off a third. So it seems my sister got herself a boyfriend after all. And I will tell you it kind of sickened me that even though she had acted like a fool, Lily came out smelling sweet again. Why did I expect it to be any different this time around?

But when I sit down across from her, I see it is different. Because Lily's true misery is finally right there on her face. She looks up at me and though she is wearing lipstick and rouge and perfume and her hair is done up nice, none of those frills can hide the plain truth of her shame at having a man like Giles feel sorry that a boy like Joe Palmer played to her vanity all for an 'A' in a community college summer school class.

I finish the orchid seat cover as we drive home that evening. With every stitch and color in place, tight and square against each other, the pattern is complete. It is full and neat—the way I knew it would be. And when she drops me off at home, Lily looks at it and says maybe she won't go dancing on Saturday night after all, that maybe it's time for her to learn some needlepoint.

I hide my smile and never say I told you so. I just reach out to her, arms open wide, ready to pick up the pieces again.

PART I

Even for July it was hot. Mona Palazolla, eleven years old, stood on the front porch near her father and two neighbors and worried about the Detroit Tigers playing in such weather. They were up 5-3 against the Senators in the sixth inning of the first game of a twilight doubleheader. She hoped they drank lots of water between innings. She was thirsty just standing still.

Mona adjusted the earpiece and tuner on her new white transistor radio as a plane flew overhead and announcer Ernie Harwell's play-by-play turned to static. She'd walked to the S&H green stamp store with her mother the week before to buy the transistor with four books of stamps. She'd pasted the stamps in the books in careful even rows, edges perfectly aligned. The plane passed and Mona relaxed, Ernie's voice settling smooth in her ear again.

A minute later, as Earl Wilson waited on deck, she heard her father over Ernie. "I'm telling you. I'm thinking of buying a g-u-n. And then I'm shooting anything that moves and is black."

She turned her transistor way down at that and, curious, crept closer to the circle of talk.

The riots had started that morning, about four miles east of Mona's west side neighborhood, and already Mayor Cavanagh talked about the National Guard and curfews and lockdowns. All up and down the block, little knots of neighbors stood close to their homes, convincing themselves they were safe.

"Tony, you don't mean that." Mrs. Keller chastised Mona's father, and then she turned and looked worriedly at her house next door, aiming an ear at the upstairs bedroom windows, wide open in the heat—her four kids, all under seven years old, were asleep. She smoked a cigarette, holding it outside the circle of conversation, and she jerked it up and down keeping Mona at bay. Mr. Gustafson, from the house on the other side of Mona's, nodded approval at her father's intention. "When will Viv be home from the hospital, Tony? She doesn't have to drive too close to the trouble, does she?"

"Too close as far as I'm concerned. I talked to her an hour ago. She'll leave soon. But we'll have to figure something out if this goes on for long." Mona didn't know if he meant the riots or her little sister Dee Dee's hospital stay, which was up to almost one week now, starting the day after Mona got her new transistor, but her mom was "Viv," and she was glad to hear that she was on her way home that night even if Dee Dee wasn't.

"How's Dee Dee doing?"

"She's a fighter. But they don't know what's wrong yet. They're doing all kinds of tests. Poor little kid, still a baby really, not even three years old—to go through this. It kills you to see her like this." Her father stared at Mrs. Keller's cigarette as he spoke, and though Mona crouched right behind it, she could tell he didn't see her. And even if he did, he'd just wish she were somebody else, somebody he missed—Dee Dee, her mom, or even her sister Rose, who knew how to make him feel better this past week.

Rose was almost eighteen and every day, when she got home from her summer job at Mr. Duffy's pharmacy, and their dad got home from his job at Chrysler Forge and Axle, they'd sit together and talk before Rose went upstairs to get ready for a date with her boyfriend Jimmy, whom she'd gone to prom with the month before. As far back as Mona could remember, Rose always had a boyfriend. When her dad and Rose talked, Mona only half listened from the kitchen, not sure she wanted to hear, but so far they hadn't said anything important anyway.

She thought maybe their dad just liked sitting there looking at Rose, who was not fat in the can like Mrs. Keller or cruddy-skinned like him or like Mona herself so skinny that her nose looked huge. Instead, Rose looked like their mother. Or at least the way their mother looked before Dee Dee went to the hospital and she quit bothering with curlers and makeup. Rose was beautiful. Sometimes Mona held up a picture of her sister to her own face and, looking in the mirror, compared features, but she couldn't see any resemblance. Fifteen minutes of Rose talking smoothed out their dad's face, which was another difference between Mona and Rose. Lately, whenever Mona talked to him, her father's forehead got all tight and pressed together, or his eyes went empty and she knew she could ask him anything and get a yes.

Mrs. Keller reached out and patted his hand. "You can send Mona my way during the day while nobody's home here. I'll be happy to keep an eye on her. She can help me with the kids." Mona crouched low at that, wondering if her father would say she was too young at eleven to baby-sit. She had watched the Keller kids that afternoon for an hour, earning the fifty cents in her pocket. She wasn't sure she wanted to do it again.

A white Mustang convertible pulled up in front of the house. A young man, Rose's date Jimmy, whistled as he turned off the ignition and stepped out of the car, and then stopped, silent, as he saw the cluster he'd have to step around to get to Rose. He walked up, arm stretched toward Mona's father. "Evening Mr. Palazolla."

"Hello, Jimmy. You know our neighbors? Mr. Gustafson? Mrs. Keller?" Her father didn't wait for a response. "Rose is inside getting ready. The mayor says there's a 9:00 P.M. curfew. That gives you kids just two hours. And I don't want Rose going out of our neighborhood tonight."

"We'll just be three blocks over—at a barbecue."

"The president is sending paratroopers."

"Just three blocks, Mr. Palazolla, I swear."

After Rose and Jimmy left and just before the streetlights came on, Mona sat on the floor in her bedroom, back against bed-frame, earphone in, transistor tuned to WJR so that Ernie Harwell could give her the play-by-play at Tiger Stadium. *"Man on, nobody out, no score in the bottom of the third. Bob Santangelo is with us at the game today. He asked us to say hello to his grandpa Joe in Livonia. So, 'hello Joe.' "*

Mona thought it would be nice if Ernie Harwell said hello to her on the radio. She liked his voice, smooth like pudding and available on schedule. She turned the pages of the *Free Press* as she listened, looking for riot news, for a hint of what started the fires and fighting, even though she knew there couldn't be any so soon. She looked for headlines that promised the right kind of trouble, passing by "Two die in car crash," "Thief caught in art heist," "Feds propose food aid package," and "Detroit schools fail national reading test." She stopped at "Coed's body found in Ann Arbor," and read the whole article because Rose was going to the University of Michigan in the fall. But she found nothing more about the riots in the paper.

After that, she reached under her mattress for her notebook, the one where she wrote down the dates and scores of all Tiger games and kept track of other things too, and she made her day's note: *July 23, 1967. Riots start. Dee Dee in hospital for five days. Made fifty cents baby-sitting. Pizza for dinner.* She heard her mother's car pull into the driveway, but she didn't go downstairs. Instead, she put down the notebook, turned down the volume on her transistor, and crossed her fingers, hoping her mother wasn't too sad and tired from being at the hospital all day to stop in and become part of the day's entry.

·   ·   ·

Mona's father lectured her as they drove to Chrysler Forge and Axle the next morning. Her mother and father didn't want her to stay home alone while the riots were going on. "Stay in the car. I'll come out at 10:00, 11:30, and 1:45 and sit with you during my breaks."

"What if I have to go to the bathroom?"

"Hold it."

Mona's father had worked at Chrysler for twenty years. For the past ten, he'd been on first shift, 7:00 to 3:30, in the cradle of the plant where huge presses heated metal and forged it into shapes that made the heavy undercarriage of a car. She didn't exactly see how sitting in a car in a parking lot all day was safer than sitting at home, but she didn't argue with her mother and father that morning when they'd told her she couldn't stay home alone during the riots and then debated what to do with her.

"I can't bring her to the hospital. They're very strict. Sixteen and over only for visiting on the wards. She'd never pass for that. They're doing construction on the main lobby—it's all torn up—so there's nowhere for her to sit there. The neighborhood is really bad, so I can't just drop her off somewhere to wait nearby, either. How about the plant?"

"She couldn't go inside, but there's security in the parking lot. I suppose she could sit in the car."

They looked at Mona then, and she looked up from her cereal and shrugged. "I don't care where I sit all day." But underneath the table, she kept her fingers crossed. She wanted to see her father's plant.

Now, an hour later, her father exited the freeway at Mt. Elliot, barely slowing down, looking at the dashboard clock almost more than the road. Just before Leland, as they passed GM's Hamtramck assembly plant, he gunned it past a line of cars and sped toward the railroad crossing a block ahead where a red warning flashed. A tinny bell clanged through the open windows, but her father drove faster toward the gate that had started to lower. They arrived at the tracks while the gate was just above the roof of the car and thumped over the crossing, jouncing high and landing so low Mona thought the railroad ties might rip out the bottom of the car. Her father looked over at her as they landed safely and he slowed the car to legal speed. "Sorry honey, but we'd have to wait twenty minutes for that freight train to cross and we don't have that kind of time this morning. Miss a minute, docked a half-hour."

Mona leaned down to pick up her lunch sack, which had skid-ded to the floorboards. "That's no fair."

"Well that's how it works." He turned right on Huber then, and there they were. "I'll park in the shade, close to the building. Then I'll move the car to the shade on the other side in the after-noon. Your mother packed you some Kool Aid," he patted a metal thermos at his side, "and you've got your sandwich and other things for lunch, and you brought some books and other things, didn't you? So you'll be fine out here."

He said it like a question and Mona wanting to answer right sang, "Kool Aid, Kool Aid, tastes great . . ." just like on TV.

"You have your transistor?"

"Yes." Mona patted her shorts pocket.

"Well, listen to that if you get bored."

"There's no game until tonight."

"Listen to something else, then. Just don't leave the car."

Her father pulled into a parking space in the first row from the building. "Okay, Mona, I'll be back out at 10:00."

Mona climbed over the seat and ducked to the backseat floor as soon as he left so the men walking by the car wouldn't see her. Bits of conversation and wispy puffs of smoke from their cigarettes slipped through the open windows. "Hey Charlie, you see those niggers throwing bricks on 12th Street last night?" "They looted my father's shoe store on Dexter." And she heard other voices too, which sounded like Negroes, "There's guys coming up from Ken-tucky with shotguns." "My mother's house burned. Now she's got nothing."

Others talked lower so all she heard was rumbling that could be black or white talking. But black or white, everybody talked of the riots. After a few minutes, a bell rang, just like on the playground at school, and Mona heard a few men, rushing by, dropping something, saying "shit" and "goddamn it," as they ran to punch in.

Then complete and sudden quiet, and she got up. Being on the floor of the car when it moved was fun. But stopped, it was just hot and uncomfortable. She looked around the huge lot, the size of four school playgrounds at least, with all the cars lined up like dominoes around the plant. She imagined them churning out even more cars inside. Sliding them down a chute on the other end, cars stacked like crackers, no room in the lot to hold them all.

On the expressway, approaching the interchange of the Chrysler and Ford, she always looked for the Firestone sign that had the number of cars made so far that year. It changed even as her mother or father drove by it at sixty miles an hour. How fast could an assembly line move to make the sign change numbers like that? Once, on *I Love Lucy*, Lucy and Ethel worked on an assembly line for chocolates, and it only took a few seconds before they fell behind and had to stuff candy in their hats and dresses and mouths. She thought of the men on the assembly line working faster and faster as they tried to keep up with the cars speeding by like chocolates, but missing a steering wheel, an engine, a door. She'd passed by auto plants her whole life. But she'd never been in one.

Mona finished reading the *Free Press*, ate her lunch, and listened to CKLW all before 8:00 A.M. Then she did a page of Mad Libs, which wasn't fun because supplying the words herself meant the silliness wasn't a surprise. Then she made a purple, pink, and yellow potholder on her blue plastic loom, weaving the nylon loops up and under, admiring her color combination. She'd give it to her mother if she saw her that evening. Then it was 9:15 and she had to go to the bathroom. She didn't think she could hold it until 10:00. Anyway, this was her chance to see cars made. She got out of the car and walked into the plant. It wasn't hard to do. She waited until the security guard at the door walked away from it to smoke a cigarette with another security guard who walked around the parking lot.

When she entered the plant, she scooted over quickly to a side hallway, far away from a woman sitting behind a long raised counter in the center of the room and making marks on a batch of papers she held. The hallway was tiled in squares of green and tan and Mona's foot in her navy blue tennis shoes fit exactly diagonally in a square so she walked zigzaggy for a while, not stepping on any cracks. Offices lined both sides of the hallway and most of the doors were open and people sat at desks with papers and coffee cups and lots of them smoked, which made her cough, quietly, so that no one would hear.

So far the plant was not interesting. She'd have to look harder, to find the good part, but not until after she went to the bathroom. She saw a LADIES sign on a door to her right and slipped inside. She left the bathroom moments later without washing her hands— no time for that while sneaking around, plus who would check? Back out in the hallway, she pushed open a door at the end of the tiled hallway, walked out to a small platform that stood six steps high over the floor of Chrysler Forge and Axle, and that was more like it.

Mona looked up at the rafters of the plant, metal beams that crisscrossed above her to hold a ceiling so high that the lights hanging from it were just dots, adding to the dimness, shining on nothing. Small panes of glass lined the wall to her far left, hundreds of squares the size of her geography book, some propped open with sticks, most painted over or so dirty they were more wall than window—the air in the plant seemed worn out, used. She heard the traffic of forklifts and small trucks moving down the cement lanes between the different clusters of people working, the buzz of power saws, the grind of gears rumbling to go and then sitting idle again, the clank of metal being dropped or sorted or stacked for picking through. The workers raised their voices over all this so that the din had a sound half-human, half-machine. The platform stood at the foot of a wide aisle that was painted with white and yellow stripes, as if it were a freeway. Every few minutes yellow and red lights above and behind her flashed, and a truck or a forklift came down the aisle loaded with sheets of steel. On either side of the aisle, and, she could tell, far down and deeper through the long length of plant, little groups of workers stood together doing one job or another that made a car.

She was almost at the bottom step when the red light flashed, and she heard a loud buzzer that went off and on, then off and on again, and she heard the sputter of an engine, closer now, and looked up to see a tractor-sized forklift coming her way, its steel tines pointing at her like spears. At the last second, it turned left down an aisle and hoisted a pallet of boxes strapped together with metal strips onto a low shelf. Ahead and to her right, but at a distance, a group of men stood, a dozen of them, backs to her, before a huge dirt-brown machine with levers and grates that opened like a submarine hatch to show rods glowing orange. Then the men, bending and lifting in sync, all doing the same motion as if they were attached to strings tugged from above, hoisted a sheet of metal, as if it were a linen tablecloth for Sunday dinner, and laid it carefully on the press.

From where she stood, looking out at the floor of the plant at all the men in work clothes and boots, their backs to her bending and reaching and performing on cue, she couldn't tell who was black and who was white and who bossed whom. Everybody looked the same.

As she stepped onto the plant floor to look more closely, she felt a hand on her shoulder and heard a voice in her ear, "Who the hell are you?" When she turned around, she faced a Negro man wearing a yellow hard hat, a short-sleeved white shirt with GEORGE MARTEL embroidered in blue on the left pocket, a right shirt pocket full of pens, and a skinny black tie. He leaned down and looked at her, and despite his question, she could tell he was more mad than really wanting to know.

Twenty minutes later, Mona sat outside George Martel's office while her father sat with him inside. They left the door open, so she didn't have to work hard to hear or see.

"Palazolla, you have to expect to get docked for this."

"I want my committeeman man here. You forced me off the floor. You're making me punch out."

"What the hell are you talking about. You've got to get your kid out of here. My god, she was on the floor, she . . ."

"Bullshit, Martel. She never came off the platform."

"Thanks to me. Be glad I found her when I did. Six more feet and she would have been flattened by a forklift. Then your damn union is suing my ass. Go ahead. Call your committeeman. File a grievance. But I'm trying to help you here. I am not writing you up. I am not busting your balls. I'm saying get her out of here and then come back and punch in. I'll call it a previously granted permission for absence. I won't note it on your record. You're not thinking straight Palazolla."

Mona's father muttered something she couldn't completely make out, but she thought she heard the word "nigger" and she saw George Martel's face switch to a deeper form of mad that made his voice lower as he stood up, "Taking into consideration your personal family trouble right now, I'll forget I heard that, but get the fuck out of here before I suspend you right now, union or not."

Mona's father walked out, his boots pounding the green and tan tile. Before she turned to follow him, she looked in again at George Martel. He stood behind his desk, hands gripping the edge, his cheeks sucked in, and his face like a stone that would turn to rubble with a blow. He looked right back at her, staring like he hated her too, not just her father.

"What the hell were you thinking, Mona?" Her father jerked the car into reverse and backed out of the parking space without looking.

"I had to go to the bathroom."

"Jesus Christ. You've got to be smarter. Because of you I have to get a lecture from that asshole. Now he thinks he did me a big favor. I don't want his favors."

"Why don't you like him?"

"He's my boss. Let me tell you something Mona, the colored people, they're just different from us. They act different. They live different." Her father clamped his lips together after he spoke, like he was afraid to let more words out.

Mona wondered how he knew that. She didn't think he'd ever even visited a Negro's home. Even if he had, lots of white people lived different from him and he didn't mind that. His own sister, her Aunt Jenny, got up on a ladder and washed her house once a year, which was a pretty different thing to do. And Mrs. Keller's sink was full of greasy dishes, and her grass needed mowing, and her kids had dirty faces, and that was different from their house too. How many other ways of different could Negroes live beyond those two? There had to be more to it than that. It took a long time to get home, because they got stopped at two railroad crossings, one with 53 cars of freight, the other 102—she counted—along the way.

Mona's father called the Negroes niggers sometimes, but only if he thought Mona couldn't hear. Otherwise he mostly said coloreds. Her mother called them Negroes. Rose said black. Dee Dee had stopped saying much before she went to the hospital, mostly she just slept or made whimpering cries, thin little bleats that Mona heard in her memory even though she didn't want to. Mrs. Keller said colored people too. Aunt Jenny said coloreds, darkies, nigger, pickanniny, and shine with no apologies or hushed voice. She said slut, hussy, asshole, polack, and chink too. The last two not, of course, when referring to Negroes. Mona thought the Negroes should pick for themselves what they would be called.

That night Mona's dad told her she had to stay at her Aunt Jenny's until the riots ended. "But why?" Mona looked up from the *Free Press* sports section, which she studied to memorize American League batting averages. Aunt Jenny was mean. When the whole family visited there, Mona managed to dart out of her way, but without Rose and Dee Dee to help distract Aunt Jenny, she doubted she could dodge her aunt. "Dad, her house is closer to the riots than our house. Do you really think I'll be safer there?" Her father admitted this was true, but Jenny was laid off for the summer from her job at GM, so at least, he said, she wouldn't be home alone all day while he and Rose worked and her mom and Dee Dee were at the hospital.

The curfew lifted the next morning at five, and they left for Aunt Jenny's soon after that so that her father could take Mona there and still make it to the plant to punch in on time. It was already light out. Mona could hardly remember the last time it had been dark. The days never ended lately. A handwritten sign propped against the pump at the Texaco station at the end of their block said it was closed due to the riots. She looked for tanks and guns and Negro people on the way to Aunt Jenny's, but all she saw were houses with cars in the driveways just like in her neighborhood. Mona knew, looking out the window of her father's Plymouth, there could be trouble in any of the houses they passed. The quiet didn't prove a thing.

Aunt Jenny leaned over the counter next to the sink when they walked in. She held a toothbrush in one hand and a jar of cleanser in the other as she scrubbed pristine grout.

"Jen, what the hell is your door doing wide open? My God. People are burning buildings and looting three miles from here."

"Let 'em try to come into my house. Let those goddamn niggers come here with a bucket of gas and try to burn me out."

"Jen. Mona's here. You want to watch what you say, please."

"She goes to school with them. She knows better than anybody what they're like."

Mona thought of Cissy Powell, who always lined up next to her on account of alphabetical order and who was one of five Negroes in her grade, but other than that seemed mostly the same as anybody else. Her father turned to her. "You listen to your Aunt Jenny, now. Help out around the house and do whatever she says. It should only be for a few days. Until the trouble stops. I'll call every night and check in with you." He held her Samsonite train case, the one Rose had given her for her tenth birthday. It was pink, but he didn't look silly holding it. He just looked tired. It made her want to cry to think of him leaving her with Aunt Jenny all alone, but no tears came out. She wasn't holding them in, so they must have evaporated under the surface of her eyes in the heat.

Once her father left, Aunt Jenny made oatmeal and then went downstairs to iron. Mona ate a little and then wandered into the living room where she went to the mantel and fingered a Hummel figurine of a little boy playing a drum. She jumped when Aunt Jenny crept up behind her. "You didn't finish breakfast and now you're going to break my curios. I swear you're just like your father—useless. He never moved off the street corner except to stir up trouble. How old are you now?"

"Eleven."

"You're lucky. When I was eleven, I worked twelve hours a day. Six hours at home cleaning and cooking for your father and all my other brothers because our mama had just died, and six hours hired out to earn money cooking and cleaning because our daddy might as well have been dead for all the good he did us. That man could drink away a paycheck faster than anybody on Hedge Street."

"I think he died when I was a baby."

"That's more good luck to you. Though I don't suppose you're feeling too lucky now with the baby dying and your older sister a damn harlot."

"Dee Dee's not a baby. And Rose is not a damn harlot." That was the first Mona had heard about Dee Dee dying, and she didn't want to hear about that from anybody, especially not from Aunt Jenny. She didn't know what a harlot was, but her aunt was always mean to Rose, so it couldn't be good.

"She's baby enough. And I know for a fact that older sister of yours thinks those cock-a-doodle-colored hot pants she wears is something she has to jump out of every time she's with a boy." Mona thought about Rose and Jimmy, Rose and Alex, Rose and

John—her boyfriends before Jimmy—and Rose and all the other boys she dated whose names Mona couldn't remember. That had always seemed a good thing. Aunt Jenny kept talking. "But you have to spend the next few days with me and that's going to be hard enough for you without worrying about your sisters, so put it out of your head and go clean up after yourself in the kitchen. And then I'll come in behind and do the job right."

"Then what?" The quiet house seemed full of more empty time than anything could fill.

"Then we'll wash some windows and floors. Then we'll play darts in the basement. Then we'll sit on the front porch and listen to that radio while I knit." She pointed to the transistor stuck in the pocket of Mona's daisy jean cutoffs. It didn't exactly sound like fun, but Mona had spent much of the past seven days home alone missing her sisters and her mother and her father and waiting by the window for somebody to come home, and it sounded like more fun than that.

On Mona's second day there, Aunt Jenny gave her a stack of *Good Housekeeping* magazines and told her to find a recipe for rainbow Jell-O that she remembered seeing months ago. It had seven layers— red, yellow, green, and orange between cream cheese–like slabs. Mona looked for a while, but then she got bored and read the articles instead. One story about eight-month-old quintuplets in Nebraska came with photos of the babies—always all five of them together, eating, sleeping, in diapers. Mona felt bad for them. Probably nobody ever looked at them one at a time. So she did, studying each baby quint alone by using her hands to block out the others. The middle one, Michelle, looked like she remembered Dee Dee looking as a baby. She put the magazine in the waistband of her shorts and when Aunt Jenny wasn't looking she went and put it under the pillow of the cot where she slept in the den. She found the Jell-O recipe in another issue.

After dinner, they sat on the porch. The riot news on her transistor was not good. At the Algiers Motel in the thirteenth precinct three men were shot dead and seven motel guests were beaten up. The radio didn't say exactly how it happened. Nobody really knew anything for sure. But then the announcer reported that a four-year-old, Tanya Blanding, while lying flat on her living room floor to avoid sniper fire, most definitely was killed by the National Guard who drove a tank and fired with a 50-caliber machine gun. Mona wondered to herself if Tanya Blanding was white or black.

When she heard the radio report, Aunt Jenny folded up her knitting and said they better go inside and watch the riots on TV instead. "I think it's getting serious." Mona nodded and followed, glad to get off the porch where somebody might shoot them before they even knew what was happening. The TV news had pictures of what was going on. The reporters talked about the tragedy that was happening to the people of Detroit, but Mona wondered since most of the faces in the riots were black, and most of the people she knew weren't. Most of the white people on the TV news were the police or the store owners who swept up glass from broken windows, but at least they were alive to do it. She studied everybody who came on the screen.

She saw a black man, he looked like her father's age, leaning back to throw a brick, his face not changing its one expression, like it was made of cement and might crack if he moved it, just like her father's face when he talked about Dee Dee, like George Martel's face as he watched her father walk away. She saw an old man, white, his shirt ripped, a streak of dirt on his cheek, holding his left arm, which was bleeding, with his right, carefully, gently, as if it were a baby he cradled, as if he wanted to cry at how much it hurt. His face was pale behind the dirt, paler even than his white skin. Then she saw another black man, this one young like Rose, and he kneeled on the street holding a man with blood on his head. The young man's face looked all caved-in and broken as he stroked the hurt man's head over and over again. Mona had seen this look on her father's face too, usually as he hugged her mother when she got home from the hospital each day, her crying, neither of them knowing Mona had snuck downstairs to watch. Maybe one face led to another—she didn't know—but none of them meant anything good, of that she was sure.

Mona heard a snort that pulled her back from the TV, where she'd inched up close. Aunt Jenny slept in her chair, the flabby skin of her throat jiggling with little snores. Mona crept closer to the TV again and then the screen was full of white men, and the reporter said they lived in a neighborhood on the far east side that was far away from the trouble. The men stood on the hoods of their cars, which were placed bumper to grill blocking entrance into their streets. Some of the men held two-by-fours, others kept one hand on the butt of a gun in a shoulder holster. Mona saw the men's faces clearly. No fires raged around them, no windows lay shattered at their feet, but their faces looked as hard as the black man with the brick in his hands.

Aunt Jenny snorted again, this time loud enough to wake herself. Mona looked away from the TV and watched as her aunt, confused by sleep, struggled up from her chair, her knitting falling from her lap. A ball of yarn rolled to the corner of the living room—a deep red trickle of wool that Mona crept after on hands and knees. When Mona handed it back to her, Aunt Jenny told her to turn off the TV and get to bed.

Awake in bed an hour later, coiled tight, knees to chest, Mona tried to remember exactly what Dee Dee looked like, and instead saw Tanya Blanding lying on her living room floor, maybe even hiding behind the couch or a chair like it was a game, but then ending up shot dead. She wondered what was wrong with Dee Dee. Aunt Jenny said she was dying and Mona thought that could be true. But maybe not. Aunt Jenny never bothered to think past the first choice of anything. Mona knew other possibilities existed. Maybe Dee Dee would just have to stay in bed all her life. Or maybe she'd come out of the hospital with only one leg or with a patch on her eye.

She took the *Good Housekeeping* magazine from under her pillow and opened it to the picture of the quintuplets. So far, her mom and dad's whispered conversations were full of questions. They didn't know what was wrong yet, but they needn't bother to whisper anymore. Sitting at Aunt Jenny's, Mona made a decision. Though she wondered what was wrong with Dee Dee, she decided *not* to know. Not to ask anybody, even Rose. She would keep quiet and wait, even as waiting got harder to do. And if they tried to tell her anything, she'd turn away. She wouldn't listen. She wouldn't try to see Dee Dee in the hospital. She wouldn't go even if they forced her. She had to offer up something important to make sure Dee Dee came home. Being alone in the dark was the best she could think of to give. She looked at the quint's picture and imagined Michelle with only one leg. She'd still be cute.

She sat up in bed and tore out the baby's picture and glued it in her notebook. She made a note under it: *July 26, 1967. Fourth day of riots. Seven people killed so far. Dee Dee in hospital for eight days. Possible things wrong with her: 1. Amputation, 2. Blindness (one or two eyes), 3. Retardation, 4. Heart murmur, 5. Other? Possible body parts affected: a. Head, b. Heart, c. Legs or arms. Tigers off.*

At 11:30 the next morning, Mona, hungry and bored, sat waiting at the living room window for Aunt Jenny to return from her doctor's appointment. Aunt Jenny had been full of warning before she left, "I should be home by one. I'll fix your lunch when I get back." She wore a red straw hat and a navy blue skirt and sweater even though it was ninety degrees outside.

"I'll fix lunch for myself. For you, too. I'll have it ready when you get home."

Aunt Jenny spit on her finger and leaned down to rub out an invisible spot on her white sandal. "You stay out of my kitchen, young lady. I'll be home soon enough to feed you."

At 11:45, Mona heard the car pull in the driveway and ran back to the window that she'd abandoned in favor of doing bicycle kicks on the floor. It was Rose, not Aunt Jenny, getting out of the car, and Mona ran out the front door and hurled herself toward her sister, chest high like a perfect pitch.

"Mona!" Rose opened her arms and caught her, twirling her around.

Mona looked up at Rose, checking, "Is everything okay?"

"Everything's fine. Well, the same at least. I told my boss I had a dentist appointment so I could take a long lunch. I thought you might want a break from the old crab apple here. Where is she?"

"She had a doctor's appointment. She won't be home until one."

"Good. Let's get out of here. I'm taking you to Top Hat for lunch. Run inside and leave a note so she doesn't worry in case she gets home early."

Mona couldn't decide which way to look as they drove away from Aunt Jenny's. At Rose who looked prettier than ever in her white pharmacy dress and hose or out the window where she might see some riots.

"Mona, we're driving away from the trouble. Don't worry. I wouldn't take you anywhere you're not supposed to be."

Mona scooted over and sat next to Rose, and Rose put her hand out and patted Mona's knee. Mona thought that when she was eighteen and driving, Dee Dee would be ten and sitting next to her. She'd reach out to pat Dee Dee's knee, too. Or the stump where her knee used to be. If it came to that.

At Top Hat, Rose ordered a sack of hamburgers at fourteen cents each. The coaster-sized burgers had five holes in them where the sizzling steam escaped while they cooked. Last time they'd been at Top Hat was for Dee Dee's second birthday. The whole family. They'd had a burger eating contest, and, figuring in for age and weight, Mona's mom, the referee, said Mona won by eating seven. Even Dee Dee had been part of it, stuffing mostly the bun in her mouth and laughing as Mona ate number five without hands. When Dee Dee started to choke, their mom said hey, hey, that's enough, even though she laughed too. Altogether, their dad said as they left, they'd eaten thirty-two burgers.

"Aren't you hungry, Mona?" Mona looked up when she heard Rose, who only picked at her second burger and leaned her chin on both her hands like her head was too heavy to stay up on its own.

"I thought I was. Maybe it's too hot to eat much." Mona reached back and lifted her hair off her neck. It curled in wet tendrils underneath where she sweated.

"The rioting is dying down. You'll probably come home in a couple of days. Here, turn around. I'll help with that." Rose reached over and twirled Mona around on her stool, holding Mona's hunk of light brown hair in her hand and dividing it into three strands.

"Why do you think they're doing it, Rose?"

"Who? Doing what?"

"The Negroes burning stuff and everybody shooting and looting."

"I don't know. Sometimes people get tired of waiting and counting on things that aren't going to happen. Sometimes you just boil up and have to *do* something."

"Maybe Mom should do something at the hospital to make Dee Dee come home." Mona winced as Rose yanked hard, tightening the braid.

"Maybe she should."

When Rose dropped her off, Mona was glad to see that Aunt Jenny's car wasn't in the driveway yet. Better not to have to explain anything to her. Right before Mona got out of the car, Rose reached over and hugged her and whispered in her ear that everything would be okay. Mona breathed in deep trying to absorb her sister's smell—part perfume, part vitamin from the pharmacy—and hung on until Rose pulled away saying she'd be late for work. Aunt Jenny didn't hug.

For the next few days, Mona and her Aunt Jenny ate, cleaned, and played darts. One day they moved all the living room furniture so Aunt Jenny could vacuum underneath, something she did every two weeks. Once the work that day was done, they listened to the news of the riots as they sat in metal rockers on the front porch.

Mona read stories from the *Free Press* out loud to Aunt Jenny, too, choosing ones that didn't make the Negroes sound too bad because Aunt Jenny was mean enough about them already.

On the sixth day of the riots, Aunt Jenny made meatloaf for dinner. Mona watched as she mixed together sticky raw meat, egg yolks, bread crumbs, and chopped onions, which Mona particularly didn't like. While they ate dinner later, Mona read Aunt Jenny a long story from the *Free Press* about the three black people who were shot to death by police at the Algiers Motel and seven others who were beaten up. It had happened a few days before on the same day Tanya Blanding got shot. The story said the Algiers Motel had always been full of narcotics and prostitutes and that the police received tips that riot-looted merchandise was being sold there. The police log for that night said that at 12:23 A.M. there had been a report of a sniper at Woodward and Euclid just north of the Algiers but that, "troopers are there, no help needed." And then at 2:21 A.M. the log read "8301 Woodward [the address of the Algiers] check for dead person." So how did *three* people die, the *Free Press* wondered? And who beat up seven more?

Aunt Jenny didn't see the need for such questions. She stood up, her dinner finished. "Anybody at a place like that deserves what he gets. A bunch of darky whores and drug addicts are no great loss to Detroit." She looked over at Mona's plate, "I want you to eat that meatloaf young lady. There's no waste allowed in this house. I don't care how much they baby you at home. You don't leave the table here until your plate is clean."

Mona ate a little more, picking around the onions, which her mother never made her eat. But she wasn't hungry. Instead, she was hot and tired and sure that her aunt would never quit picking on her. Aunt Jenny was already at the sink, hands sunk into suds, her back to the kitchen table, so Mona scooped the gummy glistening onions and the crumbling meat into her cloth napkin, folded the napkin carefully into a pouch, and put it in her pocket. She'd throw it away later, when Aunt Jenny wasn't looking. Aunt Jenny turned from the sink and stared suspiciously at Mona's plate,

"That was fast. Stay put there and keep reading to me and then when I'm done with these, I want you to dry, but only the silverware and plastic. I don't trust you not to break everything."

Mona turned the page looking for a story that would distract Aunt Jenny and, as she did, she noticed a six-inch strip that said the Ann Arbor police were investigating if the dead girl they found the week before was killed by the same person who killed another University of Michigan girl six months earlier. They'd both been last seen at a party. They'd both been placed in freshly dug shallow ditches in a wooded area about three miles apart. The story was full of words like preliminary, speculation, and unfounded theory. Mona wondered if the dead girls had sisters.

Late that night, when she was sure Aunt Jenny slept, Mona slid off her cot and took the folded-up napkin out of her pocket. Then she crept softly into the living room and deposited little bits of her leftover dinner under the furniture. Aunt Jenny wouldn't find it for another two weeks. She'd be awfully mad about it, but Mona didn't care. She'd be home safe with her sisters long before then.

All that week, Aunt Jenny went to sleep before nine, and woke up before five, and she made Mona do the same. The Tigers were on the West Coast and after paying attention to the riots all day, Mona fell asleep at night listening to Ernie Harwell as he talked about double plays and pop-ups, called third strikes and sacrifice flies, line drives and wild pitches. He told her exactly what happened without mentioning trouble in Detroit. *"Freehan scoops up a fastball in the dirt. Runner on first is off. He throws. It's a bullet to McAuliffe. He's out. Two down for the Tigers as Freehan stops the steal."* With her radio turned low on the pillow right next to her, Mona always remembered to reach out and pat it, whispering "thank you" to Ernie for delivering good news. Then she tucked herself in with one hand while she coiled herself tightly, barely taking up half the small, old, army cot.

The riot flames smoldered out, eight days after they began. Mona still listened to her radio, but it only reported spots of trouble now. Loot selling here or there; a woman who shot her husband in a house on a street just five blocks over from Aunt Jenny's. But the army was leaving Detroit, and the woman missed. That Sunday morning, Mona and Aunt Jenny watched *Meet the Press* where Detroit's Mayor Jerry Cavanagh was on. He was tired from not sleeping much during the riots he said. His voice cracked into near silence at the end of every sentence, but still he sounded mad. If we didn't give more money to the children in the cities, he said, we would have some things far worse than the Detroit riots. The last part came out an angry whisper and it sounded to Mona as if he were casting a spell. She shivered and quit listening.

The next day, the last in July, Mona's father picked her up on his way home from work during the hottest part of the afternoon when the sun attacked the street and sidewalk, flattening everything it touched. They talked about the Tigers on the drive home. Her father said Al Kaline was a jerk for busting his hand when he got mad and slammed his bat in the rack the month before, but Mona knew that, like Rose said, sometimes you just had to *do* something even if it meant you broke your own hand. She stayed quiet after they finished talking about the Tigers, hoping that her mom and Dee Dee would be home when they got there, imagining her dad planned it this way as a surprise. But her father squinted into the sun as they pulled in the driveway, and then he reached past her and opened her door, "Run and see Mrs. Keller now. She's been asking for you every day since you've been gone."

With the riots over, Mona made a different kind of list in her notebook that evening. It started with Cissy Powell from her class at school and ended with Sammy Davis, Jr., and in between it had Gates Brown, Willie Horton, Earl Wilson, and all the other black people she knew of and who she figured liked her, or at least would like her if they knew her. If she studied it, maybe she could figure out the riots. She added George Martel to the list, but crossed him off right away. She was pretty sure he didn't like her or her father.

Then she looked at the magazine picture of baby Michelle while she waited for her mother to come home, touching the little girl's cheek over and over. She hadn't seen her mother in six days and had only talked to her three times on the phone. But Aunt Jenny had shaken her awake at five that morning and they'd spent most of the day cleaning the attic, and before she heard her mother's car in the driveway, Mona fell asleep.

PART II

"Mona," Rose scrunched a white pharmacy stocking in her hands as she spoke, "I think you should go to the hospital and see Dee Dee. And then you'd at least see Mom since she won't leave Dee Dee's side. I swear it's like she's forgotten she's got another daughter."

"Two others." Mona pointed at herself, then Rose.

"I don't count. I'm going to college in a few weeks. I'm an adult now. I'm moving away from home. Mom doesn't need to worry about me."

"But only sixteen and over are allowed at the hospital. Mom and Dad said."

"Dee Dee wants to see you. Who cares what's allowed?"

"She'll see me when she gets home."

"You never even ask about her. You need to see her. You must miss her a lot. Sunday afternoon, when I go visit, I'm taking you with me. I'll sneak you in."

Mona put her hands over her ears and hummed. She'd never been in a hospital and though she was curious, she couldn't go. She needed to stick to her promise—if she gave up seeing and hearing about Dee Dee now, she was sure Dee Dee would come home and be just fine later. If she changed the rules of the bargain, something awful could happen.

Three days later, on Sunday morning, Mona got up at six so she'd know exactly where Rose was from the start. Whatever it took, she had to avoid Rose. That turned out to be easy, since Rose slept until the phone rang and woke her at ten. Even then Mona didn't have to worry, because it was Jimmy asking Rose to go swimming at Belle Isle, and Mona heard Rose tell him yes, but only if they could go straight to the hospital, which was close by, right after that.

On Monday, Mona was careful to dodge Rose in case she brought up the subject of visiting the hospital again. But by Wednesday, Rose seemed to have forgotten. She went out with Jimmy right after work that day, and when she came home on Thursday, she carried two bulky cardboard boxes and told Mona and their father that she was going to start organizing and packing her things for her move to Ann Arbor. Mona could tell she didn't need to avoid her anymore, and when she offered to help her pack, Rose put her to work folding clothes and placing them in the large green suitcase she got as a high school graduation gift in June.

Saturday was Ladies Day at Tiger Stadium and Mona and Rose took the bus down Grand River to get there. It was mid-August and the Tigers, in a four-way pennant race with Boston, Minnesota, and Chicago, hadn't been hitting well. Mona hoped she'd bring them luck. It was her first game in person. She'd only been a fan for a year, since Gates Brown came to school after last season and gave a hitting clinic and told Mona she had the most natural swing in the whole gym class. Before Dee Dee got sick, her dad had promised to take her to a game that season, even though he and her mom and Rose teased her for caring about the Tigers so much.

Her dad had been surprised that morning when Rose had offered to take Mona to the game, and then he gave Rose three dollars and hugged her while Mona sat still, staring at her Rice Krispies, fingers crossed against it being a trick or him changing his mind—praying she really was going to see Al Kaline and Willie Horton and Denny McLain in person. Maybe Gates Brown would even remember her.

On the bus to Tiger Stadium, she pestered Rose, "So we can sit anywhere in the upper deck, right? For fifty cents, right? I'm glad we're going early. Ernie says it will be a sellout." Mona had her transistor with her so she could listen to the play-by-play while she watched. That's what experienced fans did.

"Sit still Mona." Rose pulled on Mona's shorts. "We'll sit in Section 17."

"But that's the third baseline." Mona knew the sections by heart. "We should sit on the first baseline. That way we'll be closer to Kaline. He's back in the lineup. He's playing great."

"I could care less about baselines or Kaline. We're sitting in 17. You'll like it. I'll buy you a hot dog."

Mona held Rose's hand as they got off the bus and were caught in a swirl of people entering the stadium at Gate D. The peanut and pennant vendors barked demands, and when Mona tugged at Rose to stop so she could buy an official scorecard, Rose said later. Mona tried to see the field as they walked the ramp to the upper deck, but her only unobstructed view was a pair of plaid shorts when she looked ahead and mustard-, ketchup-, and beer-stained cement when she looked down. The crowd thinned as it funneled up—people splitting off to find seats or to buy scorecards or hot dogs. Mona's calves ached with the effort of keeping up with Rose, and she was about to complain when Rose stopped.

Mona looked down a long aisle carved through rows of green-painted, wooden-slatted seats. The field rested at the foot—a bowl of green glinting in the August sun. Straight, white, chalk-on-dust baselines fanned out from a pivot point at home plate. The players who speckled the outfield in warm-up hardly moved. Mona felt happy looking at that big picture of nothing wrong.

But not Rose, she looked left and right and up and down the stands, everywhere but the field. Being ladies, Mona and Rose were allowed to sit anywhere, but Rose shook her head as a bald usher in a green jacket with gold fringe on the shoulders dusted two seats in the first row, and then she tugged Mona up the cement steps painted with numbers, until they were in the last row, not good seats at all, an expanse of empty rows below them. Before Mona could complain, Rose stopped her. "Go run around. Sit wherever you want. Try to sneak down to the lower deck and get some autographs by the dugout. Just check in with me every other inning." Mona took the stairs two at a time in case Rose changed her mind.

When Mona returned during the bottom of the third, Rose was turned to the side, not even looking at the field, but instead talking to a man who sat in the seat next to her. Mona looked closer and saw Rose was not just talking to him, she had her hand on his thigh, while he massaged her shoulder. He didn't move his hand even when Mona came up behind Rose and he saw her. His name was Don and he finally stopped rubbing Rose's shoulder and patted Mona on the head just like Jimmy and Alex and John did the first time they met her, the kid sister. Mona knew for sure then that this was like a date for Rose, but different because she hadn't broken up with Jimmy, she hadn't said anything about meeting Don at Tiger Stadium, and Don didn't look too much younger than their father. None of that could be any good. Don left in the fifth inning after kissing Rose full on the lips, which Mona saw from a distance and pretended not to.

The Tigers lost to the Orioles 5-4 when Boog Powell hit a grand slam in the eighth inning. After the game, Mona and Rose waited outside Gate D for an hour, and Mona was glad about that because she got Norm Cash's autograph and saw Dick McAuliffe kiss a woman, maybe his wife, she thought, trying to remember what she'd read about him in her fan magazine. She didn't know why Rose was being so patient and letting her look for Tigers, but she wasn't about to complain. When Don came walking down the corridor toward them, shaking hands with two men wearing sweaters and loafers, and saying he'd call them about their promotional ideas on Monday when he was back in the office, Mona understood.

Walking outside the stadium, Don put his arm around Rose's shoulder and she looped hers around his waist and Mona followed behind as they went to Don's car, a convertible, in a lot on Trumbull where the old man who sat on a chair next to the PARKING 2$ sign looked at them all getting in the car together and winked at Don. When they had driven away from the traffic around the stadium and were merging fast onto the freeway, Rose slid over next to Don and he put his arm around her shoulder again. Mona turned on her transistor, plugged in the earphone, and lay on the backseat. It was her first time in a convertible, and with the upside-down view making her pleasantly dizzy, the rush of air on her face, and Ernie Harwell's voice doing the postgame wrap, she almost forgot about the loss.

Don dropped them off downtown an hour later, at a bus stop. Rose told Mona that Don did public relations for the Tigers and that she'd met him just a couple of weeks before at a party at Jimmy's parents' house. When Rose asked Mona please not to mention him to their father or to Jimmy or anybody else, Mona said, "Mention who?" and Rose laughed and hugged her and said she wished she'd thought to take Mona to a game before. That night Mona made her notebook entry longer, describing Tiger stadium and how Don and Rose kissed and made heavy breathing noises when they stopped and parked for half an hour at the Belle Isle Fountain. Then she patted baby Michelle's head and thought about how she'd take Dee Dee to a game as soon as they were old enough to ride the bus downtown alone.

It was Rose, not Mona, who ended up telling about Don. It happened the next Saturday when Mrs. Keller knocked on the Palazollas' kitchen door at 9:00 A.M. Rose wasn't home—she'd spent the night at her girlfriend Janet's house. Mona's father read the paper, and her mother, who would leave for the hospital soon, stood at the kitchen sink washing the cereal bowls. Mona stood next to her and dried the dishes, purposely bumping into her every now and then just to feel her, until finally her mother wrung out her dishrag and bent down to look at Mona closely. "Are you feeling okay, Mona? You're awfully wobbly this morning." Her mother placed the back of her hand across Mona's forehead. Mona didn't answer right away. Her mother's hand, cool from the rinse water, felt good.

Mrs. Keller's knock interrupted them. She had her boys, five-year-old Davey and two-year-old Charlie, at her side, and she asked if she could borrow Mona for half an hour. Davey was learning to ride his two-wheeler, she explained. She needed Mona to push Charlie in the stroller while she ran alongside Davey's bike. "Oh, and I wanted to tell you that we saw Rose at the game last night. Well, the girls did." Mrs. Keller had six-year-old twin daughters also.

"What game?" Mona's mother and father asked in tandem.

"The Tigers. It was family night so Ray and I took the kids. The girls saw her. She was with somebody. Jimmy, I guess—the girls made jokes about them kissing—I didn't see her myself. I was in the ladies room. She and Jimmy went and sat somewhere else after the girls called out to her."

"Jimmy is on vacation with his family. And Rose spent the night at her friend Janet's house. The girls must be mistaken." Mona's mother ran the dishcloth over the counter as she spoke.

"No. It was Rose. Ray saw her too. He's never seen Jimmy before. It's strange—he asked me if you approved of Rose going out with somebody so much older than she was, but I've always thought Rose looked mature for her age, at least compared to Jimmy."

Mona noticed that the wrinkles on her father's forehead had squinched together and he stared at the paper, but his eyes weren't moving. She reached up and touched her own forehead trying to remember her mother's cool touch there. She sensed trouble starting. Mr. Keller had seen Rose with her secret boyfriend and that couldn't be good. She hoped she didn't end up getting in trouble for not telling about Don. Her mother nudged Mona toward the door, "Go ahead, honey. Go help Mrs. Keller. I'll probably leave before you get back, but I'll see you tonight when I get home from the hospital."

A few minutes later, Mona pushed Charlie in his stroller while Mrs. Keller, crammed into pink pedal pushers, her hair wound round little blue rollers that weren't hidden by the yellow-flowered scarf she tied round her head, and holding a cigarette in her right hand, huffed and puffed alongside Davey, who pedaled halfheartedly despite his mother's order to give it his all. They were about six blocks from home when Mrs. Keller lurched to a stop and let go of the handlebars causing Davey to crash to the sidewalk. Mona, following behind with Charlie in the stroller, almost crashed into him. Stopped still, they all stared at Rose, who sat in a convertible parked on the side of the street, kissing a man whom Mona recognized as Don even though his face was smashed up close to her sister's.

When she realized she had an audience, Rose, forehead and cheeks tinted with patches of red, the strap of her sundress trailing down to her elbow, got out of the car and stared right back at them. She turned and waved good-bye to Don as he gunned the engine and then Rose walked home the long way while Mrs. Keller followed, saying she was going to be in big trouble, and jabbing her cigarette at the back of Rose's head as if she were tattooing her warning there. Mrs. Keller yanked Davey's hand—hard enough that he cried—as she walked and talked. Mona, a few steps behind, struggled with the stroller full of Charlie and the riderless bike.

When Rose didn't respond to her hollering, Mrs. Keller added, "Rose Palazolla, you should be ashamed of yourself. What are you thinking? Behind your family's back with a man old enough to be your father? Staying out all night? Lying to your parents? How could you take advantage of your parents' trust? Especially with your little sister in the hospital? Next thing you know you'll have more babies than me. I'm telling your father, young lady. Don't think I won't."

Rose ignored her, and Mrs. Keller grabbed the stroller from Mona. Pushing the stroller in front of her and dragging Davey behind, Mrs. Keller marched toward home, shaking her head and muttering. Mona, still wheeling Davey's bicycle, followed Rose.

"What are you going to do, Rose? She'll tell for sure."

"I'll tell first."

"Dad will kill you."

"Go away, Mona. It's none of your business."

Rose stuck out her chin and knotted her forehead. Mona knew that anything her sister was thinking would erupt before it would dissolve and not wanting to get hit by any debris from the explosion, she sat on Davey's bike and pedaled away. When she came to the school playground, she parked the bike and found a tennis ball in the bushes and played Russian handball against the gym wall. She couldn't get past seven, a toss behind the back with a clap under the knee, and after she missed it fourteen times she started thinking that she should go home and be there when Rose or Mrs. Keller told her father what had happened. He might get less mad with her there. Riding Davey's bike home, she realized that all this probably meant she wouldn't get to go to any more Ladies Days at Tiger Stadium.

When she got home, she went in the back door quietly. She heard shouting in the living room, first Rose, then her dad. She heard a quieter voice—her mom hadn't left for the hospital yet after all. She inched closer so she could hear and see through the half-open dining room door, but was careful to keep out of their view. She saw her dad shaking a finger at Rose, "All you've thought about all summer is yourself. You visit the hospital when it suits you. You visit if it doesn't interfere with your date." Her father curled his upper lip as he said the word "date."

"At least I think about Mona more than either of you do. You don't tell her a thing about what's going on with Dee Dee. I've kept my mouth shut because it's not my place to tell her anything. But what kind of parents are you? Mom, it's like you forgot that Mona's your daughter. I'm only eighteen—I can't be the mother around here. If I'm a liar, I learned it from you."

Mona shrank back behind the door. Why were they arguing about her? That wasn't good. They were supposed to be yelling about Rose and Don. About Rose lying and not being at Janet's like she said she was. They weren't having the right fight.

Her father yelled at Rose again, "You have the nerve to tell us how to raise a child? To question your mother *now*, with all she's going through?"

But her mother spoke up then and put her hand on his arm. "It's okay Tony. Everybody is upset. Rose, I can't be two places. I need to be with Dee Dee now. Your father has been here for Mona as much as he can be—we're doing the best we can."

"That's crap, Mom. And you know it. You think you're some saint because you never leave Dee Dee's side, but you're not. You're not being a good mother."

Mona saw her mother sink to the couch and drop her head to her chest suddenly, like her neck had a hinge in the back. Her father smacked his hands together, a sharp crack that made Mona flinch behind the door, "That's it. That's enough. You want to talk about lying? You lie to us and stay out all night while our little girl, your little sister, is in the hospital? And then have the nerve to talk like that to your mother? Get out of here. Now."

Rose pounded up the stairs to her room, and with her absence, their father paced hard, covering their small living room in just a few strides, and doubling back to do it again. When he changed direction suddenly and came toward the kitchen, Mona ran outside the back way, but not before he saw her watching.

After she returned Davey's bike to his house, Mona played some more Russian handball, this time against the side of the Kellers' house because nobody was home there. When she finally went home, her mother's car was gone and her father sat at the kitchen table, his gaze fixed out the window. "Should I make you some lunch, Dad?"

He looked at her accusingly, "What your sister did is wrong. She disgusts me. Do you understand me, young lady?" Mona nodded, though she wasn't sure which wrong thing he meant. He turned to Mona and looked at her, staring at her stomach, which was bare because she'd tied up her shirt to a midriff in the heat of the Kellers' driveway. "She leaves for school in four days. I don't want her in my sight before then. I don't want to speak to her. I don't want to hear her name in this house. Do you understand that?" Mona nodded, untying her shirt so that it covered her stomach. "And you will never go to Tiger Stadium unless I'm with you, and trust me, I'll never take you there."

He didn't say anything after that, but Mona inched out of the room slowly in case he wasn't done talking to her, not letting out her breath until she reached the living room carpet. Then she took the stairs two at a time upstairs to find out if anything else had happened to Rose. Her sister was in her bedroom, flinging sweaters, unfolded, into boxes. She had taken a bath—her hair was wrapped in a bright yellow towel, turbanlike, and she wore her pink seersucker bathrobe.

"Rose?" The bedroom door was open, and Mona looked in and watched as her sister emptied a nightstand drawer full of odds and ends—barrettes, half-full bottles of nail polish, tweezers, pencil stubs, rubber bands, a handkerchief, a pink foam-rubber curler, into a paper bag. "Why didn't you go to Janet's last night, like you said?"

"Just forget about it Mona. It's none of your business."

"Well now Dad is mad at me, too, and I didn't even do anything."

"He's not mad at you."

"Is Mom?"

Rose didn't answer at first. Instead she poured the contents of the paper bag back into the nightstand drawer and picked through it slowly, throwing away an old emery board, placing a bottle of red nail polish upside down next to the clock radio on the nightstand. "Mom and I had a different fight. I made her cry. I think Dad is more mad at me for that than for staying out all night with a guy. God, you know things are bad around here when that happens . . ." Rose laughed ruefully, and then she bent her head, unwrapped the towel from it, and rubbed her damp scalp vigorously.

"Why did you make Mom cry?"

Rose stared into the drawer full of odds and ends, talking to herself more than answering Mona. "She just stands there listening to me call her a crappy mother and lets Dad call me a whore. I can't stand it. I'd rather she did get mad."

Mona left Rose talking to herself and went to her own room to think. She was worried that Rose had messed things up for her. She didn't want her mother or her father thinking about her more than they already did. Them not noticing her much had worked right into her plan, but the longer Dee Dee was in the hospital, the harder it was getting for Mona to keep to her bargain about not seeing Dee Dee—about not hearing news, good or bad, about her little sister. Mona didn't want her mother spending more time with her at home. Not now. Not yet. Not until Dee Dee was home too and everything was back to normal and they could all just forget that anything like this summer had ever happened.

Mona avoided her father that afternoon and stayed in her room all evening. She tuned in WJR on her transistor and listened to the game. The Tigers played the Senators in Washington, and Ernie Harwell talked about the city between pitches. *"Folks, our nation's capital is just beautiful. Makes you proud to be an American. Gates Brown takes a curve. Strike two. It holds the history of our country. Jefferson, Lincoln. Great men. A great country. Uh-oh, Northrup dives back to first and barely misses being tagged out by Frank Howard. The silver fox almost got caught sleeping in the hen house. And Howard would be an awfully big hen, folks—six feet, seven inches tall, 250 pounds—that's a lot of chicken dinner. Ball three, a fastball high and wide. Full count now with two outs, men on first and third and Tigers down 5-3 in the top of the ninth. It's all up to Gates here. But really, folks, visiting Washington, D.C., you get a sense of the struggles of our forefathers. The sacrifices they made so that we can all live free and . . . Oh boy, Brown gets a piece of a curve that hangs. It's a screamer to left. Runners are off. It's going. It's going. It's gone. The Tigers go up 6-5 in the ninth. Gates Brown has come through for Detroit once again."*

The Tigers won as the Senators went down one, two, three, in the bottom of the ninth. When Mona opened her diary to note the score, she looked at her list of black people. Besides Cissy Powell and Sammy Davis, Jr., it was all baseball players.

Mona and Rose looked nothing alike until they cried. Or tried not to cry. Mona thought she could be looking in a mirror that afternoon in front of West Quad, the place Rose would live during her first year of college. She saw Rose fighting sadness as they said good-bye, struggling to keep her mouth and eyes set firm, her face quivering but taut like an umbrella opened in wind.

On Channel 4 News the night before, Sonny Elliot said they'd set a record for the hottest August 22 in Detroit. Standing in front of his weather map, he tried to make a joke about the heat and humidity, but halfway through, he petered out, wiped his forehead, and said everybody should sit very still. The sixty-mile ride to the University of Michigan in Ann Arbor that morning had been so hot, Mona almost wished she hadn't come along. Aunt Jenny and Rose sat in the front seat of Aunt Jenny's Impala. Mona sat in the back, wedged between Rose's belongings—a blue corduroy reading pillow, an Indian print bedspread, and boxes of records and clothes. She listened to Ernie Harwell's pregame show on her transistor. He said the four keys to the Tigers' success were hard work, smart plays, good pitching, and better luck. As summers go, except for the Tigers, Mona was pretty sure her luck had been bad.

Aunt Jenny was only driving because Mona had thought to ask her. Her father and Rose hadn't been in the same room for three whole days after Rose got in trouble for staying out all night, but Rose finally waited for him to get home from the hospital on Saturday night and asked him how he expected her to get to college the next day. Her father didn't answer her. He didn't yell at her. He just stared at the wall behind her, and then he went downstairs to the basement. Rose went up to her room and packed furiously, and when Mona came up later and said maybe Aunt Jenny would drive her to college and she, Mona, could call and ask, Rose only said whatever, she didn't care. Mona checked that her father was still in the basement and then she called on the kitchen phone. Aunt Jenny was suspicious. "Why isn't your father taking her?"

"Oh, he wanted to, but my mom wants him to go to the hospital and be with Dee Dee tomorrow." Mona felt bad using Dee Dee for a lie, but she wanted to help Rose.

"Well, I'll do it, but only because the little one is so sick." Mona made herself a peanut butter sandwich before she went back upstairs to tell Rose. She knocked on Rose's bedroom door, and opened it before Rose answered.

Rose had the phone to her ear. "I've really missed you, Jimmy. I'm glad you're finally back from Traverse City. When will you get to Ann Arbor? Let's get together right away. Your dorm is right next to mine, you know." Jimmy must have answered something she didn't expect because Rose flopped back on the bed like she'd been pushed. "Oh, that's a good one. You shouldn't listen to gossip. Listen, I have to go. I want to call the hospital and make sure my little sister is doing okay."

When Mona told Rose Aunt Jenny would drive her the next day, Rose didn't even thank her. She just told her to get out of the room.

Mona's mom cried as she said good-bye to Rose the next morning. Mona thought it must have been the tears that kept her from noticing how nobody else seemed too sorry, or maybe she was just too full of truth to take in any more. Aunt Jenny pestered Rose the whole ride, so she must not have completely believed Mona's lie. "You must have really done it this time, didn't you Rosie? So what was it? Did he catch you being a slut?" Rose turned and glared at Mona, like it was Mona's fault. Mona turned up her transistor so she didn't have to hear any more of Aunt Jenny's meanness. She was sorry for Rose, but she was glad Aunt Jenny wasn't yelling at her instead. Rose ignored Aunt Jenny for most of the sixty miles to Ann Arbor, staring out her window instead, as if she saw something interesting there. Rose's things, tightly packed, almost blocked Mona's view out the side windows. Until they drove past the ninety-foot-tall Uniroyal tire at the side of the expressway near Allen Park, all she could see was a three-inch strip of treetops and sky.

They arrived on campus and pulled up to Rose's dorm, making no wrong turns because Aunt Jenny had studied the map carefully before they left Detroit, determined not to waste any time. After fifteen minutes, Mona and Rose took a break from unloading Rose's things and sat together on the front fender while Aunt Jenny pushed a pile of boxes in a white canvas bin on wheels up the ramp and through the front door of the dorm. The sun scorched the asphalt at their feet and Mona lifted up her sandals every now and then for relief.

"I'm sorry how I've been these past few days, Mona. Things will be better at home without me. Dad will start being normal again to you. Dee Dee will be home soon—I'm sure of it—and that means Mom will be back too. And school starts for you in two weeks, so at least you'll have something to do. I wish I didn't have to leave so soon. You know I have to. I don't know what else to do. You know that, don't you?" That's when Mona saw herself in Rose's face. Saw the connection and looked down at the asphalt, sizzling hot, dizzy-making, instead of at her sister.

On the way home, Mona and Aunt Jenny stopped at a Howard Johnson's in Ypsilanti for lunch. Mona ordered blueberry corn toasties and a chocolate shake, and then waited for her aunt to yell at her. But Aunt Jenny just rubbed the thin, purple-tinged skin under her eyes and told the waitress to bring Mona a hamburger, too, and then she stopped and looked at Mona, "And don't put any onions on it." She reached across the table and patted Mona's hand, "You need some protein." Mona stared at her, wondering if it was possible she really cared.

PART III

In June, July, and August they hadn't labeled him a serial killer, but by September, the *Free Press* called him just that and put the

news of the Ann Arbor attacks ahead of all the stories that tried to
figure out the riots. Mona turned to the serial killer stories right
after she read about the Tigers. He'd killed three coeds so far,
strangling them the paper said, reporting on the death of Lisa Anne
Wallingham. Mona studied the girl's picture, looking for the reason the killer chose her. She was white and she had short brown
hair just like the other two girls. She was pretty, but not as pretty
as Rose. She was a sophomore at the University of Michigan in
Ann Arbor, the paper reported. The story said she had a boyfriend.
They'd been at a party. She'd danced with somebody else and the
boyfriend got mad. She left with some other guy. Nobody knew
who. That's the last they'd seen of her until she turned up dead.
Mona wondered if Rose knew you could get killed if you made
your boyfriend mad, which she often did as Mona remembered it.
The girl's black-and-white checked skirt was ripped when they
found her in a ditch just dug in the woods near campus. Mona
took the paper with her to school and read the story again during
recess. When she got home that afternoon, she found the slip of
paper where she'd written Rose's phone number in her jewelry box
and dialed carefully, her first time ever long distance.

"She's at class until nine tonight," a voice said when Mona
asked for Rose.

"Do you know what she's wearing today?" Mona wondered if
they got the *Free Press* in Ann Arbor.

"Who is this?" The voice turned suspicious and that made
Mona happy. At least this girl was being careful.

"I'm her sister. Mona. Tell her not to cut her hair. Tell her not
to wear a skirt." Mona's voice wobbled.

"What? Are you okay? You sound kind of sick."

"I'm fine. My other sister is sick. Just tell Rose about the hair
and the skirts for me."

Mona thought back to sitting on Aunt Jenny's porch while the
riots went on. She'd been scared then and worried about everybody
in Detroit, especially the people she knew. But this serial killer in
Ann Arbor made her feel even worse. Maybe it was because she

didn't get to see Rose every day. Didn't get proof that she was still alive, that nobody had ripped off her skirt and then put his hands around her neck and squeezed until she died. The serial killer only killed white girls so far.

After Mona hung up the phone with Rose's roommate, she tried to do the ten math problems Mrs. Scully assigned for homework. It was quiet in the house and that was good for concentration, but math was hard. Now that Mona was back in school, her father went to the hospital from work every day. To see Dee Dee. To see Mona's mother, who sometimes made it home before Mona went to bed. He usually came home by six or seven, and Mona had gone to him for math help twice the week before, but then she stopped. By that time of day, he got the answers wronger than she did.

Mona wished she had somebody else to help her. Last year when Mona almost failed math, Cissy Powell, who did pretty good in it, said she'd be Mona's math study partner when they came back in the fall. But Mona messed that up at recess just that morning when she followed Cissy to the far corner of the playground where she sat reading a book under a skinny elm tree.

"Hi Cissy." Cissy looked up and waved, so Mona continued, "I was thinking maybe we could sit together at lunch today."

"You don't have to butter me up, Mona. I said I'd be your math partner when Mrs. Scully does sign-up this afternoon. Don't worry. I will."

"I'm not worried. I just thought we could sit together."

"Why?" Cissy turned a page.

"I don't know. For company I guess. I have potato chips today. I can share."

"I don't eat potato chips."

"Do you eat bologna? I have that too."

"What do you want, Mona?"

"I went to Tiger Stadium for the first time this summer." Cissy turned another page, and Mona knew she was faking because it was too soon for her to have finished. "What I really want is to know about the riots."

"What about them?" Cissy looked up finally.

"Were you in them? Was your family?"

Cissy eyes got small as olive pits and she stuck her face forward and the cords in her neck got so tight, it looked like they'd twang if you touched them. Mona backed away. "I guess you just want to be alone."

In math class that afternoon when the study partner sign-up sheet went around, Cissy grabbed it first and took Billy Hunter. There was an uneven number in class, and Mrs. Scully didn't even notice that nobody signed up for Mona.

Mona gave up on her math homework though she still had five problems to go. She made herself SpaghettiOs for dinner and ate them on a TV tray while she watched *The Mike Douglas Show*. When she was done, it was only 5:30, and she was bored. She went upstairs and got the laundry out of the bathroom hamper and collected her favorite jeans from the floor in her room and went to the basement to do a couple of loads, a job she'd had since the riots.

She liked being in the basement. It was cool and dim and echoey. She separated the lights and darks, trying not to directly touch anybody's underwear. After she loaded up the washing machine, she held on to the metal pole in the middle of the room and twirled around as fast as she could while she listened to the water rush into the tub. She stopped, dizzy, when she heard the fins of the machine agitating back and forth, beating the dirt out of her family's clothes. She went back to the machine and checked to make sure she'd put in detergent, which she sometimes forgot to do.

From there, she walked to her father's workbench in the corner of the room. It was chest high to her and built of thick, solid, slabs of wood that didn't budge even when she held one leg and shook with all her might. Her father's bench vise was bolted in the corner.

It was iron gray, and it looked like two anvils, flat faces in a stand-
off, waiting to squeeze to death whatever came between them. The
vise's sliding handle—her father called it a lever or a screw—was
long and thin. Mona twirled it in its iron cuff five times and
watched the flat sides of the vise move closer together. Sometimes she watched her father working at the bench. He'd turn the
bench vise lever clockwise, tightening its grip on a two-by-four he
needed to trim, or wringing any sliver of space or bubble of air
between the uppers and the sole of an old pair of boots he'd just
mended with glue. The vise kept things together for days,
months—forever—if nobody loosened its hold.

A few days before, she'd worried as she overheard her parents
as they sat at the kitchen table, drinking coffee and saying they
had better talk to a doctor about getting special permission for
Mona to visit Dee Dee. That it had all gone on too long. That
they had never imagined something as serious as this. Mona, lurk-
ing in the hallway, shrank back. But she couldn't keep herself from
listening. Her mother said the "platelet count" was thirty thousand. Her father asked if the "pleural effusion was subsiding." They
added other words she didn't understand, "lymphocytes" and "he-
moglobin." She felt as if they'd begun to speak in some harsh
foreign language. All the words and phrases sounded ugly. Then
her father mentioned that a group of second-shift men from Chrysler Forge and Axle had gone to the hospital to donate blood, and
a little while after that her mother held up her hands and measured
off a space in the air with her index fingers saying, "Tony, it killed
me to see it. The needle was six inches long." Mona understood
this language much better, so she'd gone outside to play hide-and-
seek with Davey Keller. So far her bargain was working. She
couldn't let them ruin it by making her go to the hospital, by
telling her what was really happening, and by thinking about her
instead of Dee Dee. Dee Dee wasn't home yet, but if Mona kept
her promise, the one she'd made at Aunt Jenny's during the riots,
she was sure her little sister would be okay.

After she'd listened to that conversation, Mona had worked

hard to avoid her parents for the next two days, dodging them, especially when they were together. But then the night before last, she'd overheard them talking again, in their bedroom, after her mother had gotten home from the hospital. There were complications. Mona heard her father mention pneumonia and fluid-filled lungs, and her mother, a canceled bone marrow. Mona heard her own name, heard them saying it was time to talk to her, and that they had better do it together. She scuttled to her bedroom and moments later, as they both stood over her bed, looking down, she used all her concentration to breathe slowly and deeply, to will herself still even as she needed to reach up to them, even as she wanted more than anything to tell them not to worry, to tell them that everything would be fine. Even as she felt desperate to huddle next to her mother, to hold on to her so tightly she'd feel her bone-to-bone, to feel her mother's lips at her ear, and to hear her mother say, "You're right Mona. Everything will be fine. It really will."

Just last night, her mother had stayed even later than usual at the hospital, and Mona didn't have to fake sleep by the time she got home.

When the first load of laundry was dry, Mona heard her father come in, and she came upstairs to watch TV with him. She folded T-shirts and matched up socks, and he ate a tomato, biting into it like an apple. He said he liked eating it that way, but Mona thought it was probably because her mother wasn't there to slice it up. *Lucy* was on and her father laughed when she fell in a pool with her clothes on, but his laugh sounded thin, more like he remembered it was funny, not like he found it funny right then. As soon as it was over, her father returned to his usual look, tired and sad with twitches of mad every now and then.

Mona made her notes in her journal later that night: *Sept. 6, 1967. Tigers beat Chicago 9-7. Dee Dee in hospital 52 days. Did five of ten math problems, probably all wrong. Three girls killed so far at Rose's college.* Then she crossed off Cissy Powell from her list of black people.

.   .   .

At noon on Sunday about a week later, Mona went to the back door when she heard a knock. Mrs. Keller talked through the screen as soon as she saw Mona. "Oh, thank god you're home. Mr. Keller's mother is sick. They think it's a heart attack. We just got word. We have to go to the hospital and I need you to baby-sit for a few hours."

Mona didn't want to. She'd only begun to baby-sit at the Kellers since her mother wasn't around to say she was too young. At first, she'd liked earning the money. But after she'd done it six times, she made excuses not to go. With the four kids under seven and a puppy who peed on the carpet, their house smelled, and every surface Mona touched felt sticky. The littlest, Charlie, hung on her, tugging at her shorts or her hair, his hands hot and grimy, always reaching for notice.

If she didn't go to the Kellers', she'd ride her bike to the corner store and buy the *Free Press* with the money her dad left her, and then she'd sit at the kitchen table and read every section, even business, just to make time pass. Then she'd lie on the living room couch and watch shafts of sunlight stab the gap in the heavy drapes that her mother wanted closed so the upholstery wouldn't fade. The Tigers had already been rained out in Minnesota, so she'd turn the TV to golf, the only thing left. The tock of the clock, the click of putter on ball, the hushed gallery, and her wondering how long it would take for the day to be over. That would be her Sunday. It wouldn't be fun, but it would be better than baby-sitting at the Kellers'.

"Mona," Mrs. Keller pressed her face closer to the screen, "really honey, do you *have* to do something else today? This *is* an emergency."

"A heart attack? You said two hours, right?" Mona, cornered, gave in.

Once in the Kellers' house, she regretted it. The kids ate peanut butter and jelly and the three oldest, Davey and the six-year-old twin girls, Julie and Linda, kicked at one another under the table until their monotonous "don't do that's" and "she's kicking me's" got so loud, Mona sent them outside.

Charlie stayed in and sat under the table playing with blocks while Mona straightened the kitchen and wiped up the most recent puppy piddle. Looking for newspaper to spread on the floor, hoping Mrs. Keller would get the hint to train the dog, Mona found Sunday's *Free Press* untouched in the living room.

She picked up the front section and walked slowly to the kitchen, spreading it on the table, not the floor. Another girl killed in Ann Arbor. Her picture big on the front page. Another girl who wasn't as pretty as Rose. Another stupid girl who met somebody at a party and left with him. Then they found her dead the next day. In the picture, the girl wore tiny pearl earrings. Rose had a pair just like them. Mona was sure Rose met men at parties.

The Kellers' house with its bad smells, the whimpering puppy, grimy Charlie sucking his thumb in the corner, the September heat still leftover from August, Rose in danger—Mona needed to get out of there. Needed to talk to somebody about this killer. Needed to be sure somebody would stop him before he got to Rose. She slid Charlie out from under the table, went outside, and told the others they were going for a walk. When she opened the back gate, they hollered and shot out like roaches in sudden light.

Mona pointed them toward the police station on Warren, but after four blocks Charlie sat down and refused to walk anymore. It didn't matter. Outside in sunlight, Mona could see that the Detroit police wouldn't take a kid asking about a serial killer in Ann Arbor very seriously. They'd pat her on the head. They'd send her home. They wouldn't tell her the truth. Even if they knew it. She picked up Charlie and shifted him to her hip while she called the older kids back. They scampered toward her, sandals slapping the sidewalk as they gathered speed.

Back at the Kellers', Mona sat in the yard with them, holding Charlie heavy in her lap and leaning against the house in a strip of shade provided by the eaves. She watched as the older Kellers played a game of statues, spinning themselves into soundless shapes they hoped would tempt a buyer, casting shadows black as cats. Mona sat still as Charlie fell asleep. Dee Dee had fallen asleep in her lap just that way one afternoon about a week before she went to the hospital. Dee Dee hadn't felt well that day, and Mona had touched her little sister's head softly as she sank into sleep that seemed more like surrender than rest, the thin skin around her eyes tinged purple, a wrinkle in her forehead. Now, with so much time passed, Mona welcomed Charlie's weight, the clutch of his sticky hand, the respite from the scorch of sun.

PART IV

Bob-Lo island, an amusement park and zoo, rose from the murky water of the Detroit River about fifteen miles south of the city. Mona had gone there with her class on a field trip the year before. She liked the Tilt-A-Whirl and the llamas at the zoo, but she didn't like the ferry boat ride you had to take to get to the island. The huge old boat creaked and moaned as it made the trip downriver, passing too close to the Ford River Rouge plant, a place Mona knew from another field trip—that one two years earlier. The plant made steel and during the Ford River Rouge tour, she and her classmates had scuttled along catwalk bridges in the rafters, looking down at the glowing red hot rods of iron and steel being handled by men who ducked and flinched as the sparks flew and the flames of the fires they stoked twitched.

Memories of the Bob-Lo boat and the grim, hot, roaring plant full of men with dirt-streaked faces distorted by work were welded together in Mona's mind. She imagined the old ferry boat chugging downriver and then giving up—too tired to continue. The worn wood deck would moan and bellow and finally split in two, its creaks becoming shrieks as it threw off the passengers that weighed it down. All of them would flail in the water and scream for help, but the River Rouge steelworkers wouldn't hear over the blast of the fires they tended. It could happen. In her mind, she saw it clearly.

But Mona went to the Bob-Lo boat without complaining on the first day of October because her father and mother wanted her there. The Children's Hospital of Michigan was hosting a party on the boat. Dee Dee and her mother would attend, and the boat wouldn't even leave the dock that day, so chances were good they wouldn't all drown. Driving to the boat with her father, Mona worried that she didn't have a plan for avoiding Dee Dee, but at least it wasn't the hospital. Technically she wouldn't be breaking her bargain. And Dee Dee being allowed to come out must mean things were better. It must mean she could come home soon. Mona looked forward to it just the littlest bit, despite all the good reasons she had not to.

For instance, being on the Bob-Lo boat meant she'd miss most of the Tigers doubleheader, the last two games of the season, a matchup with the Angels that would determine the final standings. It was Sunday and that was also her day for writing Rose and making sure she was up-to-date on the latest things the killer did.

She'd talked to Rose about the killer the week before. She didn't want to scare her, but Rose needed to hear out loud how bad things were.

"Rose, in the paper it says you shouldn't walk alone to class. Even in broad daylight."

"Honey, don't worry—I skip class a lot." Rose's voice was scratchy, like she just woke up, even though it was four o'clock.

"Skip?"

"Don't worry, Mona. I never go out alone at night."

"Night has nothing to do with it. And don't cut your hair. So far he's only killed girls with short hair. Maybe you should dye it, because the last two girls had your hair color, I think. It's kind of hard to tell in the paper."

"Mona, I'll be fine. I am careful. I promise. How about you? How are you doing? When's the last time you saw Mom? You're the one everybody should be worrying about."

"There's a hospital party for all the sick kids and their families next Sunday. It's on the Bob-Lo boat. Mom and Dee Dee are coming. Me and Dad too." She didn't tell Rose that she could barely sleep or eat so nervous was she about seeing Dee Dee.

As her father drove toward the riverfront and the Bob-Lo boat that Sunday, they passed burned up shells of buildings from the riots. Shoe repair shops and corner grocery stores, drug stores and auto repair shops. Most of them were boarded up. But a few were back in business, heavy metal bars attached to their doors and windows. It didn't look to Mona like anyone would want to shop at them. When they stopped at a red light, Mona saw a lady sitting on a bench waiting for a bus. She had a sack of groceries on her lap and three more alongside her. How would she get them home? The lady sat still and straight, groceries clutched to her stomach, feet together on the sidewalk, which sparkled with bits of broken glass.

In the *Free Press* that morning, after she read the news of the serial killer, Mona read a story about the police officers who'd been investigated by their own police department and were accused of murdering two of those three men dead at the Algiers Motel during the riots. She wondered which way it would be worse to be killed. By a brick or a bullet in a crowded riot? Or by a man who took you away from a party and strangled you all alone?

Mona bit her fingernails as they drove to the Bob-Lo boat. Her father never told her to stop like her mother used to. She was afraid of how Dee Dee would look. She hadn't seen her since July 17, seventy-six days ago, almost a week before the riots started. Cissy Powell came up to Mona at school three days ago and said she'd be math partners with Mona and Billy Hunter, too, and then she asked if it were true that Dee Dee had no hair left and Mona pretended like she knew and said, "Of course not." Mona had looked at baby Michelle's picture in her notebook that night, trying to imagine Dee Dee bald, but even the little quint had strands of hair down to her earlobes.

Once at the Bob-Lo dock, a yellow-smocked woman pointed

Mona and her father toward a boat entrance where a banner welcoming the Children's Hospital of Michigan hung limp. Buses from the hospital were already parked in front of the boat and Mona could see children being lifted into wheelchairs and limping off on crutches or just walking slowly holding on to a mother's hand. Most of them were so skinny, Mona couldn't imagine how they held up their heads, which were the only things about them that were normal-sized. She saw right away that Cissy was probably right about Dee Dee's hair.

She looked in the crowd for her mother, but it was hard to pick her out. Most of the women reminded her of the things she noticed about her mother whenever she saw her at the beginning or end of the day—shoulders drooping, scuffed up shoes with worn-down heels, lipstick bitten off, hair dry with gray roots showing. Her father held her hand and pulled her up the boat ramp and then to table number twelve, where she sat and waited while he went to find Dee Dee and her mom.

After he left, a large woman came over, crouched before Mona, her eyes all pity, and handed her a ticket. "Here you are, honey. This is for a raffle. The grand prize is a new bike. Wouldn't it be fun to have a new bike once you get out of the hospital? And Bozo is coming on the boat today, too. Do you like Bozo?"

Mona looked at her own legs, skinny, but perfectly healthy, and felt for her ponytail, which was thick and curly. The woman should not have made the mistake of thinking she was sick. She took the ticket and put it in her shirt pocket, ignoring the woman's question.

Mona's table filled up with three sick kids and their moms and two other kids who looked like her, chubby, but only in comparison. The yellow-smocked adult volunteers who swarmed the boat gave all the kids, sick or not, tissue-wrapped gifts. When Mona opened hers she found a plastic bubble wand and a little bottle of dish soap, and she hoped the sick kids didn't get such stupid gifts, but she looked around and saw that everybody got the same.

Another round of volunteers moved right behind the gift-bearing ones. These dropped off aluminum foil–wrapped tubes, which turned out to be soggy hot dogs, and bags of potato chips. Bozo climbed up on stage then, and Mona's father returned.

"Sorry I took so long, Mona. I had to leave the boat and call the hospital. Your mom tried to reach us before we left the house. Dee Dee isn't feeling well enough to go out today. Luckily your mom hadn't told her about this. She would have been upset not to see you." Mona saw him look up at Bozo on stage and then back to the plastic bubble wand, the cold hot dogs, the brittle-limbed children slumped against their mothers. "But hey, there's Bozo. We'll have fun anyway."

Mona knew they wouldn't. She thought of what a waste it was to be there. She'd be better off at home writing to Rose and listening to Ernie Harwell. But her father's eyes were rimmed in pink and his white shirt was gray because at first when she did laundry, she hadn't known to separate the whites and colors, so she just nodded and said sure.

When Bozo, red nose bobbing, orange hair curving up, announced it was time for the grand-prize raffle, a yellow-smocked woman wheeled a blue banana seat bike onto the stage. Bozo trilled the bike's bell as he listed its features. "It's loaded for fun, kids. Even if you have to go back to the hospital today, think of how great it's going to be to ride around the block on your new bike next summer when you're feeling better." The sick kids at Mona's table giggled as Bozo rode the bike around the stage, his big knees hitting his tusks of hair as he pedaled.

Before he got to the bike, Bozo raffled off lots of other things that weren't so good—hard plastic baby dolls and toy guns with no parts that moved. Mona thought it mean to make the sick kids struggle to the stage to pick up such crummy prizes.

She didn't pull her ticket out of her pocket until he got to the bike and when he called her numbers she sprinted to the stage and took the steps two at a time, all healthy, healthy, healthy, and then she realized what she'd done and she slowed down, but it was too late. Standing on stage, next to Bozo, with his white-gloved hands on her shoulders, she could tell that none of the sick kids thought it fair that she had hair *and* a new bike, and she wished she hadn't looked at her ticket. On the way home, the bike in the trunk, her father said maybe she could share it with Dee Dee, which was stupid, because Dee Dee was too little to even pedal a tricycle.

They listened to the game on WJR as they drove home. Ernie Harwell reported that the Red Sox beat the Twins. That meant the Tigers had to take both games to tie for first and force a play-off with the Sox the next day. They took the first easily enough. Mona fell asleep later that night, transistor right next to her on the pillow, during the sixth inning of the second game with the Tigers up 4-2 against the Angels. *"The Tigers are looking good folks. The Motor City could sure use a pennant. It's been a long, hot summer here, and I think the good people of Detroit deserve a World Series this fall."*

She woke in the morning to find out the Tigers had lost the American League Pennant. The Red Sox were going to the World Series instead. Not winning. Coming so close. After all that. She couldn't see the good in it taking so long. And she hadn't even been awake to hear Ernie Harwell say good-bye. When she looked at her face in the bathroom mirror that morning, her skin was the color of silly putty, her eyes were slits, and her mouth drooped like a fish on a hook. It was not the face of somebody who expected anything good.

A week later, even Mona's father paid attention when another Ann Arbor girl ended up dead in a ditch. That was five girls gone and the news got bigger. Headlines. Pictures. Police interviews. Mona heard him talking to Aunt Jenny over the phone that evening. "Call and tell her not to go out alone at night." Mona shook her head at such bad advice, as if night were the problem.

When her mother came home an hour later, her father showed her the paper, but she waved it away, "No, Tony. That's too much for me right now," and even though her voice got lower, Mona backed up a little when she heard her mother mention Dee Dee. The movement caught her mother's attention and she stopped talking and reached out to hug Mona and to stroke her hair. Then she told her to go outside and ride her bike until the streetlights came on.

Mona went up to her room instead and wrote out some rules for Rose:

1. Do not wear a skirt.
2. Do not talk to men.
3. Do not walk alone.
4. Do not go to parties.
5. Do not think you are ever, for sure, safe.

She had trouble falling asleep and after a while she didn't try anymore, she just lay awake thinking about how to save Rose.

The next morning, on Sunday, her mother and father left for the hospital early. They gave Mona five dollars to order pizza for dinner, just in case, but her father said he would be home before then for sure. Mona knew he wouldn't. She didn't care. It fit her plan perfectly.

Once they left, she made a bologna sandwich and put it in her schoolbag with her homework and then she walked over to Michigan Avenue and took the bus downtown to the Greyhound station. They passed deserted Tiger Stadium on the way. Mona didn't listen to her transistor anymore. At first she thought she'd have trouble falling asleep without Ernie Harwell telling her exactly what was going on, but except for the night before, she usually fell asleep okay. She just woke up tired.

Once at the Greyhound station, across from the Bob-Lo boat dock, Mona used the pizza money to buy a round-trip ticket to Ann Arbor. She had a story ready—her mom in the bathroom while her dad parked the car—in case the ticket agent wouldn't sell to a kid, but he barely looked at her as he gave her a ticket and change.

On the way to Ann Arbor, she sat scooted forward on her seat near the back of the bus. An old man holding a loaf of bread in a worn paper bag sat down next to her just before the bus pulled away. He didn't speak English. Or maybe he did. He grunted a lot and gave her the heel from the bread, tough as meat. She had the window seat and when they passed the Uniroyal tire, she knew for sure they were going the right way, so she sat back and sucked on the bread.

If she hadn't been traveling to do something so important, her first bus trip alone would have been more exciting, though she reminded herself not to sit so close to the bathroom, which smelled bad, on the way back. She'd copied Rose's dorm room address on her geography folder that morning and she looked at it every time the bus stopped to pick up passengers. She knew the address by heart when they were still four stops away.

When the driver called "Ann Arbor, Michigan Student Union," she was already at the door, waiting to get off the bus. The first girl she asked for directions to West Quad pointed behind Mona and told her to walk two blocks that way and that she couldn't miss it.

All the way to West Quad, Mona looked at the people she passed. Most of them looked about Rose's age. They dressed the same. Jeans. The girls in peasant blouses. The boys in T-shirts. There were lots of them and they looked nice. She felt better about Rose walking around campus. A second later, she shook her head at how stupid she was. The killer would want everybody to think he was nice. After that, she looked at all the boys, especially the white ones, suspiciously. The killer probably was white because the police said the dead girls met him at a party and Mona knew most white girls wouldn't go off with a black man.

She rehearsed what she'd say to Rose when she saw her. "Rose, you must not go to parties." All the women had been raped, the paper said. And right after that it said the women's panties had been cast aside from their bodies and that their skirts were pushed up almost over their heads, so Mona knew what raped meant. "Rose, you must not wear a skirt. And don't take off your underpants." She'd give her the written rules, too, as a reminder. And she would tell her that even their dad was worried—that he was the one who asked Aunt Jenny to call.

When she got to West Quad, the front door was propped open with a stick and nobody was even at the front desk, just a sign saying, BACK IN 5 MINUTES. She shook her head, kicked away the stick, and closed the door behind her, wondering why nobody in Ann Arbor seemed to take this killer seriously, but she was glad for herself it was so easy to get in. She went up two flights of stairs to the third floor. As she walked down the dim, narrow hallway that led to room 319, she realized she didn't have a plan for if Rose wasn't home.

And she should have, because nobody answered her knock, which was tentative at first, then firm, then banging. She turned and leaned against the door and slid down until she sat on the grim brown carpet. She sat there for an hour, shaking her head no to two girls who came by and asked if they could help. After that, she decided it probably didn't matter anyway—Rose wouldn't listen to her any more than she listened to anybody else. She'd do what she wanted to do. What she *needed* to do. Just like everybody had done that whole summer. Everybody but her.

Traveling to Ann Arbor on the bus, she'd looked out the window and imagined Rose opening the door and hugging her and whispering in her ear, just like she'd imagined Rose or her mom or dad doing during the first week of life with Dee Dee in the hospital when Mona was home alone all day missing her sisters and her mother and her father and waiting by the window for somebody to come home. That was back when Mona still believed everything would be okay. Before Tanya Blanding was shot dead. Before the Angels ruined it for the Tigers.

But she wouldn't have believed Rose this time around anyway. That was the difference between then and now. Now she believed in the things she could count. She concentrated as she tallied them.

Al Kaline batted .308 for the season. The Tigers finished 91-71, one game out of first, losing to the Angels 8-5 in the very last game. The riots lasted eight days and ended with forty-three people dead and more than seven hundred injured. Earl Wilson won twenty-two games. Since July, she'd made $12.75 baby-sitting for the Kellers. The serial killer killed five girls in nine months. Her father ordered pizza for dinner eleven times since the riots. She'd seen her mother for fifteen minutes that morning and twenty-five minutes the night before. Dee Dee had been in the hospital for eighty-one days. She'd update her tally and add new things to it more often now that she couldn't listen to Ernie Harwell anymore.

She was tired and she wished she could cry, but everything inside her had dried into small powdery pieces that Rose and everybody else had scuffed to dust as they walked past her on their way to taking care of something else. Something important. Maybe just themselves.

When she left West Quad, the front door was propped open again. She left it that way, and then she crumpled her list of rules for Rose and threw it in the bushes outside the door. Rose wouldn't be murdered. Dee Dee probably would die. When she got back to Detroit, she'd ask her parents to tell her that. She felt trampled, ready for the truth.